The Prize

by

Debra Doggett

The Prize

Contact Information: info@thewildrosepress.com

Cover Art by *Rae Monet*

The Wild Rose Press
PO Box 708
Adams Basin, NY 14410-0706
Visit us at www.thewildrosepress.com

Publishing History
First Faery Rose Edition, 2008
Print ISBN 1-60154-309-3

Published in the United States of America

Oderean closed his fingers around the stone as Cardis reluctantly gave Stellan her hand. The stone began to glow, the soft yellow light gleaming through Oderean's fingers. Oderean cupped his other hand around it, eyes closed, as his lips moved in the ancient chant. When he opened his eyes and spread his fingers, a small golden cup stood in his hand.

"Each of you will drink from the golden cup as your acceptance of the challenge. Once you drink, the time for the challenge has started and there is no going back." He looked again at Stellan. "For once done, the magic cannot be undone. In three days, the decision will have been made. Cardis."

She took the cup from her father's hand and lifted it to her lips. Stellan licked his own lips as he watched her mouth slide along the rim of the cup. When she lowered it, her lips were red and moist and he nearly groaned thinking of what the next three days held. Without taking his gaze off her, he lifted the cup to his own mouth, surprised at the cool thick taste that spread across his lips. It gave him a kind of buzz, like really good alcohol, only quicker. As he lowered the cup, he stared at Cardis. She gave him an evil grin.

"Well, lowlife, the clock's ticking."

Stellan swore he heard the sound of it in his own head. *Let the games begin.*

Dedication

To Erin, Ellen and Emily,
whose love and support kept me going.
To Rick, Karen, Mallorie and my parents,
who always believed.
To Rhonda, Raquel and Rozana,
who told me what worked and what didn't.

Chapter One

Cardis heard the alarm through the haze of sleep only moments before the freighter lurched and dumped her from her warm bed. The high-pitched screech split her ears as she glanced around the darkened room, holding on to the rim of the small night table to steady herself. She rubbed her hip, thankful for what cushion the plush carpet provided.

From under the door the amber glow of the hallway's running lights shone against the black of her quarters. Pictures and knickknacks tumbled down onto the silvery carpet, nearly smacking Cardis in the head. As the craft tossed from side to side, she gripped the steel bar of the table to keep from being slung around the room.

The rocking told her the *Venetta* had taken some sort of hit to its stabilization panels. Thuds against the outer hull shook the walls. Whatever space debris was pounding them, it sounded solid and big.

She reached for the black silk robe at the foot of her bed, but it lay beyond her fingertips unless she let go of the table. Letting go would likely send her tumbling across the floor. Cardis braced her feet against the wall and cursed the dark.

"Lights on."

Her annoyance deepened when the room remained dark. No emergency power wasn't a good sign. Whatever had started them spinning must have sapped the freighter's power as well, at least enough that the immediate restart hadn't kicked in. The engine crew would be on manual without the emergency crystals. Left dark and powerless, the *Venetta* would slow to a crawl. That would definitely mean a trip back home for repairs.

Preferring not to simply hold on while being

1

scrambled around the room like an egg, Cardis struggled to her feet, using the table for support. As she strained to see enough to make her way to the door, another sound penetrated her daze. The echoes of running feet in the hallway and the shouts of the crew made her realize the amber light had changed to red. *Oh, great.* She had slipped away from her father's house and boarded the *Venetta* with the hope her absence wouldn't be noted until at least tomorrow evening. If something happened to force their return home, she would be right back in the middle of the whole mess with Wald. *So much for avoiding confrontation.*

Cardis let her eyes adjust to the dark, taking a moment to get her bearings before moving. Releasing her death grip on the table, she dropped down and crawled along the floor until her fingers bumped the wall where the door was. She slid her hand up until she found the emergency open switch. The silver door slid aside with a hum.

Flashes of red and green light illuminated the steel walls, giving eerie bursts of brightness to the dim corridor. Orders bellowed through the static from the intercom system. Bodies collided against the walls and each other as crewmembers scurried to their posts. And over all the chaos rode the smell of fear.

Cardis ignored the sense of panic spreading through her as she stood in the doorway. Swallowing hard, she stared at the faces running past her until she recognized one. She grabbed Marco's arm and pulled him to a stop. He frowned as a young technician crashed into him from behind then hurried off mumbling a short apology. Shaking his head, Marco turned to face Cardis.

"Cardis, what are you doing standing in the hallway? You don't have to answer the alarm. Go back to sleep." He started to step away from her.

Seeing the irritation and what might be worry on his face sent the first curl of fear through her.

"What is it? What's going on?"

"Marco!" Eldwyn, one of the older crewmen, paused in flight to turn back to them. "Come on! They need us on deck."

Ignoring the other man's protest, Cardis planted

herself in front of Marco so he couldn't move as she stared at him. But now what she saw on his scarred face made her tremble. If whatever was happening now put panic in Marco's eyes, then something was really wrong.

"What's going on, Marco?"

Cardis worked to keep her voice calm and even. Hysteria wouldn't help any of them right now, even if it was the main thing bubbling up in her throat. Marco patted her on the arm.

"We hit a ion storm, Cardis. It's sent us off course."

Cardis knew he sought to comfort her, as he always did. Marco had befriended her when she was a scared teen trying to prove herself among her father's crew. In the years since, he'd mentored her, taking her side when her father would have left her behind to tend to women's things. Marco was her friend and now she needed the truth from him.

"That sounds like a minor problem, Marco, not something to put panic in your eyes. What is it you're not telling me?"

Eldwyn pulled at Marco's other arm. "Let's go. They need us on deck."

Marco nodded then turned his attention back to Cardis.

"I'm not panicked, Cardis, just in a hurry. Right now I really don't have time to explain. Malachi needs me on deck. You came on this trip for a vacation, remember? Leave the worrying to us. That's what we're paid for."

Cardis looked from one man to the other. Eldwyn avoided her gaze.

"This is my father's ship, Marco. If something's wrong, I need to know it. Besides, maybe I can help."

Marco opened his mouth to argue, but a rumbling along the outer hull of the freighter echoed down the dim hallway, freezing the words in his mouth. The sound tightened Cardis' grip on his arm.

Marco eased her hand off him and pushed her gently back toward her open doorway. "We'll let you know when things have leveled out again." He patted her arm. "If you're worried, then go down below with the other passengers, Cardis. Take whatever you need from your room and go down to Level Three."

The ship lurched again, tossing the three of them against the cold metal walls. Marco started to move off but Cardis caught his sleeve once more.

"Tell me what's going on, Marco. I'm not a rookie passenger so don't send me down to the rec room as if I need a drink to steady my nerves. I can help. My father brought me on my first freighter trip when I was four and I've been on more trips than most of your current crew. I'm not a pilot, but I can certainly handle navigation backup."

"Nobody can help us now."

Cardis noticed Eldwyn's face was paler than usual. "What do you mean?"

Marco hesitated then shrugged. "You're hardheaded as always, Cardis. If you were the biddable daughter you should be, you'd move aside and let us see about putting things to right."

Cardis snorted. "If I were a biddable daughter, I wouldn't be here right now."

Marco chuckled, his face losing some of its grimness. "That's certainly true." He ran his hand through his hair and shook his head, the stark look coming back over his face. "Well, if you must know, we lost our tracking signal when the storm hit. We're not in our airspace anymore. We're ...we're in Edarian airspace."

Cardis gaped at him. "How could that happen? I mean, it's forbidden to even cross the buffer zone into their airspace, and for good reason." Fear tingled up Cardis' spine at the thought of those reasons. She leaned against the wall to steady herself. "We can't be in their airspace, we just can't."

"But we are." Eldwyn's voice shook and the sound of it added to Cardis' panic. The alarm bursts came louder and faster.

"Cardis, we've got to get up on deck." Marco's words broke through her thoughts. "Go back in your room or down below with the others. Malachi will do what he can. He's a good pilot, a really good one. If anyone can get us out of this, he can." Marco gripped Eldwyn by the arm and pushed him down the hall.

As she watched their retreating backs, Cardis fought the anxious feeling that rose inside her. The blaring voices over the intercom and the flickering red and green lights from the alarm didn't help clear her head. By all the stars and planets, what had she done? She had fled her home to escape an impossible situation only to land herself in something worse, much worse.

Shoving her way back into her quarters, she tossed on her clothing from the night before and headed to the navigation room.

****

"Is it newer than the others, Stellan?"

The boy rubbed the piece of metal, the blue-gray sheen of it glinting in the harsh Edarian daylight. He held it out to the man next to him.

"Yeah, Samuel." Stellan's finger traced the emblem on the shattered piece of the freighter's outer hull. "Probably the most up to date we've seen yet."

He handed the piece back, knowing his nephew would squirrel it away with the rest of his collection. Samuel was nearly sixteen summers old, tall and muscular with his mother's fair skin and blue eyes. Old enough, in Stellan's brother's opinion, to carry as much of the load as Hakir chose to heap on his illegitimate son. To Hakir's mind, blood wasn't enough. The boy needed to prove himself worthy of being his father's son. Stellan always wanted to tell Hakir that blood had less to do with things than conditioning. He took a long look at the faraway expression on his nephew's face and sighed. His father's neglect and his mother's pining for more had formed Samuel more than any blood tie. Together two selfish people had created another dreamer.

Stellan surveyed the scene before him. What was left of the *Venetta* lay silent and still among the rocks and scrubby green trees of Mostase Canyon like a shining star yanked out of orbit and tossed in the dirt. They'd heard her calls through the static on their pitiful comsets, seen her come spinning through their atmosphere before hitting the landscape with a shockwave that brought down two of their shelters.

"Fancy doings sure didn't help much when it came down." Samuel pocketed the piece of metal.

"No, it didn't."

Stellan prodded what was left of the freighter's

5

emblem with his foot. The vessel was definitely Adenan, likely one of the more wealthy merchants, if its cargo was any indication. Though modern in design and more technologically advanced than Stellan had ever seen, the dents and gaping holes in the ice blue hull clearly showed the beating the craft had taken from the ion storm before shattering most of its outer shell on the rocky Edarian terrain. Proof once again that civilization and Edaria weren't compatible.

The damage wasn't to the vessel alone. A breeze carried the smell of burning wood and a strange chemical aroma across the swells of the canyon. His brother's men had extinguished most of the small fires started when the fuel tanks of the vessel's thrusters exploded among the stunted trees and wild grass. Still, they would have to watch the area for the next several days to ensure no smoldering embers blazed up again. The trees often held onto tiny sparks, hiding them for days until the heat blazed up again. Even if they were lucky and no more fires started, the air would smell like smoke and fumes for days to come. Hakir would need to move his people away from the area for the next several weeks. That wouldn't put him in any better humor.

"Can we go inside?"

Stellan knew his nephew longed to see more, although he wasn't sure that was a good idea. It would only fuel the boy's curiosity. And he knew well enough from his own experience how much curiosity could weigh on you.

"Let's have a good look at the outside first."

Stellan rose and walked the length of the main piece of the wreckage. The inside of the vessel remained remarkably intact, probably due to the thick metal alloy of the hull. Still, the large holes in the *Venetta*'s sleek walls leaked out a variety of cargo, technology and people. Most of the trade wares were in one piece and all of the passengers and crew standing and breathing. That was a good sign.

What wasn't a good sign was the look his brothers shared. Martin and Hakir could almost be twins with their dark brown hair and stony green eyes. They both stood six foot five, with the broad shoulders and intimidating build of their father. Angus Tolten knew how to use his physical presence to great advantage. At a mere six one, Stellan always felt like a child around the three of them. His slender build and the golden streaked hair he inherited from his blonde mother only added to the feeling of separation.

He started over to where his two brothers stood surveying the wreckage, Samuel close on his heels. Hakir's eyes glowed as he stared at the riches scattered along the canyon floor, tossed like gold and silver coin among the weeds and rocks.

"Truly a prize this time, eh, brother?" Hakir clapped Stellan on the shoulder. "And Eustacia told me it was a foul wind blowing last night. Bah! Shows what women know."

Stellan could well imagine what Eustacia knew. His brother's wife feared most things in her world, including his brother. And this time he had to agree with her. A foul wind would begin to blow their way if he couldn't keep Hakir from treating this incident as manna from the heavens.

All of the riches had to be returned, along with the survivors, preferably intact. Or at least not marred by anything except their unfortunate landing. Their last warning from the Interstellar Council threatened dire consequences for any further complaints from the Merchants Association about Hakir's treatment of their lost vessels.

"What are you doing over here, boy?" Samuel cringed at the hard glare his father gave him. "You got no business lazing around over here. There's work to be done. Get over there and help Dalen get the boxes packed so we can move this stuff out by nightfall." He grabbed the boy's arm and gave him a shove, shaking his head as Samuel stumbled away.

Stellan glanced over at his oldest brother and sighed. He feared not even his persuasive skills would help this time. Hakir's hard green eyes were already filled with that look, the one that never boded well for anyone who got in his way. To his brother's mind, an entity like the Council was far away and easy to dismiss, especially when weighed against more riches than Edaria's meager resources would produce in several years.

Mostase Canyon had never yielded much in the way of ore or valuable minerals, but today it glittered with the wealth from the merchant's lost wares. Likely Hakir already knew the exact amount he would gain from the wreckage, had already calculated in his head what and how much it would bring him from the thugs and careless traders only too willing to carry goods forbidden to legal merchants. And willing to deal in all forms of cargo, including human. The shady underworld Hakir frequented for his business dealings encompassed a healthy slave trade.

Stellan swore under his breath as he watched his brother's men round up the vessel's survivors. Whoever piloted the craft knew what he was doing. He'd set the *Venetta* down with as little impact as possible, a feat that kept the people on board alive.

Stellan gazed at their frightened faces. Now it was his job to make sure they stayed alive. He'd made a promise to himself that he wouldn't see another captive sold as cargo to satisfy Hakir's endless greed.

Movement at the far corner of the line of survivors caught his attention. A more careful glance had him seeing red.

"Matthias!" Stellan bellowed the man's name as he covered the distance to where armed guards encircled the *Venetta*'s people.

"What?"

The older man barely glanced over his shoulder as Stellan bore down on him. The matted red beard and scraggly mustache that covered his squat face didn't mask the leer as his small dark eyes focused instead on the young girl whimpering beneath him. Matthias' bulky form pinned her thin frame to the ground.

Her black and gold uniform torn from both the crash and Matthias' assault, the girl lay frozen beneath him, her blonde hair a tumbling mass around her shoulders, her face a mask of fear. Silent tears slid from the corners of her soft blue eyes as she made small gasping noises. Matthias stroked a dirty finger down one pale cheek, chuckling as the girl's tears went fullblown.

"I'm busy here, Stellan."

Still seeing red, Stellan plowed a fist into the side of Matthias' head. The force of the blow knocked him off the girl, who scrambled back from the two men.

"Keep your hands off, Matthias."

Despite the fact his knuckles were screaming, Stellan stood over the man with a great deal of pleasure. Matthias revolted him and always had. He was a bully, preying on any who found themselves at his mercy. No matter how many times Stellan argued with his brother over the man, Hakir refused to dismiss Matthias from his guard.

"You gonna make me, Stellan?" Matthias touched a hand to his head then stared at the blood. His fingers curled into a fist.

Stellan stared him in the face. "I already did."

"Stellan!"

Ignoring the sound of his brother's voice, Stellan glared at the man on the ground in front of him. Matthias glanced behind Stellan and frowned before turning his hard gaze back on Stellan.

"For now," Matthias spat at him as he struggled to his feet. "But you and I will have a time alone one day, Stellan. You won't always be able to hide behind your brothers."

"No one's hiding now, Matthias." Stellan made the dare obvious. His hands itched for another chance at the man. He'd just as soon have this over with.

With another glance at the man striding across the field, Matthias snarled at him. "Business before pleasure, Stellan. That's Hakir's rule. So I'll have to wait." He turned to ogle the still whimpering girl. "Don't forget me, sweetheart." With one last glare at Stellan, he stomped off.

"Stellan!"

This time Stellan turned to see his middle brother Martin make his way over from the wreckage, Hakir close behind him.

"Get inside there and take a look around." Martin jerked his chin toward the piece of the vessel that remained intact.

"You're trusting me to go in there?"

Stellan knew he probably shouldn't have questioned

his good luck. Martin had to know he was dying to get a look inside the *Venetta*'s shattered walls. Technology fascinated him. But it wasn't often either of his brothers made it easy for him to indulge his fascination.

Martin scowled at him. "I don't want any of these clods out here with their sticky fingers going in there before we get a look at what it holds. Wouldn't want any of our treasure to go missing."

Hakir arched a brow as he walked up to Martin. "Are you saying my men would pick something of value up and forget to tell me about it?"

"That's exactly what I'm saying, brother. Do you have anything to say to that?"

"Only that you're a good judge of character." Hakir laughed as he slung an arm around Martin's shoulder.

"Besides," Martin said, "I'm saving you the trouble of having to beat the shit out of any of your men. That would put them out of commission for awhile and leave us shorthanded when we deal with the visitors from the Interstellar Council that this little incident will bring to our fair planet."

"And you're so sure I wouldn't pick anything up and keep it?" Stellan couldn't resist the question. There were times when his brothers' arrogance grated on him.

"No, little brother." Martin chuckled. "But I figure I'll just ask Matthias to take it away from you. He's been wanting a chance at you."

Stellan snorted. "He'd need more than chance."

"Yeah, but while the two of you are beating the shit out of each other, Martin and I will take care of the cargo." Hakir poked him in the ribs. "That'll at least distract you long enough to keep you from making your usual speeches about giving everything back."

Stellan's temper spiked as Martin and Hakir choked with laughter. Martin gave him another shove.

"Now get in there and find out what else these sky travelers have blessed us with."

Chapter Two

"Is this the finest you've ever seen, Stellan? Were the others you've seen this big? This..."

Samuel gaped at what he saw, mesmerized by the shiny equipment, the cushioned floors and textured ceilings. Even through the mess of wires and broken panels, the richness of the vessel was obvious. The outer hull was three layers thick, the inside a maze of corridors and hallways.

The intact hold of the *Venetta* held even more trade goods, a stroke of luck for which Stellan was grateful. More inanimate cargo might make his brothers more amenable to negotiating a ransom for the surviving human cargo. So long as none of the freighter's people were hurt and the emissaries from the Council agreed to the loss of the trinkets and equipment as compensation for what Hakir would call damages to the terrain, they could come out of this incident without finding themselves in the middle of a war.

He'd commandeered Samuel to help him with anything they might want to carry out of the vessel. Samuel's eyes grew wider with each step they took. The two of them wandered through what was left of the freighter, careful of loose wires and falling tiles.

"It's definitely a rich one," Stellan agreed.

He pushed aside the shattered door that led to the control room then tried not to gape as badly as Samuel. But he allowed himself several long minutes to marvel at the sleek design and well-equipped navigational panel on the upper control deck. A good pilot and good equipment. The *Venetta* had it all.

Stellan prided himself on knowing at least a little about navigational technology and telecommunication systems. The *Venetta*'s were state of the art and probably a contributing reason the crew and cargo survived the crash. He knew Hakir would scoff at the idea, saying the wreck itself proved advanced technology did no good against nature and fate. But he couldn't dismiss the longing in his own heart, or the admiration that grew with every new revelation.

Though there could be a grain of truth to his brother's pessimism, Stellan couldn't help running his fingers over the detailed fixtures at the broken control board, couldn't stop gazing in wonder at the expansive screen that would show a man the paths of the stars. *What would it be like to stand before the spread of the universe as it whizzed past you? To see something miraculous, something far beyond the constant labor it took to merely survive from day to day in Edaria's harsh environment?*

He shook his head and told himself to stop being an ass. All that stood before him was broken remnants of a life he could never aspire to. Dreaming of a life beyond the one he lived now was a costly venture, one he couldn't afford, for no treasure he knew of could buy it for him. Still, that didn't stop him from cursing the fates as he turned away from all the outside world had to offer.

"So why didn't they make it? How can something like this just fall from the sky?" Samuel's question echoed around in Stellan's own head.

"I don't know. Bad luck, I guess."

The boy nodded. "Fate. That's what my mother calls it. Things are fated to be and there's nothing we can do about them."

Stellan shook his head. *Fate, bad luck, whatever. Maybe naming what kept you from having something helped deal with the pain of the loss.*

"Come on, Samuel. We've seen enough. Let's get out of here."

As they headed back out of the freighter down one of the long corridors, they passed an opening into the personal quarters area. A door hung loose from one of the walls and the scent of sweet honey filled the air. The aroma seemed so out of character for the modern freighter it made Stellan pause.

"Wait a minute, Samuel."

Stellan moved down the corridor to the broken door. For a moment he stood and inhaled the comforting smell. Wondering what the source could be, Stellan pushed the door out of the way and stepped inside. Still gaping, Samuel followed.

The room was spacious, airy, filled with trinkets and pictures in the way some people had of filling their home spaces.

"Fancy room." Samuel gaped at the room as he picked up some of the trinkets from the floor, turning them over in his hands.

"Probably it was for the merchant's family when they traveled," Stellan mused.

"Yeah, guess my father's right. He says the rich like to bring the evidence of their wealth with them so everyone recognizes them no matter where they are."

Stellan walked to the black metal table by the broken bed. Two thick candles sat in front of a framed photograph of a man and a woman standing in a garden. The candles had burned down low, the darkened wicks like blight on the red wax. He sniffed the air around them, breathing in again the honeyed fragrance. Feeling a little ridiculous, he looked around the rest of the room.

The homey scent clashed with most of the decor. Thick silver curtains covered the tiny portals and rich carpet of the same hue blanketed the floor. One corner held a dining area, the sleek black table and chairs bolted to the floor in a neat arrangement around the food dispenser. A desk with a wide screen and some sort of intercom link sat across from the table. The bed beside him was a blend of steel and cold elegance, the twisted frame a mute testament to the intrusion of the force that jerked the freighter from its sky berth.

"Man, Amalia would like this."

Stellan turned to see Samuel fingering a robe that lay at the end of the bed. He stepped closer, closing his own hand over the bit of cloth. The garment was black silk, dark as midnight and cool to the touch. Probably like the woman who wore it, Stellan thought as he picked it up and turned it over in his hands. He caught the same honeyed fragrance that had lured him into the room as he threaded the folds of the silk through his fingers. *It must be her scent.* He thought again how different the smell seemed from the rest of the room. Then Samuel's words registered.

"Amalia?"

Samuel blushed. "She's old man Dalen's daughter. We've kind of got a thing going." He shrugged.

"I'm surprised Dalen even lets you talk to his daughter."

"Yeah, well, he doesn't know about our, um, thing. Like I told her, what her father doesn't know won't hurt him."

"More like what he doesn't know won't hurt you." Stellan shook his head. The boy was near as reckless as he'd been at that age. And way too young to be courting danger with a female. He'd have to have a long talk with Samuel and soon, before Hakir or Dalen found out about his little thing with Amalia. Best to acquaint him right away with what confusing creatures women could be.

Samuel's problem stirred reminders of his own needs. It had been way too long since he'd been confused by a woman. He'd have to see to remedying that once everything with the freighter was settled. Maybe he could coax Eustacia's little sister Phoebe into a trip to the river. The girl was as complacent as her sister, but her body was lush and pleasurable. She'd leave his passion untouched but his groin satisfied. Generally that was the best he could hope for. Little wonder he resisted all the marriage traps placed before him.

Samuel laughed a very male laugh. "Yeah, but if I was to bring her this, Amalia would make all the hurt go away."

"Have a care, boy, before you find yourself gracing Amalia's bed for the rest of your life."

Samuel shrugged. "She's a passionate thing, especially between the sheets. I could do worse."

"You're too young to know anything about passion, boy, and too inexperienced to know if you could do worse. Best take my warning."

"I'm a fast learner."

Samuel grinned at him and Stellan gave up. Young fool, he'd never seen real passion in his few years.

Stellan's thoughts wandered as the honey scent filled the air around him. Could a woman be found who had passion in her soul? His imagination fired as he wondered what it would be like to share a place such as this with a woman who wore silk and honey. What kind of woman traveled the stars with her man, keeping a spot he could call home ready and waiting? And what would that kind of woman be like in bed? Would she lie with him under the stars as he made love to her, as he took her body in his hands and gave them both pleasure? Would she ease his body with her hands, with her mouth, as they came together? Stellan bit back a groan as he felt the blood rush to his loins. He'd best see to his own body's ease and soon.

Trying to ignore the randy demands of his lower parts, Stellan ran his hand over the engraved logo on the wall. It was the seal of Adena. Bits and pieces of stories he'd heard over the years came back to him. There were rumors about the noblewomen of Adena, about the training they received in sexual pleasure even as virgins. Stellan always disregarded the stories for they gave a woman power beyond what he knew any man would allow, the power to choose their own mates. That kind of choice in the hands of a mere woman would give any man the shivers. But the legends always intrigued him for they held a promise of riches that made him long for them to be truth.

"Stellan! Get your lazy ass out here. And put down whatever it is you've pocketed."

Stellan sighed as his brother's harsh voice echoed down the corridor. Legends and dreams melted against the cold hard truth of his world. He let the robe slide from his hands. The only thing such a garment could bring him was the hope of a rich ransom to go with it, money for the woman and her husband. It wasn't likely that a wealthy woman would be traveling alone. Probably the *Venetta* was her husband's freighter. So now there would be double the ransom.

"Come on, Samuel. I hear the real world yelling for us."

As they stepped back out into the sunlight, Samuel wondered aloud.

"Do you think it will bring a lot, all the stuff I mean?"

Stellan nodded. "And if I can talk your father into ransoming the crew instead of using them for sport, it'll bring even more."

"Ransom?" Samuel eyed him dubiously.

"I know it's a hard concept for your father to understand, but the *Venetta* is a nobleman's vessel and noblemen pay for their people."

Samuel shook his head. "Do you think my father will buy that?"

"If I talk fast enough, maybe."

Samuel looked unconvinced. If he couldn't convince the boy, his chances with Hakir looked even slimmer. And any attempt would have to wait till things settled down. Stellan only hoped the Council delayed arriving until he'd had some time for persuasion.

"Well, if anyone can talk fast enough, it's you, Stellan." The boy gave him a grin. Then he glanced around him. "Still, even you will have a hard time getting their attention for any speeches now."

As much as he hated to, Stellan had to agree with Samuel. On what they pulled off the survivors alone, Hakir and Martin could let their men carouse for the better part of a month.

"Yeah. So much for getting anything else done."

"Anything else?"

"We've got to repair the levees before the spring rains come, Samuel. Even better would be to have the new dam in place before then."

Samuel snorted. "I don't think that's going to happen for awhile, Stellan."

Stellan sighed. Indeed, this unexpected treasure meant the end of any work he hoped to get out of Hakir and the others on his pet project. The dam was only half completed. When the spring rains came, the pressure would be too much for the aging levees to hold in the condition they were in now. Flooding could take out many of the small towns along the river. Any delay would be costly. It would take weeks to finish the dam, weeks that Hakir's men would idle away with their newfound wealth instead of putting their efforts anywhere else. This windfall held as many problems as its cargo would solve.

Raucous laughter pulled Stellan from his worries. The men had gathered around one of the transports. From the hoots and hollers, Stellan feared one of the crew had done exactly what he hoped they wouldn't. He pushed his way into the circle, Samuel close behind him.

"What's that he's yelling? I can't understand him."

Stellan shook his head at Samuel's question. He couldn't quite make out the words either. Maybe the man's translator wasn't working. But his hopes sank at the sight.

Four of his brother's roughest men held taut lead strings on an older man, the pilot from the looks of the gold ornamentation on his stark black uniform. The other survivors clustered in a tight circle a few feet away. Hakir's guards paid them little attention as they jeered the pilot on in his struggles.

"Why doesn't this guy give it up?" Samuel shook his head. "He can't get out of those leads. He's only going to hurt himself."

Deep slashes ran down both sleeves of the man's elegant uniform and Stellan soon saw why. While his tormentors laughed, the captive tugged at the restraints, the thin cord digging deeper into his flesh with every movement. Soon both the fabric and his arm would be shredded. Blood oozed from the lines already dug into his weathered skin. But the man continued to fight. His steel-gray hair cropped short in what had to be a regulation haircut, the man was built like a bull, short, stocky and every inch of him muscle. Enraged, he tugged again at the rigid steel strings.

"You'll not harm her!"

The man's translator must have finally kicked in. Still, the Edarian words seemed to grate in his throat, making the phrase difficult to discern through his accent. Not that his brother's men were listening. His shout only made the men laugh harder. Hakir's guards were a tough lot, Edarian born and bred, a fact that generally sparked terror in those poor victims who fell prey to his brothers' limited mercy. Stellan could've told the man his struggles would only amuse them more. Blood always stirred them and it had been a long time since they'd had the sport of a captive fighter to torment.

Before he could make any move to curb the situation, Stellan felt himself shoved forward, a dark blur rushing past him to get to Samuel. He bounced back onto his feet in time to see the blur land a stiff blow on Samuel's jaw, knocking the boy to the ground.

"Get your hands off her things, you little creep."

Stellan caught a quick glimpse of a lean golden-haired man struggling to rip something out of Samuel's hands before he ducked down low and went for the man's knees.

"Marco, watch out!"

Stellan heard the voice behind him, but the man had no time to react. Before he could turn, Stellan's blow knocked him off balance. He was on the ground with Stellan on top of him before he could make another move. Pinned in the dirt by Stellan's weight, the man still struggled.

Leaning in to hold the waving fist away from his face, Stellan glimpsed the piece of cloth the man had ripped from Samuel's grasp. It was the black silk robe. Distracted, Stellan reached for the garment. The man growled up at him.

"You keep your filthy hands off her."

Her who? Who was this female everyone kept referring to?

Stellan glared back down at him. "From the position you're in, my friend, it might be smarter if you kept your hands off my nephew."

Stellan leaned harder on the man's shoulders, frowning at the man's resistance. "Ease down, friend. You're not helping the situation any."

The man stilled but his look lost none of its malice. Stellan relaxed his hold a bit.

"I'm going to let you up and we're going to talk about this."

He pressed his knees hard into the man's ribs to emphasize his words. His efforts brought a groan. Carefully Stellan eased back, rolling onto his feet. Freed, the man leapt up and went for Stellan's throat before suddenly going limp. As he fell to the ground, Stellan stared up at Samuel, rock in hand.

"Guess he didn't want to talk, huh?"

Stellan rolled his eyes at the boy's grin. Samuel picked up the now disheveled robe.

"Shame though. Amalia would've really put out for something like this."

"Boy, if you don't get your mind off getting laid, you're gonna get us all in trouble."

Stellan resisted the urge to knock the grin off Samuel's face before he moved back to the jeering circle around the pilot. He motioned to two of the guards and gave them a curt order to keep their eye on the rest of the survivors. There would be hell to pay for their injuries. Best he break the party up now before anyone got killed. He stepped to his brother.

"We need to move off to the shelters before nightfall, Hakir. All these people will need to be fed and the amenities dealt with before then."

Hakir waved his hand at him, all of his focus on the man struggling with his guards. A grin covered his brother's hard features. Stellan leaned closer to him.

"What is this bunch all upset about?"

Martin laughed and clapped him on the shoulder. "These fine gentlemen of Adena seem to be rather upset over the dark-haired woman who is now entertaining Theran back at the shelter."

The words had their desired effect. The pilot raged forward, nearly cutting his arm in half with the lead strings.

"You'll not hurt her!"

"A woman? All of this is over a woman?" Stellan felt a sinking feeling in the pit of his stomach. He remembered the fancy quarters on the *Venetta*. Hell's bells, had the rich merchant brought his woman with him? He tried to focus around his growing sense that this whole situation was going to hell faster than a speeding starship.

"Why is Theran back entertaining a woman instead of helping with the rest?" Stellan kept his voice low so the man didn't hear and cut off his arm in his struggling.

Martin laughed again, the coarse sound of it carrying across the field along with his words.

"The bitch slapped him for a simple suggestion, so Hakir told him to take her somewhere private where he could explain the suggestion in detail."

Martin winked at his brother and Stellan stifled a groan. He shoved through the jeering men to reach the pilot, lifting his hand to ease the restraints. Hakir's shout stopped his movement.

"Hold, Stellan. The man is in those things for a reason." His brother turned the wicked smile to the pilot again. "And I am not done amusing my men just yet."

Stellan gave a reluctant nod then started to step back.

"He cannot harm her." The man tried to reach for him and winced. "He cannot."

"Easy, man. Be still before you take your arm off."

Stellan looked into the man's face. There was something curious about his struggles. He kept his voice low as he spoke. No sense inflaming Hakir anymore than necessary.

"Is the woman yours?"

The man hesitated for a moment then shook his head. His attitude made Stellan even more curious. The fellow could hardly be considered a coward due to his obvious intent to fight until he lost body parts, and there was no mistaking the concern in his eyes as well. Whoever the woman was, she was obviously important to him. Or important to his employer. It would be just his luck that Hakir insulted a noblewoman and not some lowly cook on the freighter.

"Of course she isn't his."

Stellan turned to find Martin sneering behind him. His brother stared at the man with malice, his words an obvious attempt to goad the poor struggling fool.

"She's way too pretty, way too elegant for the likes of this one. Definitely out of his league."

Martin roared with laughter as the man surged forward, hands fisted.

"Aye, easy." Hakir laughed. "She might take a liking to Theran. He can be quite attractive to a woman who's not known many real men."

Stellan turned to him in disgust. "And yet she slapped him? I would think it would take more charm than Theran has to change her mind."

"She tried to warn him." The pilot's voice brought him back around.

"Warn him? About what?" Stellan's eyes narrowed as his gaze turned back to the pilot.

The man hesitated. Stellan wondered what it was he seemed so reluctant to say.

"What's your name?"

The pilot looked at Stellan in surprise. "Malachi. Malachi Overton. I'm a pilot for Oderean Freight Lines."

"The *Venetta* was your ship?"

"No." The man hesitated, still obviously uneasy about giving out any information. "I mean, I pilot her, but I'm not the owner."

Hakir snorted. "Course he's not. The man is only a hired hand, Stellan. Why waste time talking to him?"

"Because our little brother likes to hear the sound of his own words." Martin waved a hand at Malachi. "But I have to agree with Hakir, Stellan. This one's a waste of time. I'm sure whoever does own the *Venetta* will already know what's happened to her. We'll be hearing from them shortly, so don't waste what time we have now with your words when we could be having so much more fun."

Stellan started to move back, but Malachi reached for his arm. The look in the man's eyes was wild with panic.

"She didn't want to hurt him. The slap was a warning."

Bells went off in Stellan's head. He knew, at least he thought he knew, if he had the story right, if all those crazy legends had a grain of truth to them. If they did, it could explain why the man fought so hard, what the warning might have been. With a jerk, he turned to Martin and Hakir.

"What color are this woman's eyes?"

Malachi started to protest, but Stellan cut him off with a wave of his hand. "Keep quiet, man. What color, Martin?"

"How the hell do I know?" Martin leered at him. "Wasn't her eyes we were looking at." He nudged Hakir, who gave a coarse laugh.

"Damn!" Stellan swore under his breath. "You didn't see if they were an, unusual color?"

"Like I said, that wasn't the part of her we were looking at. What's up, Stellan? You hoping to take her away from Theran by looking in her pretty little eyes and quoting some of your poetry?" Martin made kissing noises which made Hakir chuckle. "I think your pretty little verses would only make a woman built like that howl with laughter, whereas Theran's probably relieved her of those fancy clothes she's wearing and made her howl in a totally different way."

"He cannot!" Malachi struggled harder. "He cannot touch her."

Hakir crossed the distance in a heartbeat, anger mottling his face. With one hand he gripped the pilot's throat. "Why, are my men not good enough to touch the women of Adena? Is that what you're saying? Or are you afraid once she gets a taste of what a real man can do to her, she won't want to go back to the pasty faced excuses for men on Adena?"

He winked at Martin and the others as he squeezed Malachi's throat harder. The pilot's breath sputtered as he tried to talk. Hakir chuckled as he struggled, never loosening his grip on Malachi's throat. "That's it, isn't it, fellas? He's scared she'll want more of us." The men roared their approval.

Stellan's mind reeled with the thought that the legends could be true. He had to see the woman to be sure. According to the rumors, the virgins of the noble houses of Adena had most unusual eyes. Golden eyes. When they gave their virginity to a challenger their eyes would turn to their true color.

And if the rumors were true, Adenan virgins also came equipped with some kind of protective shield. If that were the case, the woman would kill Theran if he touched her. If Theran died, nothing would dissuade his brothers from taking out the rest of them and declaring war on the merchant when he came. And that would be all the incentive the Interstellar Council needed to come in and attack them. He had to act fast.

"Hakir, please take these people back to the shelters and keep them there. We need to talk about their ransom."

"And who do you think died and left you in charge, pipsqueak?"

"I'm just doing my job. You told me to handle the ransom end of things. And these folks," Stellan swept a hand around the ragged group. "They'll bring a good ransom, so long as they're still in one piece." He emphasized the last part as he stared at Malachi. "I'm going to go talk to Theran about the woman."

Uncertain, Malachi frowned at him then nodded.

Stellan took off at a run as Hakir called after him.

"I don't think Theran will appreciate the interruption, so don't come back here whining when he beats your stupid ass black and blue."

Stellan flashed an obscene gesture over his shoulder at his brother as he ran off in the direction of the shelter. He only hoped he wasn't too late.

Chapter Three

"Theran! Theran! Hold still now." The dimwit waved the rag in front of his friend, waiting for the moment to pounce.

Cardis eyed both men warily, keeping her guard up for any threatening movements. Instinct urged her to run, to hide in the pitiful shelter behind her or to flee as far and as fast as she could. But common sense told her the other one would follow. And the last thing she wanted was to see the shield come to life again. The whole scene was a horrifying visual in an ongoing nightmare. For a brief moment she wondered if she should close her eyes to see if it would all go away, if the hard-packed dirt clearing, the tumbledown shack and the snarling men would all be gone when she opened them again.

Theran was a big man, but he lay crumpled on the ground like a child. The bloody mess that had been his left arm lay not far from him. His screams tore at the remnants of Cardis' control.

The other man, Gundar, Theran had called him, alternated between glaring at her and comforting his friend. Though the bleeding stopped almost instantaneously after the shield took off his limb, the man kept pressing a filthy rag to Theran's shoulder. From what Cardis could tell, his friend's ministrations hurt as much as his injury. Theran thrashed from side to side, making Gundar have to wave the cloth around to catch him after each movement. Then he'd press hard against the wound and Theran would howl and thrash again. Cardis thought the pair of them would've been comical had the circumstances been different.

"Ah, Gundar, Gundar." Theran's good hand gripped his friend's shirt. "Help me. My arm. It's gone."

"I know, buddy. Lie still. I'm gonna take care of you."

Gundar leaned over and pressed the rag against the bloody stump. Theran's wails hit new heights.

"I don't think you should..."

Cardis bit off her words as Gundar threw down the rag and moved toward her with a growl. She pressed her back into the rough wood of the shelter and braced herself for what would happen.

"You don't think what, bitch? Do you know what I think? I think you should pay for this, here and now."

He stepped closer, hands reaching for her throat and teeth bared. Cardis felt the shield come to the surface, waiting. She closed her eyes, not wanting to watch another man be ripped apart.

"Gundar!"

The deep voice rumbled across the clearing. Startled, Cardis opened her eyes. Gundar stood frozen in front of her, hatred etched on his face. The voice rumbled again. Whoever it was, he was no lackey, for the voice held absolute command.

"Step away from her, Gundar."

Curious, Cardis gazed over toward the sound, wondering what new monster now crossed her path. She opened her mouth to warn them both then she caught a look at him. And her tongue froze to the roof of her mouth.

Holy stars in orbit, who are you?

Cardis thought she might melt where she stood. If she'd wanted to run before it was nothing compared to the need for speed flooding her now. The man who stood before her sent her danger meter into the 'just fry me and leave the ashes' zone. And he proved danger came in a more than attractive package. This man went beyond handsome. Being a virgin didn't mean Cardis had never appreciated a man's body before, but this body went above average on the appreciation meter. Like a primitive work of art from some erotic artist.

He wore the same rough fabric as the others but the simple black vest stretched across his shoulders left his muscled biceps and broad chest open to view. And the view was nice. Golden hairs sprinkled across his bronzed abs, a line of them tapering down to his waist to disappear beneath the dark material banding his hips.

His trousers were skin of some sort, giving her a shiver at a sudden erotic image of hunter and prey. They stretched over parts of him that didn't look safe at all. He was taller than her, lean and muscled in a way that told her he might not go down as easily as the other one. Gold hair with streaks of earth brown fell to his shoulders and framed his chiseled face. Skin burnt dark from the harsh Edarian suns covered high cheekbones and set off the vivid green of his eyes.

Cardis put her unusual reaction to the sight of him down to the emotional turmoil of the whole situation. Doubtless her entire nervous system had taken a beating nearly as damaging as the one the *Venetta* suffered. She felt completely out of control, a loss she detested. Even the shield that protected her seemed to operate on its own.

Taking the other thug's arm off hadn't taken conscious effort. The brute touched her and she felt a power surge under her skin. Cardis had only a moment to guide the force of it before the man burst into screams. Before she knew it, the man lay writhing on the ground with his arm tucked there beside him.

Another rumble of the stranger's deep voice captured her wayward thoughts before her fear could overwhelm her.

"Back away from her, Gundar. Now. See to Theran."

"Don't try and stop me, Stellan. The bitch ripped his arm clean off. He went to touch her and she ripped his arm off! Now I'm gonna rip a few things off of her." Gundar's face contorted with his hatred.

The man continued to cross the clearing, still staring at Gundar. "Think, man. She ripped his arm off for touching her. Do you get that?"

The stranger moved to stand between the two of them and Cardis swore the temperature of the very air around her rose. She was thankful he kept his attention on Gundar so he couldn't notice her starting to sweat. Getting out of this one's clutches would take some serious bluffing. The man stepped toward Gundar, backing him up a little.

"So what do you think she'll do to you? Do you think she'll just stand there and let you rip her apart?"

Gundar stared at her around the man's broad shoulder. Cardis could almost see his small mind trying to process that little tidbit. Best start bluffing now, just in case the cretin had more thinking capacity than she gave him credit for. Cardis folded her arms across her chest and gave him a smile.

"You'd do well to listen to him, for the next time I'm assaulted I may choose to rip off something besides an arm." Her stare dropped to his groin. "My mother always told me to start with a limb, then work my way down. It gives a foolish man time to reconsider his intentions."

Both men stared at her as if she'd grown two heads and shot flames out her nose. Perhaps she'd taken this bluffing thing a little too far. But then again, she didn't really know what her shield could do. Cardis kept the smooth smile on her face, hoping her luck would last. Finally Gundar took a step back, but not before giving her a look that promised dire retribution.

"I'll step aside, but you'd best see to her, Stellan. Hakir won't take the bitch maiming one of his men lightly."

With an oath, Gundar turned back and knelt by his friend. Muttering to himself, he picked up the rag and, without even shaking the dirt off, jammed it against Theran's shoulder. Cardis gritted her teeth as the man's screams started up again. Then she turned her attention to her newest problem.

She opted for talk. That should keep her tongue from cleaving to the roof of her mouth again. With her best haughty sneer, she looked him up and down.

"So, one of you lowlifes is capable of caution."

She gave the man her most pleasant smile. Unfortunately, she also looked him in the face. Those wild eyes pierced her with a look meant to terrify her into submission though he made no move to touch her. Instead the deep green pools tried to suck her into them. The musky scent of his skin now that he was so close to her only added to the danger she sensed in him. Everything about this man invaded her personal space. *Who in the known worlds was he?*

Gazing around him, Stellan felt his chances for stopping a war fade with each passing moment. Theran set up another round of wails and Stellan grimaced.

"Gundar, see to Theran and his, uh, wound. And make him stop that noise. Take him to Repatria."

At his words, Theran sent up an even louder round of screams

"The old witch might fix his arm, but likely that won't stop his wailing," Gundar grumbled as he lifted his wailing friend. "Hakir isn't going to like this. You know he isn't. Theran's his captain. He'll want the bitch to pay." He glared back at the woman.

Stellan couldn't argue with the truth of that statement. Hakir would want revenge, payment in kind. And the likely object of his vengeance was exactly the person Stellan wanted to make sure stayed in one piece. The one person they couldn't afford to harm. And, if the rumors of Adena's virgins were true, the one person who offered him hope.

"Just get him out of here." He waved Gundar off with one hand, thankful when the earsplitting wails dimmed.

"Your, um, medical facility can likely give him something for the pain, right?"

Her voice was strong and clear, the rich accent of Adena peppering her words. Stellan turned his gaze to rest on the object of his inner struggles, who stood, arms folded, in the doorway of Hakir's shelter. The look had his mouth watering. If ever there was a woman to travel the stars with, this was the woman.

Tall and slender, she carried herself like a queen. Definitely nobility. That was one question answered. This was no lowly freighter cook. He bested her height by maybe three or four inches, but she stared him down like a woman used to being protected. Or a woman with a magic shield. Guess that kind of accessory gave a woman a whole different outlook on men.

In spite of himself, Stellan couldn't stop staring at her. To his surprise, she wore sturdy trousers and a fitted top rather than the shapeless gown most of the women he knew wore. Even dressed like a man, she was the most beautiful woman he had ever seen. And her outfit allowed him to see quite a bit. With her arms folded across her chest, the emerald green top did little to hide the bounty of her breasts. They were quite full and pulled the shiny fabric taut. More than a mouthful, Stellan thought.

He dropped his gaze from her ample chest but that did little to slow down the lust stirring inside him. Her short top tucked in at the bottom to accent the curve of her waist. The trousers hugged her shapely hips as if they were tailored to her figure. The rich brown fabric flowed down her long legs all the way to her heavy black leather boots. Stellan nearly laughed when he glanced down at them. Her feet were almost as big as his own. It appeared there was nothing delicate or fragile about this princess.

He'd held off looking at her face until he'd feasted on the sight of the rest of her. Her face held the answer he looked for and Stellan wanted to enjoy the view as much as he could should her eyes puncture his dream and turn out to be some ordinary color. The rest of her was magnificent. Now if only her eyes held the opportunity he prayed for.

His first glance at her face had him praying harder. Her features were strong and well defined, as if carved by a great artist. High cheekbones and full red lips accented her creamy ivory skin. Short black hair spiked around the edges of her oval face. And right in the center were her eyes. Her golden eyes. From the sparks shooting out of those gold pools, Stellan could tell his inspection didn't sit well with her.

"Yoo-hoo, did you understand me?" The woman waved a hand in front of his face. "This thing worked for the other one." She tapped a finger against her ear where the tiny translator lay.

When he managed to tear his thoughts off the lower parts of his body and what they were screaming for, Stellan remembered her question. He stepped closer to her and folded his own arms across his chest.

"Why the concern, princess? Did his screams bother you? Of course, considering you're the source of those screams, it doesn't surprise me you're worried about him."

For a moment Stellan thought he saw concern on her face, but she quickly masked her expression and shrugged her shoulders.

"He was warned. The consequences of his actions are his own."

"But now you're worried about him. That's almost

touching."

She scowled at him. "Not at all. In my opinion, he's a thug who got less than he deserved. I merely thought, since he is your friend, that you would care about his welfare. And I didn't mean to offend with my suggestion, if perhaps you have a faith healer of some sort rather than a medical facility."

He saw the distaste in her expression. It was the same old story every time. Even fear didn't overcome snobbery.

"You mean some sort of backward tribal shaman who would make strange noises over him and shake branches in his face so the ignorant savages would believe the gods were appeased and his shoulder would reattach to his arm?"

The woman rolled her eyes then turned away. She gave the picture of supreme indifference standing next to the primitive wood and stone shelter, an indifference he might have believed were it not for the smoldering fury of her expression. In spite of being angry at her words and her attitude, Stellan found the contrast intriguing. What other kinds of heat lay behind that chilled sneer? And what would it take to break her control of that passion? Never one to back away from a challenge, Stellan felt a sudden urge to prick that cool exterior.

"But maybe you didn't mean to be nasty. I'm willing to give you the benefit of the doubt on that."

Her sneer deepened. "Really? How magnanimous of you."

"Just being considerate under the circumstances. After all, I suppose this whole place must seem strange to you, princess. Definitely different than what you're used to. But you know what's strange to me, darling?"

"I'd prefer you didn't use the little endearments if you want to talk to me."

He laughed. "Sure thing, princess. But you haven't given me your name yet, so I don't know who to address my questions to."

Cardis struggled against the surge of annoyance growing inside her. Part of her wanted to wipe that smarmy look off that handsome face, but that would involve touching that bronzed skin. Touching him didn't seem like a good idea. She needed to watch her step with this one.

"No, I haven't, have I. Not that it's necessary for us to be on a first name basis. Really, the only question you should have for me is whom should you contact to make arrangements to return me and my people to our home. You do have some form of communication in this place, don't you?"

"Yeah, princess. We yell real loud."

"How civilized. I should have expected that was the way things were done in such an advanced society as this."

"Glad I could help you appreciate the culture here, darling."

"And it's such a unique culture too. Little wonder I didn't know what to expect. Silly me, I've been dealing with all those other poor places where it's a simple matter for the local authorities to contact the Interstellar Council and arrange our return."

"You crash a lot of places, do you, princess?"

"That's not what I meant." Cardis gritted her teeth and smiled pleasantly. She was not going to lose control in front of this barbarian. "If there was some way you could contact the Council..."

She gave him a meaningful stare as her voice trailed off. Surely the imbecile would pick up on her constant mention of the Interstellar Council. Cardis often heard her father and the other merchants complain about the losses they suffered at the hands of the barbaric Edarians, who treated any intrusion into their world as an excuse to rob and plunder. The merchants had finally gotten the Council to issue a strong enough threat, or so they thought, after the last time a vessel was lost. That time only half the crew had been returned and none of the cargo. And the stories they told had made the Merchants Association furious. Cardis hoped the threat was as good as her father believed it to be. It might be their only hope of getting out of this mess. Her hope dimmed a little when the man shrugged.

"Well, maybe later we can get around to that. But first I need to get a little information. We can start with your name."

"My name?"

"For a start. Then we'll talk about my other question, namely how a pretty little thing like you managed to get a big old hulk like Theran down on the ground."

Now there was a topic she didn't want to discuss. At least not with him. Cardis focused her sneer somewhere below his chin, somewhere she hoped would be safe.

"And who are you? I don't want to be wasting my time with some underling who's merely trying to satisfy his curiosity. You've seen how I feel about too much curiosity."

Stellan snorted. "I don't have a lot of time to waste either, princess, and, though you may not realize it, neither do you. If you don't want to talk to me, then my brothers will be here momentarily. You remember them, the men who sent you back here with Theran for a little R&R while they finished up with the rest of your crew. I've sent Gundar back and he will get the word to them as to how your playtime turned out. It's always a tough choice for Hakir, ransom or revenge."

The implication hung in the air, shaking Cardis to the bone as her translator interpreted the guttural sounds of his Edarian dialect. The impact of the crash shocked her, but it was nothing compared to the sight of her people rounded up like cattle, even the wounded herded into pens without so much care as one would give an animal.

"So it would help, princess, if you'd explain to me how you bested Theran without working up a sweat."

He let his words hang in the air between them like a challenge, making sure to keep a careful distance between them as he paced in front of her.

The woman followed him with her cautious stare, never dropping her defensive stance. Like a wounded animal she watched him, ready to pounce at the slightest threat. Well, he had handled many a high-strung creature in his time. Perhaps a high-strung woman wouldn't be so different. He gentled his voice as he moved to her.

She dropped her arms, her hands curled into fists. Her posture moved from haughty to defensive in an instant and her stance spoke of some training. Maybe Adena's women defended their men as well as choosing their own mates.

Beneath all her bravado however, Stellan sensed nervousness, and a hint of fear. Yet she faced him like a warrior, not like the timid females he knew. For some reason that stirred him, aroused him. He must be in more need of relief than he'd thought. As he watched her, his thoughts strayed to how those dark curls would feel against his skin, how she would feel against him, under him. A nagging voice in his head told him a woman like this was not meant for a casual coupling or a single night of pleasure. The Adenan legends referred to the virgins as the golden prize. And a prize was meant to be kept.

The image of the room on board the *Venetta* struck him. He could picture himself there, with her. The thought surprised him. He'd never felt any great yen to have a family of his own, to take on that responsibility. No woman had ever tugged at his heart or at his need enough for him to consider yoking himself to her.

Yet the thought of having this woman and all that went with her, a woman who knew and rode among the stars, appealed to him. As did the thought of getting his hands on her body. If he took the stories he'd heard to be truth and accepted the risk she presented, he would have a chance to know the feel of that flawless skin, to see all the beauty hidden beneath her warrior clothing. The honeyed scent from the room on the freighter came back to him and he wondered if the risk might be worth it to have that smell on his skin, to have the chance to keep the kind of wealth and power she represented. It meant risking everything, including his life. Could one woman be worth that much?

Knowing he'd best get to the business at hand before his body took over and he ended up like Theran, Stellan stepped closer to the woman.

"Now back to my questions, princess."

"Cardis."

"What?"

"My name is Cardis. My father owns the *Venetta*. And I'm not a princess."

"Lady Cardis." He gave her a mock bow. "Let me bid you a warm welcome. May your stay here on Edaria be pleasant and...interesting."

"And brief. You forgot brief. And it's just Cardis. There is no title attached to it."

"Ah, Adena's nobility goes for the common touch, I see."

"Nobility? No, I told you, I'm only the daughter of a merchant, a poor businessman trying to earn a living for his family in an honest manner."

"A poor but honest woman whom the men on board the *Venetta* were willing to take a beating for. Funny, I didn't notice your friend Marco tackling Hakir's guard for any of the other women who were being threatened, didn't see your pilot, Malachi, I believe his name was, ready to rip his own arm off to save any other woman on board the *Venetta*."

At his words, the image of Malachi's beaten face floated before Cardis. He'd tried to protect her, to keep the brutes from hauling her off for sport as they had two of the other women on board. Part of her wanted to tell this stranger it wasn't out of some awe for her station they'd risked themselves. He and Marco feared what would happen to the rest of them should one of the brutes attack her and die from the force of her shield. Cardis hadn't really understood the power the shield wielded but they must have. Seeing the magic burst to life had been an impressive first lesson.

"They are honorable men, who felt they owed my father the job of protecting me. I am Cardis Oderean, just a merchant's daughter, no more."

"Very well then, Just Cardis, I'm Stellan, youngest son to Angus Tolten, the late headman of this province and brother to Hakir, his heir and new headman, which makes him leader to the barbarian horde that ravaged your freighter."

Cardis snorted. "Such a lineage is hardly something to boast of."

"Oh, it's not a boast, Just Cardis. It's a warning. Best you deal with me than with them, especially once they see what you've done to Theran."

"As I said, my father is an honorable man. He would expect fair treatment for his crew under such circumstances as these. No matter how barbaric your customs, attacking a lone woman, let alone his daughter, would be something he would not expect nor would he forgive such an offense."

Stellan arched a brow. "And he has the clout to retaliate, I take it. Hardly the kind of power a poor but honest businessman would wield."

Damn the man. He was smarter than he looked. "Had anything more happened, my father would turn to the Council for recompense. The Council protects its people. Your brothers should be grateful for my warning to their man. I could've done worse."

"Then I would give you a warning, Cardis. My brothers will not share your judgment on this little incident with Theran. Believe me, gratitude for your restraint isn't even in the realm of possibility."

"And they will take their anger out on me, even with the threat of retaliation by my father and the Council?"

"On you, and on your people. Something tells me your pilot and some of his crew would not deal well with what might happen to you. Any resistance on their part, even in defense of you, and they will suffer for it. Dealing with me is the best option you have at this point. So there isn't much time for you and me to talk this out. As I said, my brothers will be here shortly. No magic tricks will save you from them then, for they will not give you the opportunity to use them."

"Magic tricks? I don't think your friend would see what happened as a trick. It was a warning, as I've told you. And besides, what do you know of magic?" She glanced around her with obvious disdain. "Although I suppose magic is what suspicious little minds believe of things they cannot comprehend. Things such as a woman defending herself from a brute who wanted to get his jollies by raping her. This barren wilderness boasts not even the slightest amenities nor the most basic of technology. The smallest trick would seem like magic in this place."

Stellan shrugged. "Maybe I spoke from more knowledge than you give me credit for."

Cardis rolled her eyes. "I doubt that."

He stepped closer and the invasion sent Cardis' danger meter spiraling. His voice was low and guttural when he spoke, tingling along her skin.

"Maybe I know things you don't want me to know. Things you would keep secret because they would put you at risk."

She tried to shake off the strange feeling his nearness sent through her. "I can't see how I'd be more at risk than I am now. The savagery this place is synonymous with is used to terrify small children throughout the known realms. What could you possibly know that would change my situation to a more risky one?"

He circled her, a slow, casual inspection that heated her even from a distance.

"For one thing, I know where you come from."

Determined to find her usual control, Cardis glared at him. "Now that wouldn't take a great deal of intelligence, nor is it hardly any great news flash. Our freighter bore Adena's emblem as well as my father's insignia, so you wouldn't even need to be able to read to understand that much."

She returned the long look of inspection, ending with a sneer as her gaze landed again on his face. "Although it may have gone better for you if you could claim not to know the owner or where we came from."

He smiled. Tired of dealing with her frazzled nerves and his obvious attempt to intimidate her, Cardis stepped toward him and poked a finger in his chest.

"As a matter of fact, my dear lowlife, it would be better for you to slobber and drool and pretend you know nothing, for my father will come for us. And that is something you should be very worried about. He will already know what has happened here and he does not look kindly on thieves and brigands. Our distress signal had time to reach him before our vessel crashed, so he would also know our coordinates. Your little wilderness is not prepared to deal with what he and the Interstellar Council will do if all of our people and our cargo are not released immediately."

Taking a step back, she gave him a smug smile.

Against his will, Stellan admired her. She looked magnificent, all righteous indignation and outrage. Her breasts heaved against the fabric of her top, stretching it tight across with a view that made his mouth water as he thought of the peaks of her nipples under the shiny cloth, thought of taking those breasts in his mouth to taste that honey sweetness he could still smell. A perverse part of him wanted very much to turn that smug look into the glazed look of satisfaction. To make her moan with the feel of his hands on that tight lithe body. And if he had the story right, the Virgin Challenge was all about exactly that.

From the reaction of his body to the thought of touching her, seducing her wouldn't be a hardship. That part of the challenge held definite appeal. And sex was an area where his confidence was high. Those two thoughts made the risk more palatable. Now to get the issue settled before his brothers arrived.

Stellan stepped back and leaned against the railing in front of the shelter. He smiled at her as he looked her up and down once more.

"I also know what you are."

"What I am? You mean, a way for you to extort more money from an honest merchant? A way for you and those cretins you call brothers to make yourselves rich off the labor and industry of others?"

"Well, that might be open for debate, but for now we'll focus on the answer I've come up with about you. You're a different sort of woman, princess."

"Different?"

"Yeah. What happened here tells me that. I come back here to make sure you're okay and to my surprise I find it's Theran I need to rescue."

"Surprise? You allow this ruffian to carry me off to a shack far away from all the others and you're surprised to find I defended myself?"

"Well now, I do apologize for the poor surroundings. I'm sure they're much less than you're used to. This shelter is one we use on those occasions when some errant freighter manages to land here."

She snorted. "You're worried about the surroundings?

Stellan shrugged as if she'd captured his meaning. Though he'd teased her, he'd heard enough about Adena to know a building such as this one probably wouldn't even be used by their animals. Likely this woman had never even been near a shelter so rough. She probably rated the whole place as primitive, people and buildings included.

He stared at the building behind her, trying to see the place as she would. The structure provided shelter for basic survival and little more, its weathered exterior covering an interior that boasted a fireplace, a solid roof and minimal toilet facilities. Not that any of their homes provided many more amenities. His brother's scorn for technology kept life pretty hard for all of them. But the elegant woman in front of him didn't need to know that.

He pushed away from the fence, moving toward her again. She tensed, but kept still.

"But as to just defending yourself, I think what happened here is a little more than that."

"Really?"

Stellan raked his gaze up and down her as he circled around her. Convincing her of her dire circumstances would go a long way to aiding him in making the challenge.

"Yeah, really. I'm going to take a step closer to you, but it's not a threat, so you can relax."

"Relax? I hardly think so." She raised her hands just a bit. "And we can talk from a distance so there's no need for you to come any closer."

"You'd do better to remember you don't control this situation, princess. This is my territory, not yours, and what I need is for me to determine, not you."

She arched a dark brow at him. "You say something like that after saying you want me to relax?"

He gave her a hard look. "I don't want to lose any body parts because you misinterpreted my intentions."

"I believe you people have made your intentions perfectly clear since you responded to our misfortune by taking us captive instead of helping us."

"Edaria has faced a number of threats recently from those outside her borders. We've grown cautious when dealing with outsiders."

"Cautious? You mean greedy."

"Whatever. But right now I want a better look at your face so I'm going to step closer."

"My face? Why do you need to get closer to look at my face when you can see it from where you are? I thought you said you know what I am. So we don't need to get better acquainted." She stepped back from him.

Stellan ignored her words and took another step toward her. Sunlight played across her features, illuminating her golden eyes until they glowed against her creamy skin. He found the sight fascinating. Her obvious annoyance at his continued staring fascinated him as well. She looked like she wanted to rip a piece off of him, but he knew her shield wouldn't harm him unless he attacked her.

"We need to talk. I have some questions I want answers to. Answers that will help me decide how best to help you out of your little, um, situation."

"Situation?" She tapped her foot impatiently. "I'd call it a little more than a situation."

The sight of Theran's missing shoulder kept Stellan's movements slow and careful, his voice calm. But he knew he didn't have much time. Gundar would take the word to Hakir that his man was injured. Once his brothers arrived, there would be no chance to talk to the woman. He had to make a decision and quickly. Could he base his future on a legend?

"Perhaps you'd rather I refer to it as a challenge?"

Chapter Four

"A challenge?"

Cardis echoed his words, her heart in her throat. She thought she spotted a flash of something in those wild green eyes, a kind of satisfaction at her reaction to his statement. But that was ridiculous. There was no way this barbarian could know anything about the Virgin Challenge. Edaria didn't communicate with the rest of the realm. *Did they?* The smile he gave her wasn't reassuring at all.

"Does that word bother you, princess? I would think it's a word you've grown used to." He circled her, the heat on his face burning its way across her skin. By the time he made it back around to face her, Cardis felt singed. Then he gave her that smile again and her brain melted.

"A woman like you, one who rides around the stars in that fancy ship of your father's. Why, I bet you've traveled more places than lots of your own people. Surely you've faced other challenges before."

Was it just her imagination that he emphasized the word challenge? Cardis tossed her head and tried to look somewhere beyond his shoulder. If she could focus her wayward thoughts on open space, maybe the sight of him wouldn't freeze her brain cells. And if there were just a few of those cells left working, her words would come out coherent. She plastered her best bored look on her face.

"Of course I've dealt with other difficulties in other situations. And those difficulties could indeed be considered challenges." She tried to let the word slide out of her mouth as if it were totally unimportant. "But you must know Edaria is, um, unique. There aren't many places as backward as your home."

He chuckled. *Didn't he realize she was insulting him?*

"I don't think we've exactly put our best foot forward during your visit here, princess. I'd like to think there's a way to make amends for that oversight."

"Really?" Cardis' hopes jumped. Maybe the barbarian was going to help her. "Does that mean you're willing to contact my father immediately and arrange transport off this rock for me and my people?"

She folded her arms across her chest and glared at him. This time he laughed outright.

"Take it down a notch, darling. You don't have to play the queen with me. I'm already convinced, remember?" He shrugged. "But whether or not your cargo is returned isn't up to me. That would be Hakir's decision. And he's gonna be pretty pissed about what happened to Theran. So you and I need to do some negotiating before he gets here or else things are gonna get really ugly really quick."

"Look, I'm fed up with being bullied." Her hopes dashed, Cardis threaded her fingers through her short curls. *Why couldn't she get control of this situation?*

"Bullied?" He gave her a quizzical look.

"Yes, bullied. You're not as direct as that one," she pointed off in the direction Gundar and Theran had taken, "since you come at me with words instead of your fists. Or perhaps you have more attachment to your limbs than they did."

"As you said, I'm a lowlife capable of caution."

"Whatever. The result's the same. First that ignorant brother of yours allows that thug Theran to come back here with the intention of doing no telling what to me. Then you come along claiming to want to rescue me from a situation I never should have been in, in the first place.

"And you don't want to be rescued?"

He leaned back against the railing again with an air of calm that tore at Cardis' control.

"What rescue? All you've done so far is tell me how badly things will go for me if I don't cooperate with you. Well you know what? I don't cooperate with thugs, no matter what weapon they use."

"Seems to me all I've done so far is to ask you for some answers."

Cardis couldn't stem the low growl in her throat. *Was the man really that obtuse?* "For answers to questions

41

with no relevance to my current situation."

"Why don't you let me be the judge of how relevant my questions are?"

Cardis stared at the man standing before her. No matter how much she wanted to hate him, no matter how frustrated he made her, she had to admit it wasn't a hardship to look at him. Why in all the known worlds she would be attracted to some hardheaded backward barbarian with a fast tongue was beyond her. And even if he did look good enough to lick, how did that help her? Being attractive wasn't enough reason to consider someone trustworthy.

Still she had little else to go on and very much to lose. Maybe the barbarian wasn't lying and he meant to help her. At least he hadn't tried to attack her or threaten her with lurid remarks about what he would do to her once he got her trousers off. And he had driven off the thug and his sidekick. What did she have to lose by listening to him? She needed to learn the measure of this man, of what he might be capable of doing to her and for her.

"I suppose that means you have more irrelevant questions for me. You do seem to like to hear yourself talk."

"I've been told that before."

The man must really have a thick skin for he seemed unoffended by her words. He took a step toward her and she lifted her hands warily.

Her gaze caught his again and she couldn't stop staring at his eyes. The way they pulled at her surprised her, as if they called to her to come on some adventure that would take her to places like she'd never seen. Her mother constantly reprimanded her for the way she courted danger. Cardis thought she best keep those warnings in mind, for when she looked at the man standing before her she swore she heard danger calling her name.

Maybe it was the sound of her mother's voice in her ears or maybe it was her fear returning, but Cardis reined in her careless thoughts. All of her people were in a dangerous, life or death situation. Now was not the time to gamble with any of their safety because some good-looking rogue gave her a 'come fly with me baby' look. Best to remember this rogue didn't play fair. He continued to move toward her and all her senses went on alert.

"Let me see your arm."

"First my face, now my arm. What are you doing, putting a value on me one piece at a time?"

As soon as the words were out of her mouth, Cardis regretted them. Maybe the savage was going to give her back to her father one piece at a time.

He held up both hands to make it obvious he wasn't threatening her. "Take it easy, now."

"I would rather not be touched."

"And I would rather have my questions answered before my brothers arrive."

The reminder wasn't really what Cardis wanted to hear. With what she hoped was a look of complete indifference, she extended her arm, letting him grasp it with his hand. His skin was warm, heated by the sun, but his fingers were rough and they scraped along her skin as he slid her sleeve back from her wrist. The sensation sent a tingle through her.

Stellan watched her face as he tugged the sleeve back. He didn't want to relax and end up minus an arm or worse. She bit her lip, but allowed the touch. Stellan felt the slight tremble and wondered if it came from her or from him. The feel of her skin against his made him feel shaky. He told himself it was only the thought of what she could mean to his life, to his future. His gaze trailed down her arm to her wrist. What he saw there brought a smile to his face.

Cardis tried to tug her arm away but he held on tight. His fingers traced the outline of the small tattoo, the tiny crossed swords giving him proof of her connection to Adena's noble families. Paired with her golden eyes, it was all the evidence he needed to stake his challenge on. For the first time in years, hope rose in Stellan. Keeping his hand on her arm, he looked up into her face.

"And I know what you are."

Stellan knew he repeated himself, but his mind reeled at the idea that the legend could be true. Standing before him could be his way out of the dead-end future that awaited him on Edaria. Standing before him could be the beginning of a whole new life. Stellan tipped her chin up with one hand and stared at her eyes. Her golden eyes. Could it really be true? Could fortune have smiled on him this way?

Cardis jerked her chin from his grasp.

"Don't touch me. I told you I'd rather not be touched."

She took a step back, her voice clipped and cold as she viewed him with a disdain that made Stellan want to smile. If only the woman knew how he really wanted to touch her. Bet her princess to peasant demeanor would freak at the thoughts going through his head at this moment. Her lip curled as she started to speak to him, making him hope telepathy wasn't a tool the Adenans had mastered. He had to live long enough to make his challenge.

"You are fortunate my control is good enough that you are not missing a body part as well. My patience has already been sorely tested."

He laughed. Stellan felt something free itself inside of him and he knew it was hope. There could be no doubt she was of Adena's royal house. None other than a princess could be so arrogant. And that fact gave him hope that the rest was true as well. He felt like shouting, but he kept his voice even and calm. No sense scaring her off before he had the chance to make his challenge. But poking at her might be sort of fun. He shook his finger at her as if she were a naughty child, rewarded by the outraged scowl on her face.

"No, my prize, you can't rip any of my parts off just yet."

Cardis' eyes narrowed at his words and she took another step back. Stellan stepped closer.

"I haven't done anything to threaten you, Cardis, and you can't use your magic shield unless you're threatened. I told you I knew things about you. And about the force you used to rip Theran up. Only if faced with an attacker will the magic reach out and protect you. Not when faced with a lover. Or a potential lover. I believe that's the way the challenge works, isn't it?"

A deep red blush covered her cheeks at his words, a reaction Stellan found oddly charming. And revealing.

Only a virgin would find such a mild statement cause for blushing. At any rate, it put her at a loss for words.

Besides," Stellan brushed by her, letting his hand trail down her wrist, wanting to touch that flawless skin before she moved away. It felt soft and silky against his roughened fingers. "I'm willing to wager you'll find my parts offer you more if they are still attached to me. And in working order."

Stellan leaned his face close to her hair and breathed in the scent of her. She jerked back from him.

"Don't sniff me either. Why do you have to be so close to me?"

Cardis wished he would back up and let her breathe. Maybe if more oxygen got to her brain, it would begin to work again. Or at least put out more intelligent thoughts than yummy. The only impulse it radiated now was the urge to take her tongue and lick along the stubbled line of his jaw. If the man tasted half as good as he looked, she could stave off hunger for months.

"I don't know, princess. Just some weird impulse." With a smile he stroked a hand through the short black curls. "And, being an impulsive kind of guy, I decided to follow it."

As he dropped his arm, his fingers brushed her breast and she trembled. She scowled at him, but all he did was chuckle.

"I told you my parts would offer more if they stayed attached."

She glanced down at his groin and sneered.

"Your parts hold no interest for me."

"Liar."

The word echoed like a challenge in the air as he circled her, his confident grin widening as Cardis stared at him.

"Excuse me?"

Cardis felt sure she hadn't heard him correctly. Her brain no longer appeared in working order for the ruffian standing in front of her didn't compute at all. Everything that had happened, everything she knew about this godforsaken place and the people who inhabited it told her she should keep her distance from any and all of them and run like hell at the first opportunity.

Yet her brain froze as she stared at him. It issued no commands to her feet to flee, offered no start button for her shield so she could protect herself from, well, from having to stare at him, something she sensed should register high on the virgin danger meter. Thankfully, she couldn't lose her virginity through what she was thinking. The man would have to touch a whole lot more of her than he had so far and that would never happen. Cardis had a fleeting moment of disappointment at the thought. Further proof her brain had died.

"What part didn't you understand, princess? Tell me and I'll be glad to repeat it."

"Never mind. Best you step back or I might misinterpret your intentions and you lose one of those body parts you seem so proud of."

"Oh, I don't think you misinterpreted my intentions at all, princess. I think you got the message loud and clear. And the message was mutual. That's why I'm still intact. Like I said, there are rules that go along with your magic shield."

"What does one of your kind know of my magic shield?" Cardis clamped her mouth shut quickly and Stellan chuckled. She glared at him. "Again with your suspicious rambling about magic. Little more than one would expect from such a backward place and a backward people."

"Too late, Cardis, you've already given me the truth I needed. By your own admission you have the magic shield that is talked about as the possession of Adena's virgins. Did you truly expect me to believe you ripped Theran apart by sheer force?"

"Your kind might believe anything. Edaria isn't known for its high intellectual culture." Cardis shrugged, hoping the words pricked some of the confidence from his grin. "And Adenan women are trained in all forms of protective arts, including the use of weaponry," she added smugly. "We can take care of ourselves."

"So your men don't have to?"

"Our men don't have egos so fragile that women have to appear helpless to make them feel strong." *Take that, you barbarian.* Cardis smirked at him, sure her brain would unfreeze any second now.

46

He laughed. "Sweetheart, all men have egos that enjoy being stroked by a beautiful woman. No amount of civilization changes that."

Cardis gritted her teeth in frustration. "Let's go back to your babbling. For the sake of argument, I'll agree that I didn't hurt your friend by brute force. Not that he didn't deserve what he got."

Stellan stepped away from her and Cardis let out the breath she'd been holding. But her reprieve was short-lived. With an easy movement of his hips that had her riveted to the lower half of his body, Stellan seated himself on the low stone wall in front of the shelter. She felt a strange dampness in a spot of her body she'd rather not think about.

He folded his arms across his chest as if he hadn't a care in the world. His gaze wandered insolently over her. The look on her face told him it annoyed her and for some reason that amused him.

"Okay, for the sake of argument, I'll agree with you. Cute as your muscles are, I don't think they're what you used to protect yourself."

He chuckled at her growl. Poking at this woman would be fun, even if dangerous fun. And it had been a long time since he'd done anything really fun.

"You see, the stories I've heard about Adenan virgins are much more complicated than that. Like I told you before, I know a great deal about you, princess."

"Obviously not, for I'm not a princess. I believe I already told you that. Perhaps it was too much information for your small mind to remember. I'll try again. My father is a merchant, a simple businessman." Cardis enunciated each word carefully.

"From Adena. A noble merchant. And you, princess, are from a noble house. A noble house of Adena."

"I give up. Believe what you will. Since you've made it a point to tell me how little time we have to discuss how you're going to help me and my people, I suppose you're going somewhere with all this chatter. Unless you just like hearing the sound of your own voice and your offer of help was an empty boast that would let you rattle on for a while."

"Oh, indeed, I am going somewhere with it. Maybe

even places I've only dreamed about until now. For there's more to this story I've heard about the women of the noble houses of Adena. A part I listened to with a great deal of wonder."

"Really? I would think a grown man no longer listened to stories. Perhaps the men of Adena don't prolong their childhood the way your kind does."

"Well, princess, this story is definitely not for the young ones. This is a story of Adena's virgins. And of what a man gains if he deflowers them."

He pushed off from the wall, perversely delighted by the wary look she gave him as he walked toward her.

"You see, this story says that if a man gains the virginity of a woman from Adena, he gains her wealth and her lineage as well. An Adena virgin is referred to as the golden prize." He touched a finger to her cheek. "Golden, because of her eyes. Her eyes are gold until she gifts a man with her virginity. Once he seduces her, her eyes gain their natural color. It's quite a story."

She swatted his hand away. "I can see the story enchanted your narrow mind and dazzled the greed in you. But from your words I'd say you failed to read the entire story. You left out the part about what happens to the challenger who tries but fails to seduce the Adena virgin. The part about the consequences of that failure for the poor gambler who risks it all and loses."

"Well, princess, I don't really see that part as important to the story at all, at least not in my case."

"Really? And why is that? From the way you've been rambling, one would think you planned on testing out this story. If so, I would think consequences such as death or a lifetime of slavery would keep you from putting your foot in your mouth. Or rather from putting your life in my hands."

Stellan let his lips almost brush her skin when he whispered in her ear. "It's your body I want to put in my hands. Or under my hands." He leaned back with a satisfied smile when he saw the flush on her face. "And that's something I don't plan on failing at, so those consequences aren't really important at all."

Cardis gritted her teeth and closed her eyes. Maybe if she blocked the idiot's face from her sight her mind would begin to work again. *Why oh why couldn't she have been born with her mother's skill at handling men?*

With a modicum of control back in her voice, Cardis opened her eyes and took a deep breath.

"I believe I was wrong in saying you were capable of caution. You cannot have thought this through at all."

Maybe if she told him the truth, with special emphasis on the consequences of failure, he'd stop his babbling and this conversation wouldn't head in the direction she feared he wanted to take it. She hadn't come across a potential challenger yet she couldn't persuade away from their goal once she put her mind to it. Usually it only required tact and careful discouragement. With a barbarian she probably should use blunt and easily defined words.

"All right, yes, I know these stories too. What you're babbling about is referred to as challenging for seduction. The man makes the challenge but he is not the judge of the end result of his efforts, the woman is. In other words, dear lowlife, you don't get to decide if you win, I do. And should you lose, pretty much a foregone conclusion in your case, there are only two choices of punishment, death or enslavement, both of which alter the course of your life quite drastically. That's the challenge you seem so interested in making."

"A challenge I believe I'm more than up to winning."

"You? Win the challenge of seducing me into giving you my virginity and my wealth and my lineage?" Cardis made her shock as obvious as possible. "I was completely wrong about you. You're a simpleton, a slow-wit. Your keeper must be searching for you even as we speak. One of your kind cannot begin to know the art of seduction. From the sample of technique I've already been subjected to by the other fine specimen of Edarian manhood, I would judge that you people rut like dogs, mindless mating with no finesse, no skill. To charm a woman, to romance her, to bring her to breathless fulfillment sexually, such a thing would be utterly beyond you."

Stellan's fingers threaded through her hair, massaging her scalp with heat that curled down her neck and across her skin. He leaned in again to touch her neck with his lips, his warm breath in her ear sending shivers through her. *Did the man whisper secret spells of his own magic into her brain?* Cardis feared he'd done something for her thoughts scattered like the wind and all she could do was enjoy the feel of him next to her.

"And maybe you, virgin that you are, don't really know what would bring you to breathless sexual fulfillment."

As Cardis struggled to find her common sense, Stellan trailed a finger down her cheek then rubbed it across her lips. If she continued letting him touch her, there was no telling what might happen. More from self-defense than outrage, she slapped at his hand. Obliging, he stepped back.

"If you don't know what would give you that fulfillment, how can you judge that I wouldn't? Only the opportunity to prove it would show which of us is right and which one is wrong." He smiled at her. It was a look that went way beyond anything friendly. "Perhaps I'm more learned than Theran. Maybe I have skills he didn't."

Cardis swallowed hard and tried to rid her mind of several extremely erotic images his words conjured up. *Did a barbarian get trained in sexual skills?* Cardis rubbed her hand across her forehead, praying the friction would kickstart her brain. She found her voice where it was hiding in the back of her throat and prayed words would attach themselves once she opened her mouth.

"It wouldn't take much to be more proficient than your unfortunate friend. But let me warn you, there's a time limit on this challenge. You only have three days to prove this skill you boast of, too short a time to depend on limited abilities. No matter how learned you may think you are, the vast tutelage you've likely gotten from your brothers would hardly get you through one day before you use up all your tricks and end up resorting to brute force. And that I do not have to stand for. I am not a bitch in heat to allow my body to be used in such a way. Adena's virgins come prepared to protect themselves, as you've already seen."

She ran the same insolent stare he had given her over him. He smiled back at her and it grated on her taut nerves. The man had a mischievous glint in his eyes. The idiot wasn't taking this seriously. Cardis wanted to yell at him that just because she hadn't blasted him so far shouldn't give him any sense of security. She was tired, she'd been traumatized. There were a hundred reasons for her outrageous reaction to him, none of them having to do with the fact that he was the most appetizing thing she'd seen in eons, maybe in all her life.

"And what about enjoying themselves? Are Adena's virgins prepared for that too?"

"Well, of course we're taught all about sexual enjoyment and technique. That's how...."

Cardis glared at him as she realized what she'd been about to rattle off. If he'd had any doubts about who and what she was, her careless tongue had erased them for him. Suddenly she'd become her own worst enemy. She gave him a smug smile.

"But all that really is irrelevant, at least for you. As I said, the woman is the judge of the challenge."

Cardis hoped her reminder swayed him away from this topic. No matter that he was a barbarian, the thought of executing a man who failed in a challenge for her didn't sit well with her conscience. And a man who looked this good was probably one of the few chances the women of Edaria had of enjoying a marriage bed. And of producing offspring with a modicum of intelligence. What right did she have to take him out of the gene pool because he failed the stupid challenge? A bad result could alter Edaria's whole genetic future. Besides, she'd already been traumatized by seeing the other one injured and he'd more than deserved it. This kind of situation was exactly why she'd always maneuvered her way out of any possible challenges or threats. Couldn't the fools understand she didn't want this? Somehow she had to steer this idiot away from the whole idea of a challenge. She had to make him see the sheer impossibility of it, the foolishness of taking such a risk. And she had to keep him from touching her again. When he moved toward her again with his hand lifted, she stepped back. He smiled at her.

"A man who doesn't take the risk stands little chance of succeeding, now does he, princess?"

"Calculating the risks involved would be a good start. Do you really want to take that kind of chance?"

"If I take the chance then I wouldn't be planning on

failing."

"You don't plan on failing, huh? And what, pray tell, would lead you to believe you could succeed in such an endeavor?"

His hand reached for her again and Cardis forced herself to be still. She watched him closely, hoping her words hadn't pushed him to try to force her. Ripping one man apart today was enough for her frazzled nerves. But he only trailed his fingers down her arm.

It was a silly movement, hardly anything erotic or stimulating. But the feel of his warm skin against hers sent a tingling through her. She glanced into his eyes and then away from the smile they held.

He chuckled softly as his fingers continued their slow circle around her arm. She swore she smelled the sun on him, hot and steamy, rising off his skin in waves that threatened her with the promise of a coming wildfire. A fire that would burn away what little control she had left.

He leaned so close Cardis felt his breath against her mouth. For a moment she thought he would kiss her. But his lips brushed past hers to touch her hair. She was so caught up in watching every movement he made that she almost jumped when he whispered in her ear.

"I have a certain reputation among the women here. They've gone away satisfied."

Trying to regain at least a little of her dignity, Cardis stepped back from him and cleared her throat. Without any help from her errant brain, she coaxed her facial muscles into a semblance of a sneer.

"What you mean is they've gone away in one piece without any bleeding. That was probably all it took for them to smile at you as they left."

"Nevertheless, if I issue the challenge, you must allow it. I read that part of the story too."

"You seem harmless enough, or should I say brainless enough. You honestly believe I could be seduced into giving up the greatest treasure I have to one of your kind? You take too grave a risk. Such a jest isn't even worth a smile. For your own sake, I'm willing to let you reconsider your words. I won't hold them against you should you come to your senses now."

Stellan looked at her, at the way her breasts heaved

with indignation, at the way her mouth crooked when she sneered at him, at the way her golden eyes went hazy when he got near her. She was most definitely a prize. There was little enough in his future here to risk, though she didn't need to know that. Let her think him arrogant. Better than knowing him desperate. She was his way out. To be truthful, she was his only hope. All he had to do was make the challenge. Live or die, it would be a glorious three days. Three days alone with her, three days with her full permission to have his hands all over that body. And if he succeeded, then the risk would pay off in the wealth and status that would never be his otherwise. When weighed against the empty future that lay before him, such a prize was worth the risk. Most definitely.

Before he could answer her, Stellan heard shouts from behind him. Their time had run out. It was one challenge or the other, either seduction or persuasion, golden eyes or his brother's temper. Both risks had their consequences, but only one offered him a future. Stellan knew his decision had been made when Hakir's voice boomed across the field as he rounded the curve to the clearing.

"Where is the bitch?"

Stellan stepped in front of Cardis before Hakir could get to her.

"Get out of the way, Stellan. I've no desire to hurt you but the murderous bitch will pay dear for injuring my man."

"No, Hakir, you can't do this. She's the merchant's daughter."

Hakir shoved him aside, intent on getting to Cardis. Stellan grabbed his arm and swung him around.

"The daughter of the owner of the freighter. Hell, the owner of the whole line and one of the noble houses of Adena. The man you're going to have to negotiate with to keep the cargo without a fight. There will be no negotiations if you harm his daughter."

"What do I care for negotiations? Those are your precious worry, Stellan. Let the man fight me for what he scattered all over my canyon." Hakir looked past him to Cardis, malice on his face. "And if teaching this bitch a lesson first brings that fight on, then so be it."

"You don't understand, Hakir. She's protected by her lineage."

"Her rich father isn't here to pamper her or protect her. I run Edaria. Her fancy lineage means nothing here."

Stellan caught Hakir's arm as he brushed past him. "Yes, it does. It means she cannot be touched in any way. There's more to this than you know. You can't threaten her. That's what the pilot was trying to tell you."

"The hell I can't." Hakir reached a hand out for Cardis' throat. Stellan caught him just before he touched her.

"No, Hakir, you..."

Before he could get the words out, Stellan felt the magic rise. Like liquid fire it flowed from Cardis' fingertips to his brother's outstretched hand. With a sudden growl of pain, Hakir pulled his hand back.

"What the bloody hell..."

"I tried to tell you. You can't touch her. She's protected because of who she is, because of who her family is."

"Hakir! Hakir!"

Both of them turned to see Samuel flying down the road to the shelter. The boy was running as if the armies of hell were chasing him. Hakir growled at the sight of him. When Samuel reached him, he grabbed him by the neck and shook him.

"What the hell are you doing leaving your post, boy? You're supposed to be on lookout. I'll thrash you within an inch of your life for leaving your post."

The boy's eyes bulged as Hakir lifted a hand, but he finally got his mouth to work again. "They're coming, Hakir. I came to warn you they're coming."

"Who's coming?" Stellan pulled the boy from Hakir's grip. "Catch your breath, Samuel, and tell us who's coming."

The boy swallowed hard and kept his face turned to Stellan. "Rich men, the ones who carry the banner of Adena."

"My father." Cardis folded her arms as she looked at Stellan. "He has come for me and for his property. You had best say prayers to whatever deity cares for this place for my father does not suffer fools gladly."

Chapter Five

If the amount of hardware Cardis' father and his party carried was any indication, there was no need for prayers. They would all be blown to bits before they got the first words out of their mouths. Stellan tried not to gape at the men who walked toward them, each one outfitted with military gear that would take out a small town.

Seven rows of armed men stretched across the clearing in perfect formation, laser weapons strapped to their sides. Each carried a small stun gun in their hands. In spite of the size, Stellan bet each gun would take out three of Hakir's men before they ever cleared their ancient weapons out of the holsters.

He watched the advancing army, each man well over six feet tall, muscled and garbed in the black and green uniform of the Interstellar Council, and his desperation grew. The row of men in front wore red bands around their arms, an adornment Stellan knew meant they were a combat unit. Cardis' father came prepared for war.

Two small transports fronted the army, their armored covers glinting in the sunlight as they glided across the rocky terrain. A cadre of guards rode on the sides of the vehicles. Hakir motioned his men forward, putting a hand on Martin's arm when he started to move up.

"Stay here, brother. Watch my back. I don't trust these fancy martinets to not have something tricky up their sleeves."

Martin nodded, glancing around as Hakir strode through his men to stand at their head. Stellan inched up behind him, Cardis' hand gripped firmly in his. He hoped she kept her mouth shut.

"Shouldn't you all be running about now?"

So much for his hopes. The woman had no sense of timing. Stellan squeezed her hand and prayed she'd take the hint. Instead she hissed at him. He turned his attention to Martin.

"He brought a lot of people with him."

"This bigshot's got himself a personal army, all the better to let our men blow off some steam." Martin spat on the ground and grinned.

"It's not his army, brother. Those are guards from the Council. They mean business, Martin."

"Don't worry, little brother, we'll put you in the rear. Short as you are, they likely won't notice you."

Stellan held onto his temper. "Now isn't the time for a fight, Martin. We're outgunned here, with these guys. They could blow us all to the next star system."

"But they won't." Martin grinned at him.

"I wouldn't underestimate my father if I were you." Cardis gave him a cool stare. "He's better equipped and better staffed than you. And he won't hesitate."

"Oh, but he will." Martin gave her a knowing look. Stellan shoved Cardis behind him.

"That's good, Stellan. Keep her hidden. But she's still the reason we've got nothing to fear from all the fancy weaponry shining in the sun out there. Her father will hesitate. He'll most definitely hesitate."

"What do you mean?" Cardis shoved her way around Stellan.

"He means your father won't risk harming you and the others." He stepped around Cardis, blocking her from Martin's view. The less she had to do with this the better. "Isn't that what you're trying to tell her, Martin?"

"That's it exactly, little brother. So long as we've got men with weapons trained on his precious people, her father will hesitate all we want him to."

Stellan shook his head. "He won't wait forever, Martin. If Hakir is too stubborn, sooner or later he will make a move."

"Why, Stellan," Martin looked at him in mock shock. "You're the one who's always saying how loyal these merchants are to their people. Are you saying they'd risk their precious cargo for a little firefight with us?"

Stellan gritted his teeth in frustration. He had to hold off a fight until he had time to make his challenge. Cardis shoved around him again. He stepped in front of her and she snarled at his back. "Okay, forget about the people from the *Venetta*. Think about the women in the shelters, Martin, the people in the outlands, our people. Think about what you're doing to them before you help Hakir start a war."

Martin shoved him aside. "Get out of the way, Stellan. The men have things in hand."

He strode past Stellan without waiting for an answer. Cardis pushed him from behind and Stellan turned in time to catch her I-told-you-so glare.

"That's far enough." Hakir's voice halted the movement of the men and vehicles. "You've crossed the borders into my territory carrying weapons and armor enough to start a war, so state your business and be quick about it. Or else I'll take your presence here as an unwanted intrusion into Edaria's affairs and respond to it as such."

From the lead transport emerged an older man dressed in an elegant black uniform. He stood even with Hakir in height, with cropped gray hair and a military bearing. Around his waist he carried a laser weapon and several stunners. On the calves of both legs were sheaths that held blades at least eight inches long and across his back was a wicked looking sword. Advanced and backward weaponry. A man prepared for anything. Stellan's hopes flagged a bit.

The man strode to the front of the lines and faced Hakir. Stellan felt a sinking feeling in the pit of his stomach as he noticed something familiar about the man's arrogant stance.

"I am Alden Oderean. I am here for the return of my people and my cargo."

Stellan's courage faltered for a moment. *Why did the man have to actually come himself? And be so well-armed about it?* Most of the merchants left the recovery of their vessels to the Council guard. Stellan racked his brain for any other tidbits about the virgin legends. Did their fathers come equipped with any sort of magic shield that obliterated any unsuitable suitors who challenged for their daughters? Of course, Oderean had come equipped to do away with him in quite a few ways, none needing magical help.

Oderean didn't spare a glance for anyone but Hakir. "Due to an unfortunate accident, they were forced to land here in your territory. I appreciate the assistance you've given them in their difficult circumstances." The words carried more challenge than gratitude.

Hakir glared at the army in front of him. "This is the way you show your appreciation? Looks more like you came here to take, not to ask."

Oderean gave him a cold look. "I'm a businessman. When I go into a situation where I do not know all the facts, I go prepared for whatever may happen. Since there has been no diplomatic correspondence with your territory for many years, I had no idea what I may find when I arrived. If your intentions are honorable, then I mean no offense and would hope none was taken."

Hakir rested his hand on the long blade belted at his waist. "Oh, I've taken offense all right. I've taken offense at having to clean up the mess your freighter made of my canyon. I've taken offense at the damage done to my territory and my people by having your vessel and your cargo scattered all over my land. Your people made a mess here and now you show up armed to the teeth and expect me to hand everything and everyone back over to you without any recompense for those damages. I take offense at that, indeed I do. You can take your arrogance and your army and shove them both up your stuffy ass. When you're ready to come back alone and speak to me about this situation your people have created here, then maybe we'll have something to negotiate."

Hakir started to turn away. Oderean's men moved toward him and the Edarians all unsheathed their blades. Oderean waved his men back.

"Negotiate? What would there be to negotiate when the property you hold and the people you've enslaved belong to me?"

Hakir turned back to stare at him. A cold smile covered his hard face.

"Why, as I said, the damages I have incurred because of your property."

Oderean looked him up and down. "I am not given to blackmail. There are interstellar rules which even Edaria must abide by. And those rules allow me to ransom my people without further threat from you."

"You're in our territory now and the rules that apply are the ones we choose, so get off your high horse or we'll show you personally how things are going to be."

"No!"

Stellan's voice carried across the open courtyard. He walked out, dragging Cardis behind him.

"There is another matter that may have some bearing on this situation, Oderean." Stellan hoped his voice sounded more confident than he felt. He straightened his shoulders and faced Cardis' father.

The merchant's gaze narrowed on Stellan, a hard look covering his patrician features. "I do not know who you are, but that's my daughter you're manhandling, boy, and I suggest you release her immediately."

Stellan's hand slid down to hold Cardis'. "I'm not trying to harm her, sir. In fact, I'm challenging for her."

Cardis smacked him on the arm with her other hand. "You idiot!"

"A challenge?" Oderean stared at him for a moment. "Have you any understanding of what you are saying?"

"Yes, I do, sir. I know exactly what I'm saying. And I know the risk involved."

"Risk?" Hakir stepped in front of him. "Stellan, what are you doing? What are you talking about? Challenge for what?"

"For her wealth and her lineage. I have three days to seduce her, three days to convince Cardis to gift me with her virginity in order to win the right to wed her."

"Wed her? Three days?" Hakir looked from Stellan to Cardis and back to his brother. "With her? Stellan, are you sure?"

"I can't believe I'm about to say this." Cardis glared at Hakir, who snarled back at her. She jerked her hand out of Stellan's. "Listen to your brother, lowlife, you don't understand what you're risking."

"What are you risking, Stellan?" Hakir looked at Cardis with suspicion.

"His life, that's what." Cardis folded her arms across

her chest in triumph. Surely the ogre would forbid his foolish brother from going through with this farce.

Stellan caught her hand once more and shoved her behind him, ignoring both the glare the movement earned him from Oderean and the thump Cardis gave him. The woman just couldn't keep her hands off of him. He swallowed the grin that came with that thought. A little more fast talking and he'd have the next three days to fulfill his fantasies. And maybe a few fantasies she didn't know she had. He faced his brother.

"Let me handle this, Hakir. I think I have a way for us all to profit." Stellan turned back to Cardis' father.

"I know what I'm asking, sir. I know what the challenge is and I'm ready to face it."

"Stupid, stupid, stupid," Cardis muttered as she stepped from behind his back.

"You say you understand what the risk is, what the challenge involves?" Oderean looked from him to Cardis.

Stellan nodded. Cardis rolled her eyes and groaned.

"And you would make that challenge anyway, when it's obvious how my daughter feels about it from the commotion she's putting up right now?"

Again Stellan nodded. "I'm willing to take that risk, sir. I'm challenging for your daughter's virginity, right here, right now."

Cardis shook her head. "Give it up, Father. I have tried to get this moron to see the idiocy of his words, but he thinks he knows what he is doing. Let us leave this place before he goes any further with this insane babbling."

Cardis jerked at her arm, but Stellan's grip was firm. She ran her other hand through her hair in frustration.

"You cannot mean to go on with this. Let me go, I demand it."

"I have challenged for you, woman, and you must allow it." Stellan turned to Oderean. "Is that not so?"

Oderean nodded. "It is so. If you insist upon it, Cardis must allow the challenge. But I urge you to consider her words. Cardis will be the judge and you have only three days to accomplish your seduction. It would not seem promising that she is discouraging you from making such a decision."

"Nonetheless I am making a formal challenge for your daughter, in front of these witnesses." Stellan waved a hand around the clearing.

"Ahh!" Cardis pressed her fingertips against her eyes and shook her head. "Fool! I am telling you now you will fail. You can never succeed in this."

"Stellan, what the hell are you talking about? What kind of mess are you getting yourself into? Let me deal with this. We can ransom the hellion and be satisfied with enough gold." Hakir spat on the ground, narrowly missing Cardis' feet. "We have the upper hand now."

Stellan shook his head. "I am challenging for your daughter, Oderean, according to the rules of Adena. A challenge she cannot turn down."

H gave Oderean a look and the older man nodded.

"As it seems there is no persuading you from it, I believe my daughter has a challenger."

"No!" A young man rushed from the ranks of the Council guard to grasp Oderean's arm. "You cannot allow this! I came for Cardis." He turned to face Cardis and there was no mistaking the look of sheer adoration on his face. "I came for you, Cardis, to make the challenge that would allow us to be together forever. You must not have known of my feelings, for you left on the freighter before I could say the words yesterday. You didn't know how I feel, how I can make you feel."

"I knew, Wald." Cardis' voice was a gentle whisper. "I left so you would not make such a challenge. I tried to make you see, to make you understand that it cannot be. You must not risk your future, your life on a challenge you cannot win."

Wald shook his head. "You don't mean that, Cardis. You care for me, I know you do."

"Friendship, Wald, it's only friendship I feel. Not the passion it would take to seduce me. I left because I couldn't let you risk such a thing, nor would I put myself in the position of living a lie to save you from the consequences."

"But..."

"Enough!" Hakir's roar cut the boy's answer off. "I can't listen to any more of this mewling and whining. Get a hold of yourself, boy, a man doesn't beg a woman like

61

that. It's enough to make me puke." He shook his head in disgust.

"It doesn't matter anyway." Stellan folded his arms across his chest and stared at Cardis. "I made the challenge first. It's me that will spend the next three days with you. The boy will have to wait." He winked at Cardis. "And be satisfied with attending our marriage feast."

Cardis snarled at him before she covered her face with her hands. When she looked up she spoke as calmly and slowly as she could. "Did you not hear a word I said? I'm giving you the chance to save your miserable life, though it might be kinder of me to end it than leave you in this place. You cannot win." She stretched out the words to emphasize them.

"Ah, but I can try, princess. You can't deny me that."

"What is all this craziness? What do you think you're doing?" Martin shoved his way through the cluster of men around them. "Stellan, I say we take them all and what they have on them. We could use some new weapons. And those they left behind will pay dear to see them again." Martin glared at Oderean's men.

"You are an even greater fool than your brother and he has pushed the limits of stupidity." Cardis sneered at him and Hakir moved toward her, fists clenched.

"Look here, bitch, no woman talks to me or mine like that in my own territory."

Stellan reached for his arm. "No, Hakir, I know what I'm doing." For once, I do, Stellan thought.

"No, Oderean." Wald moved to stand in front of the merchant. "Even if Cardis will not allow my challenge, I must protest. You cannot allow this barbarian to be alone with Cardis, to soil her with his filthy...."

"Hey, brat!" Martin moved toward Wald with a growl. "Remember whose courtyard you're standing in and keep your foul words to yourself or I'll make you eat them."

Stellan reached for him as Martin started past him, fists cocked.

"Wald." Oderean moved the boy to one side, out of harm's way. "This man has made the challenge and it will be honored. Cardis is the one who will judge and her shield will protect her. It is the way it has to be."

"Shield? What shield?" Hakir looked from Stellan to

Oderean. "What manner of trick are you talking about?"

"It's all right, Hakir. It only means I cannot rape her. But as I have no plans to do that anyway, there's nothing to worry about."

"You have much to worry about, you idiot," Cardis sneered. Stellan only smiled at her. She bared her teeth at him, unable to stifle the growl.

Oderean nodded to Stellan. "I would give you one last warning if I may. I have not lightly called my daughter Adena's oldest virgin."

"The oldest virgin?" Stellan worked hard to suppress the chuckle.

"What are you trying to do, foist off on my brother a woman who doesn't even like men?" Hakir looked her up and down with more distaste than before. "Is that your way of cheating, of fixing this challenge business so Stellan will lose?"

Cardis groaned. Now her humiliation was complete. She wondered once again why there were men in the world. The uses she'd come up with for them so far didn't seem all that important. Her married friends all laughed at her when she told them that, but she figured it was a way of covering up for their poor choices.

Cardis glared at the man she'd hoped came to save her. Her father's little nickname had been the source of several embarrassing encounters. He gave her a smile. Disgusted, Cardis closed her eyes, not wanting to see the smirks on the Council guards' faces.

"Uh, exactly how old is your daughter?" Stellan managed to swallow the chuckle.

"Answer that one, Father, and I'll tell Mother about the little side trip to the Mattering constellation you took last March."

Oderean cleared his throat. "It isn't only age that's the issue. Cardis has allowed no challenge until now. You might want to consider that there is a reason for her refusals. A reason that may not bode well for you."

"I won't change my mind, sir, no matter how old she is."

Oderean stared at him a moment, a hint of amusement in his eyes. "Very well, then, Stellan, is it?"

"Yes, sir. My father, Angus Tolten, was the headman

of Edaria, as was his father before him. My brother Hakir is headman now, but my lineage is good. I am not a man of wealth and nobility as you, but I'm not a peasant either."

Oderean looked at him a moment, then nodded. "I see. Well, Stellan, son of Angus Tolten, you've challenged for my daughter and for the next three days, it will be Cardis who judges you."

"Judges him? No woman judges a man." Hakir snarled at Cardis. She smiled back.

"Your brother has issued a challenge to my daughter according to the rules of our people. For the next three days, he will try to seduce her into giving him her virginity. Should he succeed, he will wed my daughter, acquiring her wealth and her lineage as a wedding gift. Should he fail, the consequences are death or slavery, the choice being in Cardis' hands, as is the outcome of the challenge. The sole judge of your brother's efforts is my daughter, the woman he hopes to gain."

"What is this garbage?" Hakir turned to Stellan.

"Hakir, trust me, it will work." Stellan gave him a grin. "And the risk is worth the prize. You know the women love me. I can do this."

Hakir looked from his brother to Cardis and back again. "Are you sure of that, Stellan?"

"It's three days of sex, Hakir." Stellan grinned at him. "I am sure."

"Three days of sex, huh?" Hakir looked Cardis up and down. "And she isn't going to rip you up like she did Theran?"

"I said sex, Hakir, not rape. The challenge depends on my powers of persuasion as well."

Hakir snorted. "I should've known there was talking involved." An odd gleam came into his eyes. "And you gain her wealth if you win this?"

Stellan nodded, sure that the look in his brother's eye didn't bode well for his plan. But he had to have Hakir's agreement to allow the time for his challenge or none of them would gain. He could deal with his brother's greed after he'd won his prize.

Hakir nodded as he gave Cardis a look that made her feel like a sow about to be purchased. "All right, Stellan,

I'll agree to this."

Oderean pierced him with a look. "You will agree to a truce during the time of the challenge? As the leader of these people?"

"For three days, aye."

"And my people will be protected during that time of truce? And their needs seen to? Will you allow us to use our medical facilities to treat the wounded?"

Hakir nodded. "Aye, they'll be protected. And you may see to them. We'll have a truce. And in three days we'll discuss the reparations. Agreed?"

Oderean nodded. "Agreed."

"Then the challenge is accepted?" Stellan moved to stand before Oderean.

"Yes, the challenge is accepted, or it will be when the ceremony is completed." Oderean looked at him. "But I must ask one last time, so there's no misunderstanding should this go badly for you."

"And it will." Cardis mumbled.

"Once I prepare the cup and you and Cardis drink from it, there is no going back. Should you fail to seduce my daughter, you will pay the penalty. The magic will see that you do."

Stellan nodded. "I understand."

Cardis snorted. "I doubt that very much. Whatever compliment I gave you about your thinking ability was premature. You've just given your life away."

"Maybe it's you who will be giving something away, princess."

Stellan winked at her. Cardis covered her face with her hands and moaned. She considered it an extreme show of control not to stick her tongue out at him. In three days, the fool may wish he had his own magic shield if he planned to tempt her control much more. She wondered if the challenge said anything about her ripping him apart with her bare hands, or a blunt instrument. *Could irritating her with words be considered attacking her?*

Her father's movements caught her gaze and she reined in her wayward thoughts. Oderean pulled a plain gray stone from his pocket.

"Cardis, stand before your challenger."

Cardis dropped her hands from her face as she moved to stand in front of Stellan. "Stupid move, lowlife, stupid, stupid move."

Stellan smiled at her. She hissed at him.

"Give him your hand, daughter."

Oderean closed his fingers around the stone as Cardis reluctantly gave Stellan her hand. The stone began to glow, the soft yellow light gleaming through Oderean's fingers. Oderean cupped his other hand around it, eyes closed, as his lips moved in the ancient chant. When he opened his eyes and spread his fingers, a small golden cup stood in his hand.

"Each of you will drink from the golden cup as your acceptance of the challenge. Once you drink, the time for the challenge has started and there is no going back." He looked again at Stellan. "For once done, the magic cannot be undone. In three days, the decision will have been made. Cardis."

She took the cup from her father's hand and lifted it to her lips. Stellan licked his own lips as he watched her mouth slide along the rim of the cup. When she lowered it, her lips were red and moist and he nearly groaned thinking of what the next three days held. Without taking his gaze off her, he lifted the cup to his own mouth, surprised at the cool thick taste that spread across his lips. It gave him a kind of buzz, like really good alcohol, only quicker. As he lowered the cup, he stared at Cardis. She gave him an evil grin.

"Well, lowlife, the clock's ticking."

Stellan swore he heard the sound of it in his own head. *Let the games begin.*

Chapter Six

"Barbaric moron."

Cardis swore under her breath as another branch struck her. If the idiot thought he could seduce her by wearing her down physically then throwing a few moves at her, he was sadly mistaken. By the time they stopped walking, all she would want was a soft bed and a quiet room.

"I'm walking through a bad dream to get to a nightmare."

Cardis shook her head. At first she hadn't believed him when he led her away from the shelter that was primitive enough by her standards. Did the man think she would enjoy spending the night in the woods? Or maybe he believed she would be so fearful she would throw herself at him so he could protect her. That was probably it, seduction by terror.

At least the physical exercise put some of her worries out of her mind. Cardis knew her father would see that the rest of the crew and the passengers were taken care of properly. He had enough men with him to ensure their safety no matter what Stellan's barbaric brothers wanted. And the Council would back him up. Whatever deal they arrived at regarding the cargo was another matter. But that was her father's worry too. All she had to worry about was spending the night in bed with a stranger. She was beginning to wonder if Adena didn't have some barbaric traditions of its own.

"What the hell were you thinking?"

She kept her voice low as she glanced at Stellan's back as he walked ahead of her. It might not be a good idea at all for her to know what he was thinking. Could she count on the fact that he wasn't the brute his brothers

67

were? After all, appearances could be deceiving. Her shield protected her from physical harm, but it would do nothing to help her with the awkwardness of the whole thing. Tonight she would be more intimate with this man than with anyone she had ever known. And she knew absolutely nothing about him.

Nothing except the fact he fills out those leather pants extremely well. Now where had that thought come from? Maybe staring at his butt wasn't such a good idea.

"Shit!"

Cardis cursed the stars, the fates and anything else that would listen as she slammed into yet another mass of snaky green vines. Forget what Stellan was thinking. What had she been thinking? How could a single, albeit well-formed piece of a strange man's anatomy sap all common sense from her? She should be mortified, horrified, traumatized. Not hypnotized by the way his muscles rippled along his back as he walked. That vest didn't cover nearly enough of him for her sanity. And she used to be a sane woman.

Since her coming of age, she'd avoided any possible challenges for she knew they would turn out badly. It wasn't that men weren't nice or that she had no interest in sex. The thought of sex appealed to her. But the thought of giving away her independence in exchange for sex definitely did not appeal to her. Thanks to Adena's wacky concepts, she had to choose one or the other.

Cardis didn't want a husband, any husband. All through her teen years she'd studied hard to learn her father's business, even going so far as to prepare to test for a navigator's license. Not that her father had ever let her take the test. But with time she knew she could convince him.

Granted, her parents at first considered her interest in interstellar flight and Adena's merchant trade an indulgence they humored her in. But circumstances changed with her brother's death four years ago. Stefan was her father's heir and the one groomed to take over Oderean Freight Lines. With him gone, her father turned more and more to her growing expertise and skill. In the last two years, she'd taken over the management of many of the local routes. She knew the ins and outs of the merchant trade better than many of the merchants themselves. It was the life she wanted.

Her parents weren't the only ones determined to persuade her otherwise. One by one Cardis watched her friends marry, each of them becoming extensions of their husbands. All their dreams melted into a sheltered life of gardening and childrearing. They never even set foot off Adena anymore, never had time to be spontaneous or impulsive. Besides, they tsked to her gently when she urged them to join her, their husbands were waiting at home. She would understand when she found her own mate.

"Hah! Not likely. Not if I can help it."

Stellan turned back to glance at her. She bared her teeth at him. He shook his head and turned back around. Nope, not if she could help it. The barbarian would find he'd risked his miserable life for nothing. And she refused to feel guilty about it. At least she was going to try her best not to.

Guilt or no, Cardis swore it wasn't going to be her fate to end up enslaved to a husband who ran off to the stars while she stayed home tending some squalling baby and figuring out what color to paint the new nursery. If only she could've convinced this arrogant barbarian not to take such a hopeless risk. Now she was stuck in a position she'd vowed never to be in. The thought of a man, even a barbarian, ending up losing his life or his freedom because she didn't want to marry made her cringe. Being stuck in a challenge left her with the choice of either marrying a man she didn't love just to save his life or becoming the reason for his ruin.

On top of all her other worries, she felt unprepared. Her mother spent little time on how to endure an unwanted challenge. Both of them assumed Cardis would control who did and didn't challenge for her. Oh, how she wished her mother was here now to give her some advice. But she was alone, in a strange place and only her own feelings to guide her. Walking behind a man she firmly believed she should be running away from instead. And her feelings were beginning to run amok, taking her sanity with them.

She bit off an oath as she stubbed her toe on another

rock. The place appeared to be nothing but rocks held together with a few vines. What had she been thinking to let him drag her off like this? Her life was among the stars. Nature girl, she was not.

As they left the clearing, Stellan had given her a moment for a quick goodbye to her father and even grudgingly allowed another tearful plea from Wald before yanking her off down what he claimed was a trail. The little exchange with Wald might have been the reason for his impatience to get going, although the fact she had pointed out the clock was ticking could have hurried him along, too.

If she had known where he intended to set off to, she would've put a quick stop to his plans. Instead, she told him there was no need to rush, for all the extra moments in the world wouldn't help him in his foolish cause. That remark only brought her another of his grins. The man had to be simpleminded. Maybe his brothers bashed him on the head too many times as a child. From the looks of the two of them, it was easy to believe any level of abuse.

"Ow!"

The gnarled root caught Cardis' foot as she stumbled back from the branch. Before she could catch herself, she landed hard on her backside.

"What happened?" Stellan stopped his steady pace to glance back over his shoulder.

"What happened? What happened? I would think you could tell from the position I'm in what happened. Now help me up."

With a sigh she couldn't help but hear, he walked back to where she sat. She swore if he gave her one of those stupid grins now, she would yank him down beside her. He must have seen her thoughts written on her face for he reached a hand down and caught her in a firm grip and pulled her to her feet. Not even a hint of a grin split his features. Cardis thought there might be actual worry on his face. They hadn't covered the rules on what happened to him if she didn't survive the challenge period. Good to see there was a chink in his confidence.

"Did you fall?"

She gave him a look she hoped told him how idiotic she thought that question was.

"Since one of us is familiar with the path we're taking and one of us is not, then one of us is at a distinct disadvantage, something that makes keeping up with the other one of us a little difficult. Besides," She brushed the leaves and twigs off her pants and stomped her feet to shake the dirt off her shoes. "Racing through the woods is not my idea of the way I prefer to travel."

"If you wanted me to slow down, you should've said something."

"Obviously, you didn't hear the things I was saying, or you'd know exactly what I wanted you to do, at least to yourself. You'd also know what I think of your attempt at seduction so far."

"I'm trying to get to that, the seduction I mean. That's why I was hurrying, so we could be alone at the cabin."

The cabin? Would that be a step up or down from what he had called the shelter? Probably best not to worry about that.

"We're alone now, and believe me, what I'm thinking is not going to help your cause. Why in the hell are we walking, anyway?"

Stellan racked his brain for an answer that wouldn't give her an opening to tell him once again how he was going to fail miserably. *Because I wanted to get you away from the others and alone with me as fast as I could.* He cleared his throat and shoved the thought away. It wouldn't help him to look like an anxious boy. He settled on the truth.

"By the time we'd gotten horses and gear together, it would've been nightfall and too late for us to get away. I didn't think you wanted to spend the night with me, doing what we were going to be doing, surrounded by everyone else, including your father and Wald."

He made a face when he said Wald's name, he couldn't help it. The boy had made it obvious he planned to dance on Stellan's grave four days from now.

"Horses? Gear? Do you mean to tell me that's the only means of transportation in this backward territory? What about the transports you had my people on?"

Stellan grimaced. "Those were, um, commandeered from some, uh, visitors who came...."

"You mean they were stolen from some other unfortunate victims."

"Something like that. And Hakir doesn't like to let them out of his sight."

"I'll bet. Someone might steal them, like some crazed woman who's been forced to walk for miles and miles."

Stellan rolled his eyes. "We've only gone a few miles."

Cardis glared at him. "And how much further do we have to go before we find some rudimentary shelter that we can spend the first of these oh so exciting nights in?"

Stellan was beginning to wonder if the reason she hadn't had a challenger so far is that most of them got to know her too well beforehand. He had heard every word she said on their walk, none of them complimentary in the least. In fact some of them had been quite inflammatory. The woman obviously wasn't used to exercising caution in her speech. Either that or it was a deliberate attempt to bait him so she could use her shield to rip him apart. She probably wouldn't even take the parts back to his brothers. She'd just leave pieces of him along the trail to feed the wild animals that roamed this area. That would no doubt make her smile.

She certainly hadn't done much smiling so far. Each time he'd looked back to check on her she sneered at him. The more time they spent together the more certain prickly aspects of her personality came clearly into focus. It was a good thing he didn't share his brothers' quick temper. And a good thing he was used to abuse. No matter how beautiful she was, it would take a man with a whole lot of incentive to take a chance on spending three days in her company, win or lose. *And I've certainly got that kind of incentive.* As he took her hand, he reminded himself it was three days of sex, just three days of sex. He pasted a smile on his face.

"It's only another mile or so to the tavern. We can get some supplies there and then it's a short distance to the cabin."

Cardis made a face at him. It took more effort than she really wanted to spend to move even her facial muscles, but the childish action made her feel better. No way was she buying that fake smile of his. His calculations didn't add up to a short distance. She considered herself a pretty active person, but walking miles at a time wasn't part of her activities. Not unless it was on a treadmill. Certainly not as a means of transportation.

And this hadn't been easy walking. It might not have been as much distance as her aching body told her, but they had covered some of the roughest terrain she had ever been in. Up and down hills, crawling over rocks and sliding down hillsides on her ass she had gotten an up close and personal view of Edaria. Wilderness was a mild term for it. The entire place appeared made of rocks and grit and little else. And there was a definite altitude difference. She felt it every time she tried to catch her breath. The air in this place was like every other amenity, hard to come by.

"You don't have to drag me."

She tugged her hand out of his grip and leaned against a rock, grimacing as the rough stone scraped her back. Stellan eyed her with what she could only describe as caution. Good. He should be careful of her. And with her. This was going to be a long three days.

"Look, we're not far from the river. There's a glen, kind of off the trail, not too far up ahead. We can rest there. I brought a little food, and the water in the inlet there is really good. After a bit, you should feel like going on."

So it was water she heard in the distance. The sound had seemed to follow them for the last hour. Given the barrenness of the land around her, Cardis figured it was the sound of the wind in the rocks. She stretched her aching limbs and waved him ahead of her.

"Lead the way, my captain. Only try not to lose me before we get there."

****

Stellan held his breath as they entered the glen, fearful he would stumble or trip and fall in front of her. The sight of her stretching her elegant arms, the rich fabric of her shirt pulled taut over her generous breasts and a hint of creamy skin exposed to his view had left him dumbstruck, barely able to put one foot in front of the other. She'd even bent over, he guessed to work the kinks out of her legs, giving him a sight of her backside that

73

made his mouth water. He had concentrated so hard on how he was going to get her out of those clothes during their walk that he had almost forgotten the prize underneath them. It took great effort on his part, effort aided by the memory of Theran's missing arm, to turn and start walking rather than sliding his hands under her shirt and letting himself touch. If he didn't come up with any better ideas for seduction than a full frontal attack his cause was lost, not to mention his body parts.

Working the pack off his back, Stellan dropped to his knees by the edge of the inlet. He hoped the water was cold. Cold was definitely what he needed.

Cardis sighed as she dropped down by the water. The spot was really beautiful, although she would never let Stellan know it, an oasis of color and charm set against the stark landscape like a painting hung in a barren room. Nice to know there was something besides rocks on this planet. The peace of it surprised her and bumped her opinion of Edaria up a notch.

Branching off from the main flow, the river formed a small inlet that eddied away from the harsher terrain. Trees not much taller than she was shaded the banks with thick leafy branches. Thick clusters of vivid red flowers grew under their spreading limbs. Tiny sprigs of purple covered the grassy area and blooms of yellow and white burst from the branches of small shrubs scattered around the glen.

The water was surprisingly clear. Cardis saw all the way to the bottom when she leaned over. Tiny multicolored fish darted among the grasses and rocks.

She breathed in the rich scent of the flowers. The wild spread of their colors bore little resemblance to the ordered paths of her mother's gardens. Indeed, whatever hand had scattered the plants must have desired them to grow at their own whim. Never would her mother or any other Adenan woman she knew have permitted such chaos.

Sheltered from the harsh rays of the twin suns and tucked away next to the river, the glen offered a restful spot for travelers. Cardis wondered if many people passed this way or if isolation was the norm all over Edaria. They had seen no one during their walk, but, in spite of all her complaining, it actually had been only a couple of hours since they left the shelter. She stretched her arms out behind her on the grass and looked around.

There was something primeval about the mossy trees with their low-lying branches that skimmed the water's surface in an almost loving touch. She had nearly relaxed when Stellan moved by her to dip two cups into the water. His wild green eyes caught her gaze as he leaned back on his heels to offer her a cup. All pretense of relaxation evaporated.

This close to him, Cardis smelled heat and man, the musky scent of his skin warmed by the hot sun. Rather than finding the odor offensive, the smell, combined with the sight of sweat glistening off the golden hairs that covered his chest, sent a spiral of plain old lust through her. Cardis dropped her mouth to the cup, certain if she wasn't looking at him that her brain would shift back into usable mode. He rose and walked back to his pack.

"There's food and like I said, the water here is actually good to drink."

She stared past him to the cloth he'd spread under a tree.

"I wondered how we would find a food dispenser way out here. I thought we'd have to wait until we got to, to wherever we were going for the night."

"I grabbed a little of what Eustacia and the others had cooked for the men. It's nothing elaborate, but it should hold us until we stop for the night."

Until they stop where he could start his seduction. The thought stole some of Cardis' appetite. She tried to remember all the things her mother told her should she face such a challenge, but all she could focus on was the man in front of her. Maybe she should try and hold a conversation with him.

"Eustacia?"

"My brother Hakir's wife. She and her women brought food to the cap...to the rest of your people while I was packing our stuff and you were saying your goodbyes."

Cardis had a vague recollection of a tiny, timid creature who stared at her only to quickly move away each time Cardis stared back.

"The little dark-haired woman who nodded at your brother every time he shouted something to her?"

"Yeah, that's her. She's a little shy around strangers."

Shy? Cardis swallowed her reply to that ludicrous statement. The woman hadn't been able to look any one of the passengers from the *Venetta* in the eye and she'd practically leaped out of the way whenever Cardis got within shouting distance of her. Of course, she'd jumped every time her husband spoke to her as well, so maybe it had nothing to do with strangers at all.

Deciding that conversation might tax her ability to remain civil, Cardis leaned back against a tree and watched Stellan as he moved around. He pulled more items from his pack, laying food out on a cloth. The heat, the quiet, the wildness of it appeared not to bother him at all.

Of course it doesn't, he's a barbarian. This is all he's used to. And he's not the one whose world's been turned upside down.

A twinge of self-pity hit her. Cardis brushed it away and frowned at him. She was going to have to do this and there was no sense putting it off.

"Do we really have time to linger here?" Her question had him turning to give her an odd look. "I mean, if we're going to get to some, uh, shelter before night comes?"

He pulled out the last of the food items and tossed his knapsack aside. "We've got time. It really isn't as far as it seems. We'll get there before dark."

As if he read her thoughts, Stellan paused in his preparations and smiled at her. The look made her wonder about him. Cardis knew she needed to get past her fear, past the trauma of the wreck and the capture and all the rest that had happened since yesterday, if she wanted to get through what lay before her. And what lay before her was this man.

In spite of the rough garb, Stellan wasn't hard to look at. He bore that bad boy look of danger that attracted some women, although she would never have considered herself the type to fall for it. Like a wild animal that tempted them to tame him if they could. She didn't think Stellan would take well to a whip and a chair. The visual that thought conjured in her head brought up all kinds of interesting ideas. Cardis had aspired to many things as a child, but never a wild animal tamer.

For the last few hours she had masked her nervousness with contempt. But sooner or later he would touch her, intimately, and she would have to let him. To avoid any charges of unfair treatment during his challenge, she would have to let him touch her however, and wherever he wanted to. And as much as he wanted to.

Truthfully, she'd considered botching the challenge so she could let him off when he cried foul. But the fool would probably insist on three more days to make up for it. No way would he let her off that easily. She'd have to play fair and let him have his chance. It was only three days.

"Are you getting hungry, princess?"

He rose and stretched like a long, lean cat as he turned toward her and Cardis wondered if she should reconsider. Maybe a whip? Sex toys had been one of her mother's least favorite topics. The woman blushed every time they started to cover that area. Now Cardis feared there might be a few things she was going to wish Mother had covered with more detail.

Cardis wondered what she might need to know tonight as he moved around. What did a man like him consider fair play when it came to sex? A man whose whole world revolved around male satisfaction. What would excite a barbarian? And would she live through it? *It's only three days, Cardis. You can make it through three days.*

Chapter Seven

"Had enough?"

Cardis had to swallow before she could answer Stellan's query. The food tasted better than she'd expected. Since she found it edible, she ate her fill. No telling when the man would feed her again.

"Walking must give you an appetite, princess."

She arched a brow at him. "Are you calling me a pig?"

"No, ma'am. Just commenting on the obvious benefits of walking."

Cardis frowned at his attempt to swallow the smile on his face. What did it matter if he thought her a glutton? All the more reason for him to regret challenging for her.

"You know I can't tell if you're a fast thinker or if your tongue gets you into trouble so often you're used to coming up with excuses to save yourself."

"I prefer to think of myself as adaptable, darling. Good in any situation."

He gave her a wink. Cardis shook her head as she stood and brushed the crumbs from her top.

"Then adapt to this. Not even the thought that I might get fat and lazy as I grow old will get you out of the consequences of this challenge you've made. Although," she stared at him thoughtfully, "adaptability would be a good asset if I send you to one of those pleasure houses on Darmon Three for your enslavement." She shrugged. "Something to think about."

"Pleasure houses? Exactly what does a virgin know about pleasure houses?"

Cardis smiled at him. "Enough to know you'd be worth a fortune there. You'd be a profitable trade for me."

"A profitable trade?"

Cardis laughed at the horrified look on his face. "My father is a good teacher. There's a reason Oderean Freight Lines has stayed in business so long. I come from a long line of talented merchants."

She sauntered over to the riverbank, leaving Stellan gaping behind her. Over the rush of the water she heard him mumbling to himself. As she seated herself by the bank she chuckled. Some things were still under her control. Her hunger satisfied and her pride confirmed, Cardis let herself relax enough to enjoy her surroundings. The glen was a beautiful spot, the first real oasis she'd seen in Edaria. She leaned over to dip her hand in the water.

Stealing occasional glances at Cardis over his shoulder, Stellan tossed the rest of the food into his weathered knapsack. The woman was perverse, that was all there was to it. A body meant for pleasure wrapped around a diabolical brain meant for profit. What kind of unnatural combination was that? He groaned softly as he glimpsed her cute little backside when she stretched a hand out to play in the water. At least if he lost this challenge as she kept telling him he would, it wouldn't matter, for his mind would be gone. He'd be lucky to remember his own name by the time she was done with him.

"All packed up?"

Stellan cursed under his breath when he jumped at the sound of her voice. When did the woman sneak up on him? One minute he couldn't keep his eyes off her, the next she was scaring the shit out of him by sneaking up on him. What in hell was happening to him?

He looked over in time to catch her grin. She knelt down by him and flicked water into his face. The woman was definitely perverse. It was a trait he admired. With a grin of his own, he reached for her hand.

"Ready to do some more walking?"

Cardis groaned as he tugged her to her feet. "How would you feel about carrying me?"

"How would you feel about spending the night here? We've already stayed longer than I'd planned." He pulled her against him, his hands gliding along the curve of her hips. "We could get right to the seduction stuff."

Cardis took a step back. What she'd felt that close to a certain part of his anatomy told her the seduction would take seconds if she didn't put some distance between them. She definitely wasn't ready for sex under the stars yet. "You say it's only another mile or so?"

Stellan chuckled. "Okay, so we go on. If you want to wash up before we go...." He pointed to the water.

"Wash up?"

"Yeah, you've got a little food left on your face."

"Where?"

"Here." Stellan licked his thumb and rubbed it over her chin. Her skin was smooth and warm. He lifted his gaze to find her staring at him and the sight of those golden eyes turned his brain to mush. His other hand slid down her arm to rest on her hip while his thumb brushed over her face in slower and slower circles, his fingers tracing the flawless angles of her features. Her hip bumped against his as she stumbled a bit and the contact was almost painful. As was his cock, which was now harder than the rocks around him. The feel of her body against his made all the important parts stand up and take notice. He tried to remind his wayward parts that if they could only get her attention, there might be a reward in it for them. Nothing like a team effort to capture a win.

Deciding to plunge ahead was hardly a radical move. Stellan didn't think he could've moved away from her if his life depended on it. He leaned in close and let himself taste her, encouraged when he noticed she held her breath as his lips brushed along the line of her jaw. The sweet honeyed scent of her filled his senses and he let his lips trail along the line his fingers had wandered. Having that sweetness on the tip of his tongue made him want to groan with pleasure. When he pressed his lips to her eyelids, he heard her sigh. He rocked back on his feet and grinned at her, thoroughly enjoying the hazy look in her golden eyes.

"Just wanted to make sure I got it all."

He could tell his team had scored several points when she had to clear her throat three times before words came out.

"Thanks, but maybe I'd better wash up everywhere, I mean, wash off my face, you know, and other stuff."

"I've probably got a rag in my pack. Let me look." Stellan gave her a quick smile before he walked away. *Just call me Mr. Handy.*

Cardis nodded as she rose to her feet, then realized Stellan had already turned away from her. Coordinating her movements with the thoughts in her head appeared beyond her. She stumbled over to the water and found herself hoping it was cold. Cold was definitely what she needed.

She squatted by the stream and stared at her reflection as she listened to the sounds of Stellan rummaging in his pack. Maybe she could find enough air to get some much needed oxygen to her brain while he wasn't next to her. Before she had a chance to inhale deeply, he was back, kneeling beside her, dipping a small cloth into the water. At first he held it out to Cardis, then he pulled his hand back. Squeezing the cloth until water dripped through his fingers, Stellan sat back on his heels and looked at her.

"What?"

Cardis felt his stare all the way down to her toes. And she felt the hunger in it. That didn't surprise her. What surprised her was the matching hunger that filled her. As a slow smile spread across his face, the hunger sent pangs of sheer lust through her belly. And lower.

"So have you really scared off all your other challengers?"

"I haven't had any other challengers. My, suitors if you will, never made a challenge."

He nodded. "So it's like I thought then."

"What?"

"The men on Adena are cowards."

Cardis frowned at him. "They were intelligent enough to understand a challenge would be futile. So they respected my wishes."

"I thought the idea of the challenge was persuasion."

"They knew I would be the judge and I wouldn't be persuaded. That makes them smart, not cowardly."

"They let a virgin decide that, did they? Cowards."

"I'm not inexperienced around men." She gave him an annoyed glare. "Being a virgin just means I've never been to bed with a man. It doesn't mean I can't tell when

I'm attracted to one."

"How many of these suitors did you let get this close?"

Stellan leaned in as he whispered the words. His lips grazed the delicate skin of her neck then moved up to her mouth. He captured her lips with his own, forcing them apart with his tongue. She shivered at the feel of him inside her mouth, at the warmth spreading through her from his possession.

Stellan deepened the kiss, pulling her against that hot, hard body of his, making her shake with growing excitement at the feel of certain parts of his body pressed against her.

None of the others had ever gotten this close, but she'd never tell him that. If he knew how truly virgin she was, she'd be toast. Stellan pulled back with a lingering tug at her lips then grinned at her.

"None of them got that close, huh?"

She scowled at him. "Pawing each other wasn't part of the typical courtship."

"Things must be really different on Adena."

"I doubt it. Men appear to be the same all over from my experience."

"From your vast experience?"

"From my travels, I mean." She snarled at him, knowing he mocked her. "Your gender isn't hard to read. And as far as my suitors went, I knew what they wanted."

"Which was?"

"What you want. The whole reason you're willing to put your life on the line to make this challenge. Virgin or not, I'm not so dumb as to think it's my body all of you are after."

"You really are a virgin, aren't you?"

"No. I mean, yes, I am really a virgin and yes, I know men like sex."

"I've known a few women who liked it too."

Cardis blushed. "What I'm trying to say is sex is available without making a challenge for it. So a man only has one reason to go through this outrageous ritual."

"Which is?"

"Wealth, status, whatever it is they think to gain from marrying into a powerful family. All the goodies they want plus the knowledge of having a sure thing at home waiting for them. Someone to be a brood mare to carry on their name for the next generation of cretins to perpetuate this archaic ritual."

"You're pretty jaded for someone so young, princess. Of course," he grinned at her. "I'm not exactly sure how old you are."

Cardis rolled her eyes as she stood. "I think we should get going. We're wasting time here. And you're dripping on me." She pointed to the wet cloth in his hand. "Are you holding that thing for a reason?"

Stellan's lips broke into that slow smile she was getting used to as she continued to stare at him. He rose to his feet and she swore some force pulled her toward him. There was no denying something sizzled in the air between them. But she couldn't be attracted to this man. She just couldn't. After all, she didn't know him. Her mother's admonishments about sex rang in her ears. *It's a physical act, Cardis, an act that's meant to be enjoyed even if the partner is temporary. Not every man will make an acceptable mate.*

Stellan thought Cardis must be the most easily readable person he had ever met. All her emotions played across her lovely face for the whole world to see. He wondered if there was anything she'd ever wanted to keep hidden. Her father had referred to her as Adena's oldest virgin. Adenan men must be dumber than he'd thought. Or bigger cowards. What had happened to make her so cynical? Why would a woman who so obviously wanted to be touched resist the opportunity to have what she wanted? Was she truly that stubborn? Would it cost him his life to find out? He unfolded the cloth in his hand, shaking water drops on both of them. She frowned at him.

"I thought I'd help you again, princess, since it was so much fun the first time."

He reached out to touch her with the cloth, careful to keep it between his hand and her bare skin. He would never admit it to her, but being this close to her, close enough to see his own reflection in her eyes, shook him. She was the most beautiful woman he had ever seen, that he could ever imagine existing. And he wanted her, wanted all of her with a fierceness he hadn't known he possessed. That thought sobered him. There hadn't been much he'd allowed himself to want these last few years. He'd learned to live with disappointment. So why was he risking so much on a woman he knew so little about? A woman who held all the cards in this gamble. Then he looked in her golden eyes again. If he died a fool, he'd die a happy one.

With a slow motion, Stellan slid the cloth along her cheeks, gliding it down her neck and around, so that his hand cupped her neck from behind.

"To cool you off."

She sneered at him. "I thought the idea was to heat me up." *Oh, smart move, Cardis. Like the man needs ideas.*

For once he didn't give her a goofy grin. "Give me your hand, Cardis."

"Why?"

"Because I want to take you right here and if I don't change what I'm doing that just might happen."

"Take me? Oh, well, I thought that was the idea. Of course, I hadn't planned on being outside...."

"Uh-uh." His thumb rubbed the outline of her lips and Cardis shivered at the sensual contact. Stellan got a great deal of gratification from her reaction, enough to tell him he should pull her into his fantasy. Acquaint her with that breathless sexual satisfaction she talked about. He tipped her chin up with his finger so her gaze met his.

"Don't be too disappointed, darling. We'll be here one day, you and I, in this place, and I'll take you, right here by the water. I'll lay you down in these flowers and ride you till we both come screaming. Or I'll slide you into the water, slip inside you while you float here and take you over and over again, until you can't know any more pleasure, can't stand 'cause your legs are so weak. But I'm not going to waste this spot if we're only going part of the way. We'll be back, Cardis, and when we are you'll like the fact that we're outside. Count on it."

He grasped her hand in his. "But for now, I want to show you what I'm going to do to you when we get to the cabin and we're alone for the night. What I'm going to make you feel when I get the chance to touch you like I want to touch you. So watch closely."

Stellan turned her to face the water. "Lean back against me and watch the water. Don't think, Cardis, just feel."

Cardis swallowed hard. She hadn't really expected pretty words, but neither had she expected words that made her quiver inside. The water rippled softly, making her image go all blurry. Much like his hands made her feel. Then he took her hand in his and slid it up under the stretchy fabric of her top.

Cardis stared hard at the reflection in the clear water. Of all the things she'd expected, to have him touch her like this hadn't even crossed her mind. She tried not to jolt when he pressed her open palm to her breast. Guiding her fingers, he rubbed them across her nipple, drew her thumb and forefinger together to pull at the sensitive nub. Cardis felt the peak stiffen. His hot breath blew against her neck and the fact that his breathing wasn't quite steady made each movement somehow more erotic. Her top covered their hands so she couldn't see anything. But she could feel. She could definitely feel. Stellan leaned close to her ear.

"I'm going to touch you all over, feel every part of you until I know all there is to know about your body and what makes you tingle, what makes you scream with pleasure."

Cardis didn't know whether to blush or moan at the feel of her own fingers massaging her breast. It was incredibly erotic to have him manipulate her movements to give herself pleasure, like a game of sexual hide and seek. And Stellan seemed to know exactly what spots to seek.

He moved her other hand to the other breast and stroked it till her nipple hardened. Then he pulled her hand out and lifted her finger to his mouth. Slow and easy, he glided his tongue along the pad of her finger then slid her hand back to her breast. With the wet tip he circled her finger back and forth across her nipple.

"I'm going to taste you, taste all of those sweet hidden parts of you that no man has touched, those parts that have been waiting for my lips. I'm going to make love to you, bring you to that breathless satisfaction you long for without ever touching you with my hands. I'm going to show you how beautiful you are with my mouth but it won't be with words."

Stellan guided her hand down under the waistband of her trousers and rubbed it down her belly, stopping to dip her finger into her belly button. This time Cardis did groan. All her mother's careful lessons faded into oblivion as this total stranger set her on fire with her own hand. What in the world was happening to her?

She knew, technically, exactly what he was doing. She could quote all the known erogenous zones from memory, could name all the spots on her body with both medical and slang terminology. But all her study hadn't prepared her for the real thing, for having a man standing behind her, the heat of him, the thickness of him pressing into her backside as he stroked the front of her until she wanted to cry, to scream.

"I'm going to show you how much fun it can be to touch each other. I'm going to teach you how to play with a man, princess."

He bent over and brushed his lips against her neck and Cardis nearly jumped out of her skin. Stellan chuckled as he moved her hands to her hips. "After all, that's why they call it foreplay. And I've got lots of toys for us to play with."

Toys? What kind of toys? Before she could worry too much, Stellan slid her hand down the front of her trousers to her crotch and pressed her fingers against the sensitive spot. She felt her own dampness as he eased her fingertips through the moist curls over her mound.

"See? We haven't even really gotten started and already you've worked up a sweat." He splayed her fingers out, using them one by one to massage her clit. "You're going to get to know me so well, to know what I can do to you, what pleasure I can give you, that all it's going to take is for you to think of me and you'll go damp."

Stellan continued to work her fingers back and forth, building a friction with the rhythm of his movements that made her breath catch in her throat. Without conscious thought, Cardis rubbed back against him, the thick feel of him against her adding heat to the fire.

"In the middle of your garden party, or as you're dressing for some fancy event, I'll walk in and your body will tighten and release that sweet cream that will guide me into you, into where you and I both find release. Years from now, when you're a little old woman, nearly worn out from all the sex the horny old man you're married to has given you, I'll walk in the room, leaning on my cane, and you'll stare at me across the kitchen and feel yourself grow wet, know that you're waiting for me to give you the pleasure that only I can."

Stellan pressed the heel of her hand inward sharply and Cardis gasped as the climax hit her. Her legs spasmed as waves of liquid pleasure spread through her like a wildfire. Heedless of anything else, Cardis clamped her thighs around his hand, tried to keep him there so the pleasure wouldn't stop. Stellan obliged her by stroking her swollen clit, keeping the pleasure building until she collapsed against him breathless. As she leaned against his chest, he continued to rub her skin, to run his fingers through her hair as he whispered nonsense words in her ear.

Several minutes later, when she could breathe again, Cardis pulled away from him. She was both mortified and incredibly satisfied. Her thoughts jumbled around in her brain, her nerves screamed and her skin still tingled. Never in her wildest dreams had she pictured herself standing in a spot like this, next to a man who'd just made her whole body light up this way.

Slowly and with more effort than she was comfortable with, she walked away from him. Confused and still breathless from his assault, she waited for her body to regain some sense of control while her brain screamed at her to run, far and fast. This man had more tricks than she'd counted on. She turned to find he'd moved up behind her.

"Warmed up any, princess?" He took both her wrists in his hands to steady her.

Cardis took several deep breaths before she spoke, not wanting to risk a voice that might not work. "You don't have to hold me up. I need to sit for a minute, that's all."

"I kinda like it when you lean on me." He eased her closer. "Kinda like how you sound a little breathless." Stellan leaned back from her to stare at her face. Yep, he was wearing that grin. "Must be what's keeping you from bitching at me about something."

She pushed away from his chest, working hard to keep the grin off her own face.

"Well, you let me catch my breath, then we'll see if there's not something I need to be bitching about."

"Oh, I'm sure you'll find something." Stellan swung her up in his arms.

"I didn't mean I wasn't able to walk."

"Relax, I'm just gonna put you on this rock here while I get us some more water and get you that cool cloth to wipe off all that sweat," he grinned broader, "you seem to have worked up."

He seated her gently on a large boulder. Cardis watched him as he strode to the water to moisten the cloth again. Looking at him made her hot all over. *Remember who and what he is, Cardis. You're a normal woman. It's not a miracle for him to make you feel passion.*

Stellan squeezed out the cloth and started to wipe her face.

"I can do it myself." Cardis tried not to notice how childish the words sounded.

"Sure thing, princess." He handed the rag to her.

A shot of guilt made her regret her bad manners. "Thank you."

"No problem, ma'am. I aim to please." Stellan moved back to his pack, shoving what was left of the food items back in.

"Here, let me help you." Cardis jumped off the rock. She gathered the last of the food and started to shove it in his pack.

"It's okay. I can do it myself." Stellan mocked her with the words as he tugged the pack from her grasp.

"What in the world have you got in there?" Cardis jerked back on the pack, laughing. As it slung from her hand, the contents spilled out on the ground. Her jaw tightened at what she saw.

"You took those off the *Venetta*."

"Thanks for the help, darling." Stellan yanked the pack out of her hand.

"You stole them." Cardis pointed to the five wrapped white containers lying scattered on the ground. "Those medkits are part of my father's cargo. They're very expensive and hard to come by. Those have been bought and paid for by the distributor on Larius Three."

"Yeah, well he won't miss a few of them." Stellan knelt and stuffed the kits back in the pack.

"That's not the point. They don't belong to you. They're my father's merchandise, his property." Cardis wrapped both hands around the pack. Stellan glared at her.

"Well then, he can file a complaint with the Council, can't he? They can add it to the others."

He yanked the pack from her grasp and slapped it shut. Hefting it onto his back, he turned to walk away. Cardis gripped his arm and spun him around.

"You hypocrite! You blather on about how you want to negotiate a return, how you want to protect the cargo of the vessels that end up here and make sure it gets back to the merchants, when all the time you're thinking about what you can take and sell, what profit you can make from our cargo. You're nothing more than a thief, no better than those miscreant brothers of yours."

For a moment he stared at her and Cardis wondered if her words had overstepped her safety. But it wasn't only anger in his eyes. She'd swear there was hurt as well. Cardis shoved away the guilt. The truth hurt, didn't it? And all she'd done was tell him the truth.

Stellan lifted her hand from his arm, his voice quiet when he spoke.

"Looks like you found something to bitch about again, princess."

Without looking back, he turned and strode off down the path.

Chapter Eight

They walked in silence for a long time after leaving the river. Torn between the commitment of the challenge and her anger at him, Cardis got a headache trying to sort out what to do before Stellan put his hands on her again. The bottom line was, he would put those large, warm hands on her again and there was nothing she could do about that. *And apparently no way she could control her rebellious body's response.* The challenge didn't require him to be a saint. Still, his actions made her feel a little less guilty about the end result.

Stellan kept his back to her while they walked, putting some distance between them. *Good, he should have trouble facing her.* Although it would've been better if he'd just realized the gulf between them before he risked so much.

Caught up in the ranting going on in her head, Cardis nearly missed seeing Stellan turn.

"Hey, wait a minute!" She stumbled over a root in her haste to catch up with him. "Ow, dammit!"

Stellan walked back to her and rested his pack on the ground as he stared at her foot. "Sorry, princess, I didn't realize you couldn't keep up."

"I can keep up," she snapped at him.

"Not if you break your ankle." Stellan knelt down and ran his hand over her foot.

Cardis stepped back to put her foot, and the rest of her body, out of his reach. "I didn't break my ankle. I just tripped, which I wouldn't have done if you hadn't run so far ahead I couldn't watch you and watch where I'm going."

"How did I know it would be my fault," Stellan muttered.

She scowled at him. "It's not a race, you know."

He cocked a brow at her. "Isn't it? I seem to remember someone saying the clock was ticking." He lifted the pack and tossed it over his shoulder. "Besides, I want to get to the cabin before dark. The path can be a little rocky when you're not familiar with it.

"And that would make it different from the rest of this trip how?"

Stellan couldn't help himself. He laughed. The woman wouldn't give an inch. The more he talked to her, the more he felt like he was on the losing end of a boxing match. He stared at her, let himself have a long hard look at the woman in front of him. Her golden eyes spit fire at him, her creamy-colored cheeks flushed with indignation. Hands on her hips, she snarled at him as he continued his appraisal. He put on his most serious expression, one he hoped oozed confidence and safety.

"I just meant it'd be easier for you in the daylight."

She snorted. Stellan managed to hide his amusement, an emotion he felt sure Cardis wouldn't appreciate. She seemed to hate it when he grinned at her, a fact that confused and amused him.

Since he'd been old enough to know what to do with a woman, Stellan had never really spent much time in their company. The painful memories of his mother faded as he grew up and the tepid images of the majority of Edarian females changed his concept of the gender.

He knew he gave more pleasure than most men of his world, knew he treated them with more courtesy than they received from others. But in his heart, they bothered him. He grew tired of their cast-down eyes, of their quiet acquiescence. They offered him their body but without passion, without joy. Now, standing right in front of him with a frown on her face and fire in her eyes, was passion bundled in a package that made his body stand up and pay attention. A package that hated him, hated everything about him. He shook his head. Fate a indeed a wicked trickster.

"Nothing about this place is easy," Cardis mumbled as she bent over to pat the dust off her legs.

The movement gave Stellan a delicious view of her ass, tightly outlined against the fabric of her pants. Her shirt shifted forward, exposing a line of creamy skin. As he swallowed the groan, he wanted to tell her she was so wrong about that. It was incredibly easy for his body to respond to her. No matter what the woman did or how much she bitched, even the sight of her shot his body into overdrive. Easy as can be.

"I'll make you a deal, darling." Stellan hoisted his knapsack back onto his shoulder. "If you'll keep up, I'll slow down. But not too much. We need to make it to Barron's Fort before much longer."

"So we are going to be near a town of some sort?"

He reached for her hand, surprised when she let him take it. "What's the worry, princess? You've got your shield for protection. I think it's me who should be worried."

"You? What do you have to worry about?"

"Well, we've already had our first fight. And you didn't exactly listen to my explanation then. And you are a virgin. Since the whole goal of tonight is for me to jump your bones, I don't want anything to get misinterpreted."

"Jump my bones?"

"Just an expression, darling. One of the less crude ones I could've used."

"Not a very sexy image."

"I don't know." He stopped and turned to face her. His gaze traveled up and down the length of her. "You've got some nice looking bones, princess."

Cardis frowned at him. "Still not a sexy image. How alluring is a skeleton?"

He laughed. "You've got me there." His look moved slower this time, taking in every inch of her. Something in those deep green pools made her shiver. "Maybe it's what's covering those bones that's got me going."

Cardis blushed. "Let's get back to this settlement you talked about. Are my flesh and bones going to have shelter tonight?"

Visions of sleeping out among the rocks and the wild animals did nothing to calm her nerves. Or maybe the man didn't intend to let her sleep. Right now she didn't know which would be worse.

Stellan stepped closer to her. "Don't worry, darling. I'll make sure you stay warm tonight."

He leaned in before Cardis had time to think, planting his lips on hers in a kiss that had her reaching out her hands to steady herself. Unfortunately her fingers landed on his shoulders. The feel of his warm skin pressed against hers did nothing to ease her nerves. She pulled out of his embrace.

"I think we need to focus on making time, so we get to where we're going."

"Oh, darling, I was making time. And I was headed exactly where I wanted to go."

"Well, you know what I meant. We need to, that is, I'd like to get to wherever, or to whatever place, you have planned for tonight."

Cardis didn't think she'd ever felt so flustered. The amusement on his face didn't help. Where had all her poise gone? For that matter, where had all her sanity gone? *Back away from the sexy man, Cardis, and take a deep breath.*

"So it's on to Barron's Fort then." Stellan kept her fingers locked in his grasp, giving her hand a little tug to get her feet going.

"Barron's Fort?" Maybe a little conversation would help her focus. "So it's a military outpost."

"Not exactly, although it was founded by a soldier."

"By a soldier? He was alone?"

"Seems this particular soldier had a pretty high opinion of himself."

"Proof he was an Edarian male."

"No harm in having self-confidence, princess. A confident man knows he can get the job done."

Shut up, Cardis, just shut up. Don't give him any more openings. He laughed when she pulled her hand from his grip.

"Anyway, as I was saying, this particular soldier decided he had too much skill and talent to be a lowly foot soldier for the headman of his province. Unfortunately, the headman didn't seem to recognize his vast talents and never promoted him. So the soldier decided to strike out on his own, to set up his own province where he would rule."

"And he came here so he could rule the people living here."

"Well, he came here, but there was a slight problem with his plan. At the time, nobody else lived here."

"I can see where that would create difficulties."

"Yeah, it's kind of hard to be a king if you don't have any subjects. Nevertheless, being the talented guy he was, Soldier Barron didn't let that insignificant detail deter him from his well-laid plan."

"What confident male would." Cardis rolled her eyes.

"Exactly."

Stellan reached for her hand again, wrapping his fingers around hers before she could protest. He raised her palm to his lips and pressed a kiss into the center of it. The feel of her warm soft skin against his made his body spark. Cardis scowled at him as she tugged on her hand. Stellan tightened his grip around her fingers.

"Why do you always have to keep touching me?"

Stellan arched a brow at her. "I thought that was sort of why you and I were together." He laughed as her scowl deepened. "But for now, we're coming to another rocky place. I don't want you falling again."

"You don't have to kiss me to keep me from falling."

"I know. That's just a fringe benefit. You don't have to thank me for it."

He smiled at her. Cardis gave him a dirty look, but didn't pull her hand away. Stellan considered that a small victory. Buoyed by it, he started off down the trail again.

"So anyway, deciding he'd worry about a little thing like subjects later, Soldier Barron decides to build himself a palace. But he runs into yet another problem."

"This guy's not having much luck, is he?"

"If he wanted luck, the fool would never have come here. But that's beside the point. This problem he didn't really recognize until he'd finished building his new palace. As the only kind of dwelling he'd ever built before was of the military variety, his palace resembled his previous carpentry efforts."

"He built himself a fort and not a palace."

"Exactly. And a very sturdy fort too."

"But not a very kingly fort."

"No. It was pretty much the standard foot soldier type fort. But it was the best he could do and winter was coming. So Soldier Barron settled into his fort and waited for his people to arrive. To pass the time, he took up a hobby, one he'd gotten pretty good at during those long nights of soldiering when all there was to do was sit around and wait."

"And this hobby was?"

"Sculpture. Soldier Barron apparently had quite a knack for carving. Since no one else was using the wood around him, he had plenty of material to work with. So he carved, all winter long. By the time spring came, he'd carved himself another item that every king needs."

"Which was?"

"An army."

"Sounds like a good use of his time. So now he's sitting around his fort that masquerades as his palace with a wooden army for him to command. You're right, if this guy wanted luck he came to the wrong place."

"Now, you never know. Maybe things turned out better for him here than they would have if he'd kept to soldiering. He could've died in the very next battle and all of his talent would've been lost."

"Are you telling me all his carvings are still around?"

"Certainly. When the people finally came, they found Barron's fortress, manned by his wooden guards, each one of them posed in the position of some daily routine. Why Barron even kept a journal, giving all of his guards' names and duties. There was one little problem he couldn't deal with though."

"Only one, huh?"

"Well, at least one. Soldier Barron lived to a ripe old age. The folks who found him figured he was probably well over a hundred from the dates in his journal."

"Found him?"

"What was left of him. That was the problem. His wooden guards couldn't bury him, so he lay where he died for several years, until some folks traveling through the area looking for a place to settle found him. Once they'd seen the valley and the readymade fortress they could spend the first winter in, they decided to stay in Barron's home. When they spread out from the old fort, they took the wooden guards with them. Every house in town has one. And they've held up well over the years too."

"So they named the town after him."

"Uh-huh. His story's been passed down for years. Guy's probably gotten more glory for carving wooden soldiers than he ever would've in battle."

Cardis paused in her stride, caught by the laughter twinkling in his eyes. Stellan stopped beside her.

"What?"

"You're a sucker for stories, aren't you?"

"Stories can tell you a lot about things, princess." He stared at her out of those wild green eyes and Cardis wondered what other stories lay behind them. "And sometimes, they tell you what's true."

He started whistling again as he headed off down the path, leaving her staring at his back with more worries than ever. Who was this stranger she had to deal with? First he was a savage barbarian, holding her and her people hostage in a strange land, a thief who looked only to what profit could be gained, then a reckless gambler pushing to acquire her wealth and her lineage by challenging for her, then a seductive demon turning her mind and her body to mush with the touch of his hands. Now the chameleon became a storyteller, enchanting her with odd anecdotes and humorous histories about a land he so clearly loved. How was she to decide anything when she couldn't even pin down his character from moment to moment?

****

The setting suns seemed determined to race them to their destination. As Stellan's pace quickened, Cardis realized they probably weren't going to make it to their shelter before dark. Still he pushed them on.

"Watch out!"

Stellan held out his hand as Cardis slid down yet another rocky hillside. She was sure her butt had pebbles embedded in it after the ridiculous number of times she'd plopped down on it to make her way across the rocky terrain. Not to mention the cuts and scrapes on her hands and arms. When his warm skin made contact with her sore palm she had the fleeting temptation to yank him down beside her. But she was far too tired to exert that kind of energy.

As she pushed herself back to her feet, she gazed around. There were lights ahead, and a number of buildings she couldn't really tell much about from this distance. They stood at the edge of some sort of town.

"Are we there yet?"

She didn't care how whiny the question sounded. Every part of her was too tired to care. Stellan pointed ahead of them as he took her hand and helped her down the rest of the hillside.

"Down there."

A roughhewn trail led to the back of a ramshackle wooden building. It was square and plain, with windows set along one wall that poured light out through the dirty panes. From what Cardis could see, the surroundings appeared to be in the same rundown condition. Withered green trees barely as tall as her waist bent over the path. She would've called them bushes, but with such sparse branches the name seemed like a lie. More rocks lined the walkway, with scruffy weeds poking out in clumps here and there.

Standing guard beside the back door like a mighty warrior was a wooden soldier nearly seven feet tall. He had an ugly face and a weird-looking pointed hat. Grasped in his oaken hands was a weapon that resembled an old-time pike with a wicked looking point at one end. Cardis shook her head at the sight of it. Thank goodness the whole thing was wood. Stellan pulled to a halt at the head of the trail.

"If you want to take a rest here while I head into town it would make things faster."

Cardis nodded, still busy sucking in enough air to fill her starved lungs. She could tell her amiable reaction surprised him.

"You think you'll be okay here for a bit?" Stellan stared at her, obviously torn between leaving her and getting what they needed.

Better than I would be in there. The noise blasting out of the roughhewn building told her a crowd filled the inside. With the way she felt now, the fewer people she dealt with the better. A few moments alone might clear her head and give her back some needed balance.

"Are you going in there?" She nodded toward the shabby building.

"Yeah. It's a tavern, but they should have what we're

after."

"A tavern? Is that like a consumption station?"

"Uh, more of a community gathering spot. But Owen will have food and a few other things we might need. It won't take long."

"Sure thing. I'll be right here when you get back." *Provided nothing eats me while you're gone.* Cardis waved him off with a limp smile.

With another cautious peek at her face, Stellan headed down the trail.

Gazing down to look for a safe spot, Cardis walked around until she found one reasonably free of debris. Her butt hurt badly enough without dropping down on another rock. Weary beyond belief, she lowered her aching body to the ground. Pleased to find nothing poking in her sore backside, she settled herself against a pathetic looking tree. She hoped its strength could hold her.

Her thoughts drifted aimlessly through her tired brain as she took stock of her surroundings. Cardis had seen a few planets that remained backward and basic, but a cursory look around this village told her Edaria redefined primitive.

A burst of noise and laughter had her turning to the windows of the rundown tavern. Through the grimy glass she watched as Stellan entered, moving among the gathered crowd with the ease of familiarity. Something about seeing him mirrored against the rough wood walls and rowdy people made her take a long hard look. He moved with the confidence of a man in his element.

She couldn't deny how attractive Stellan was on a purely physical level. But she also couldn't deny the man had something extra, a sort of innate magnetism that drew a woman in, made her want on that same physical level. And he was definitely drawing her down to his level, because it seemed all she had to do was look at him and she wanted.

As Cardis watched, Stellan strode through the room like he owned the place. People seemed happy to see him, especially the women. One of the women serving drinks to the people at the tables quickly dropped her tray and moved to hug him. Her hands wandered all over his body, one of them even easing its way along the band of

Stellan's pants, an action Cardis found totally inappropriate. She tried to tell herself it was just that the woman's blatant touches were unseemly, completely brazen. Then the harpy stood up on her toes and planted a kiss on Stellan that went beyond brazen.

The sudden stab of fury shocked Cardis. Her hands actually curled into fists before she told herself there was no way she could justify going in there and using them on the hussy. And why should she? There was nothing between her and Stellan except a risk he'd been dumb enough and greedy enough to take. The man was a barbarian, a male for whom a civilized monogamous relationship was beyond comprehension. Without waiting to see Stellan's reaction, Cardis closed her eyes and leaned back against the tree.

"Primitive in every way," she muttered. If she stayed in this place much longer, she'd become barbaric herself. "Come on, Cardis, pull yourself together."

Opening her eyes, she turned her attention to the inanimate structures around her, careful not to stare at the windows in front of her. Now that she was closer she could tell a little more about the place.

Buildings designed to provide the most rudimentary type of shelter dotted the landscape. The river she'd heard while they walked along the trail burst out of a grove of trees to encircle the edge of the town. Although there was an open space in what could have been the center of the small community, the buildings had no design or plan she could discern. Some faced the open space while other doorways faced away. A series of paths connected them, but the grassy trails wandered without any apparent order. The whole place looked like it had been constructed according to whim.

Beside most of the houses were tiny gardens, much of their contents wilted and bent over. With all the water available from the river so close by, their neglect made no sense. But then much about this place made no sense.

Cardis glanced around for what could be considered basic necessities, a landing pad, a radio tower, food silos, anything. Her search came up empty. The only building that didn't appear to be living space was the rundown tavern. And the only structure that appeared to have any sort of technological component was a half-built system of pyramids that ran across the river by the edge of town. It appeared to be some type of dam, or at least the beginnings of one. From the sound of the raging water a dam would be a good thing.

There were other things that would be good as well. Cardis' sense of order had her outlining what it would take to upgrade the living conditions in this backward place. It was the type of exercise she enjoyed. Often when she traveled, she'd spend hours laying out in her mind how to improve the areas she saw. Edaria was a blank slate screaming for technology.

As she sifted through the ideas running around in her head, Cardis remembered engineering designs that would make food production a snap with the power from the raging river and a few minor tech components. The additions of greenhouses and fertilizers would make even Edaria's rocky terrain double its production. The people of Barron's Fort would have a dependable supply of food with half the work involved now.

The walls of most of the structures appeared to be constructed of wood, weathered and beaten to a disheveled state. Several had roofs in desperate need of repair. Cardis wondered why they would use such fragile materials to build. Darvian steel was lightweight and virtually indestructible under any weather conditions. Structures built from it held out the heat in summer and the cold in winter, providing a climate controlled environment that made life pleasant and durable.

Thinking about pleasant environments reminded her of the structure they were headed to. The cabin. Even the word sounded primitive. If town lacked any amenities and the cabin was further away even yet, then there was no telling what kind of structure she could be stuck in. For the first time she began to wonder what kind of wild animals roamed the landscape of Edaria. If they were anywhere near as dangerous as the men who inhabited this place, then whatever shelter they found had better be really sturdy. She cast a doubtful frown at the ramshackle buildings in front of her.

The door to the tavern flew open and a high-pitched giggle intruded on Cardis' thoughts.

"No, Ruen, there's nobody out here. We'll be all alone."

Cardis watched the young couple in the harsh light from the tavern. She pressed herself back against the tree. The last thing she wanted was to be spotted. No telling what these people would do if they thought she was snooping around their town.

"Exactly..." The man leaned in to nuzzle the girl's neck, producing another of the ear-splitting giggles. "Come on, Savilla, don't you trust me?"

"We shouldn't be out here alone."

The man pressed her back against a tree. With a knowing grin, he leaned in to kiss any further protest from her lips. The girl let him ravage her a long full moment before she shoved him away. Cardis held her breath and hoped the twit didn't giggle again. The sound made her want to gag. The man nuzzled her neck, letting his hands play with the tiny buttons on her dress.

"I'm going away, Savilla. Feelan is taking me on as a trader with his group. I might be gone a long time before his ship comes back this way again. Don't you want to see me off with a proper goodbye?"

Talk about making her gag. For a moment Cardis entertained the idea of revealing her presence to save all of them any more embarrassment. But the thought of explaining the reason for her presence there made her rethink the idea.

"A proper goodbye?" The girl's whine grated on Cardis' nerves. "But you told me I was special, that you and I had something special."

And you bought that line? Cardis snorted.

"We do." The man grasped her hand, pressing her fingers to the front of his laced pants. "And I have something special for you, something for you to remember me by when I'm gone."

He shoved his hips against her and the girl melted against his chest. The laughing twit let him sweep her into his arms and pull her off around the rambling building, blessedly out of her sight. As the sound of their footsteps faded, Cardis swore under her breath. Another one brainless enough to fall for it. The girl was an idiot to have taken such feeble bait.

The thought brought Cardis' musings back to her own dilemma. She remembered the way the serving woman's hands roamed Stellan's body, the bold way she stroked her fingers along his pants as if to ask if his cock could come out and play. Was that what would happen when they reached this cabin, that Stellan would want her to throw herself at him with just a wink and a nod from him? Was Stellan counting on a night to remember?

"Not by a long shot, mister," Cardis mumbled. "I'm not some stupid giggling girl to fall so quickly or so easily."

Cardis found some comfort in the echo of her words on the twilight air. She'd be no man's wife, no man's golden prize. Her life would be of her own making. What happened would happen and she would deal with it. One thing she refused to do was let herself be turned to mush again. If the fool thought her easy after what happened at the river, he'd best think again. One little lapse didn't change a thing between them, nor did it change the circumstances that brought them together. She needed to remember who and what he was. And he needed to be reminded of who and what she was. Before they went any further with this seduction thing, she meant to let him know his task was still monumental. The brief bout of insanity she'd had when he put his hands on her for the first time came merely from inexperience and all the trauma of the day. Now she was ready for him and he wouldn't find her such an easy target again.

By the time Stellan came out of the tavern, physical discomfort and anger over men in general had worked Cardis into a state of nerves. She'd bitten off two of her nails and started on the third when Stellan grasped her hand. He pulled her to her feet.

"Time to go, princess." He tipped her chin up and peered at her face. The light from the tavern door stung her eyes and she shielded them with her other hand.

"Everything okay?"

Cardis jerked her hand from his grip. "Certainly. After all, it's at least every other day I find myself shipwrecked in some godforsaken wilderness, forced into an intimate challenge for all that I am by a backward barbarian, dragged through said wilderness by the aforementioned barbarian and left waiting outside some rundown shack, alone with my thoughts about what might happen to me, until my charming host comes back to claim me for the night. What could be wrong?"

She slammed by him only to be brought up short by the girl standing in the shadows. A young boy stood beside her, both of them holding bags. Their looks were anything but friendly as they gave her the once over.

They were little more than children, the girl a year or two older than the boy. The resemblance between them was striking and Cardis wondered if they were siblings. Both had blonde hair, the girl's caught up in a braid wrapped round her head as if in an attempt to make herself look grown-up. Her worn dress pulled tight across her front to accent the beginnings of breasts. A necklace of colored stone hung around her neck. She looked from Cardis to Stellan. Cardis couldn't help but notice the adoration on her face when she turned to Stellan. For some reason the sight of it annoyed her. Did every female in this place fall for him? Cardis stared at them coolly. The girl returned the frigid look as her gaze went up and down Cardis.

"She isn't pretty, Stellan." The girl wrinkled her nose as if she found the sight of Cardis distasteful.

"Kara!" Stellan looked at the girl in shock. "What would your mother say about your manners?"

"Well, she isn't." The girl glared at Cardis as she tossed the bag to the ground. Without another word, she turned and stomped off.

With a look of sheer bafflement, Stellan turned to the boy.

"Nathan, what's gotten into your sister?"

The boy shrugged his shoulders in an imitation of his sister.

"She's had her nose out of joint ever since Willem Nicholas told her she was pretty."

"Willem's been courting Kara?"

"He wants to. Kara screamed at Pa for nearly an hour last night when he told her he'd wed her off to old man Narian afore he would Willem."

Stellan shook his head. "That's 'cause he knows Willem's not much more than pretty words. Your sister would have a hard road with him."

"You could take up with her."

"What?"

The boy glanced at Stellan, then at the ground. "Kara always wanted you to look her way, Stellan. And Papa would favor you even more than old man Narian."

"Me?" Stellan gaped at him.

"Yeah. Papa likes you. Mama, too for that matter. And Kara said if she had to wed an old man, at least you'd provide well for her. And you looked nice enough. She'd have a few years before you got the paunch and lost your hair."

Cardis couldn't keep the laugh in although she did try. The look of consternation on Stellan's face was priceless. He glared at her before turning his gaze back on the boy.

"Thank you, Nathan." Stellan yanked the bag from the boy's hand. "Tell your mother thanks for the food."

The boy nodded as he slouched off toward the tavern. Cardis continued chuckling as Stellan picked up the bag Kara had dropped.

"You think that's funny, do you, princess?"

"Oh, come on, you've got to see the humor in it. The girl's hardly old enough to be contemplating a courtship, much less a marriage."

"Oh, really? For your information, her sister wed when she was but a year older than Kara is now."

Cardis stared at him. Shock covered her face and Stellan cursed his careless tongue.

"You're joking. Why, she's hardly more than a baby."

She sputtered for a moment as she saw the truth in his eyes. Her temper spiked. Was there no female on this planet who was safe from the males here?

"What kind of parent would send a child that age to a marriage bed?"

"One without many options." Stellan looked at her and Cardis bit off her retort at the warning in his eyes. "Not everyone can afford to be the oldest virgin, darling."

"But that's, that's so...." She tried to calm the anger raging inside her.

"Barbaric. Yeah, I know."

He hefted the bags in one hand, the other gripped

around Cardis' fingers as if he feared she would run. His grim smile met the shock in her eyes head-on.

"Don't judge what you don't understand too quickly, princess. Kara's parents love her, they want good things for her. At least, as good as Edaria offers."

"And the best thing for her is to let a little girl go from playing with dolls to playing with a husband."

"They'll pick a good man for her. And I wouldn't let Kara hear you call her a little girl. She wouldn't appreciate it."

He started to walk away but Cardis held her ground.

"What about her dreams? What about what she wants?"

"How do you know a husband isn't what she wants?"

"Because," Cardis spluttered. "Because she's too young, because she hasn't seen anything else, known anything else, because...."

"Because it isn't what you want?"

Cardis' retort stuck in her throat as she stared at him. There was no grin on his face now. His gaze bored into her as if he saw into her soul. She wanted to snarl at him. After all, she hadn't deceived him. She'd told him this was too risky, that he couldn't succeed. Before she could think of how to answer him, he turned away, letting go of her hand and hoisting the bags onto his shoulder.

"Like I said, princess. Don't judge too quickly what you don't understand."

Chapter Nine

"This is it?"

Stellan's hopes fell at the tone of her voice. It wasn't a happy sound. The comment was the first thing she'd said since they left Barron's Fort.

They'd made it to the cabin as the suns were setting, which left enough light to get a good look at the structure as they approached. From the expression on Cardis' face, Stellan felt pretty sure that wasn't a good thing. Total darkness might have kept some of the less positive features of the place under wraps until morning.

All the way there, Stellan mentally kicked himself for putting his foot in his mouth about Kara. He knew Cardis saw them all as nothing but a bunch of primitive uncultured barbarians, barely above the level of savages and instead of telling her something positive, he'd only added to that image. Now they'd arrived at his home for what was going to be an even more nerve-wracking experience and the woman couldn't stop gaping in horror. If he'd hoped for any assistance in winning her over from the natural beauty around her, he was guessing he was shit outta luck. He walked past her to the door.

"It's home, safe and snug." He gave her a jovial smile. She frowned at him. "Equipped with your own personal guard, princess."

Stellan pointed to the wooden statue menacing the doorway. Cardis rolled her eyes.

"He's a little short, isn't he? The one at the tavern must've been at least seven feet tall."

Stellan glanced at the statue. He'd picked the shortest one of the bunch, amused by the fierce expression on the bearded wooden face. The guard was only around five feet tall, but his teeth were bared and his weapon towered over him by a foot. *Couldn't the woman tell how fierce this guy was?*

"Hey, he's short, but stocky. Look at those muscles, at that terrifying expression on his face. Anybody'd be scared of this guy."

Cardis stared at him then shook her head as she brushed past him headed for the door. *Yep, she wasn't going to be seduced by her surroundings.* Stellan tried to keep the smile on his face.

The last rains had swelled the wood around the doorjamb. Stellan heaved his shoulder against the heavy wooden door to force it open. Part of him hoped she watched him so she could see how strong he was. Part hoped she was occupied elsewhere so she wouldn't ask why it took brute force to get the door open. He couldn't even put up a good defense by telling her his home was a typical structure for Edaria. In fact, his place bore many amenities that others didn't have. But he knew it paled in comparison to what she was used to, so he kept his mouth shut. He didn't want to have to answer any more questions than he had to. Cardis didn't have to know this was about as high as their technology went.

He shoved the door back and waved her in with a flourish. "After you, princess."

Cardis inched her way through the door, peering in before each step as if she feared what might jump out at her. Stellan toyed with the idea of giving her a little shove to get her inside. What did the woman think was going to happen? He hadn't led her anywhere dangerous so far. Well, that wasn't quite true, but if he left out the sexual realm he'd been really careful where he took her. Trying to give her a little encouragement, Stellan put a hand on her back. Cardis jumped as if he'd hit her.

"What?"

"What? Nothing. I was just trying to help you inside."

"Oh. I thought you meant to watch out for something. Don't help me, okay?"

"Sure thing, darling."

Stellan pushed past her into the room. At least the place was clean. He'd sent Samuel ahead of him to the tavern to ask Alberta to see to that. He would've asked the boy to purchase their supplies as well, but Samuel wasn't to be trusted around money. It was the only trait he shared with his father, although with Samuel it was more from distraction than greed. The boy hardly ever saw real money. If Stellan had handed the boy coin, neither message would've reached Alberta.

"See." He turned to her, amused that she still stood in the doorway. "It's perfectly safe to come inside."

Cardis stepped over the threshold and peered around. "It's sort of dark in here, isn't it?"

"I can fix that."

Stellan crossed his fingers and prayed as he hit the switch on the wall. To his relief, light flooded the room. He decided right then and there to reward Samuel with coin for remembering to kick on the generator. And to give Alberta more than one extra coin for what the light revealed.

His message had been simple, asking her to add a woman's touch. It turned out to have been a wise remark. Gone was his 'here lives a single man' décor, replaced by those small touches that made a house become a home. He almost didn't recognize his solitary dwelling beneath the comforting additions his friend had placed throughout the rooms.

The whole cabin was clean and sweet smelling. Alberta had placed wildflowers in vases around the front room. Stellan blessed the old woman's artistic bent as he smiled at the handmade rugs on the floor, the embroidered tapestry on the wall, the clever arrangement of colored stones and candles on the table by the fireplace.

A quick peek through the doorway to the bedroom had him smiling. A cloth spread of vibrant hues of blue and green covered the heavy wooden bed and more vases of flowers stood on the bedside tables, their rich colors dazzling in the fading rays of light coming through the windows. He smelled the scent of the thick woodsberry candles Alberta made in her kitchen and his hopes soared. It might not rival Adena's wealthy homes, but Cardis had to see the beauty in it. This was the beauty of Edaria, the beauty of his world and that was what he had to seduce her with. That, and a few other things he hoped she found beautiful.

Stellan pulled his thoughts together as he ushered

his prize inside. Her perpetual sneer was gone for once, but what replaced it made him just as nervous. She looked like a captive walking to the execution block. He wracked his brain for something to say to her, something to ease her mind. But he drew a blank. Was this what bridegrooms went through on their first night together? How in the hell did they get through it without sending their bride screaming from the room?

He couldn't share his thoughts with her. The only words tumbling around in his head right now were things he felt sure would not put her at ease. Especially not if he backed them up with the actions his body screamed for. So he kept quiet. His time was limited and he'd do anything he could to aid his challenge, even if it was only to shut up. Now that they were here, though, he had best start coming up with some good ideas and quick.

Cardis walked around the room, rubbing her arms with both hands.

"Why is it so cold in here?"

"Yeah, sorry about that. The place has been closed up for awhile. I didn't have Alberta start a fire since I wasn't sure when we'd get here. I've been gone for several days, even before your, uh, mishap and the nights are usually pretty cool during this season."

"But what about the climate control? Is the regulator broken?"

"Uh, no." *More like nonexistent.* Stellan thought it better to keep the answer to the first question to himself. He tried not to let her remarks discourage him. "Give me a moment and I'll have a fire going. It won't take long to warm up in here once I get some heat started."

"A fire?" She gave him a puzzled look. "You want to start a fire?"

In more ways than one. "Just watch and learn, princess. You're about to see a demonstration of Edarian technology at its finest."

Ignoring the snort that followed his words, Stellan went to the large fireplace that lined most of one wall. He felt her staring at him as he pulled wood from the box next to the hearth and scooped aside the ashes scattered over the bricks. Maybe polite manners kept her from asking what he knew was on the tip of her tongue.

Although she certainly hadn't worried about being polite up until now. From the corner of his eye he saw her standing uncomfortably in the center of the room. Her gaze scanned the walls, the floor, even the ceiling.

"This is your home?"

"Yes." Stellan laid the wood the way his grandfather taught him out of long habit. It was more decoration than efficiency, but Einarr had believed the method as important as the end result. So Stellan stacked the larger pieces in the rising v-shape, the tinder cradled inside its boundaries. He struck the flintstone, the sparks catching at once. His grandfather would be proud. He sat back on his heels, hands held out to the struggling flames. It felt good to be home, no matter how unusual the circumstances.

"Or at least, most of the time it is. I try not to be gone too long, and during the winter I'm here pretty much all the time. The weather isn't good for traveling then."

"So you don't live near your brothers? "

"No." He rose and turned to her. "There, it's going. Give it a minute and things should start warming up." *With any luck, lots of things would warm up.*

As his need feasted on her, Stellan realized he didn't need any fire to warm him up. One look at this woman and his body jumpstarted just from the view. He'd been busy the last few weeks, but he'd hardly been celibate. So why did this woman yank his chain so hard with just a glimpse of her? Even clothed, the sight of her made his hormones spark like the engine on a starship.

The memory of the feel of her skin as he pleasured her with her own hand, of the tiny gasps and whimpers she'd made as he drove her to feel what kind of satisfaction he could give her rammed itself into his brain, sending lust through every fiber of his being. If he lost this challenge, it sure wouldn't be from not putting enough into it. His whole body clamored for action. *Go, team, go.*

He strode past her to the kitchen before she got a good look at his groin and ran screaming. Cardis moved closer to the fire. *Or was it further away from him?* She stood with her backside to the flames while she continued her appraisal of his home, her hands idly rubbing her bottom as if to warm it. It was on the tip of his tongue to offer to do that for her, but he didn't think she'd appreciate it. He tried to busy himself in the kitchen, hoping she didn't notice the sideways looks he kept giving her. At least one of them should appear comfortable here.

"You chose a spot a good distance from your brothers. Was that intentional?"

"Well, you know, all kids move away from home someday. You got the stars, princess, I have Barron's Fort. And this place had, shall we say, sentimental value. Not to mention a readymade home waiting for me."

"You inherited this place?"

Stellan gave her credit for not sneering when she said it. He could tell the effort cost her.

"Yeah. Barron's Fort is where my mother was from. This was her home, the one she grew up in." He waved a hand around him. "So here I am, home sweet home."

"You came back here after she died?"

"Not right after. I came back only a few years ago. After my father died." Stellan thrust away the painful memories. "I visited at first, took care of what had been hers. Finally I decided to stay. It wasn't a hard choice. I still have people here in the village, and I'm comfortable here."

"People?"

"You know, family. Relatives."

"So you moved away from family to be near family."

"I guess you could put it that way. Odd, I know, but that's the way I am. I'm sure you've figured that out by now." He winked at her.

"I have noticed you're somewhat, different."

"Well, at least you didn't say strange. Different can be good. As a matter of fact, I'm sure it's different where you're from. Everyone probably lives in their own mansion, huh?"

"Hmm." She nodded absently as she turned toward the growing fire to warm the front side of her. "What you did here, your fire," she waved a hand at the blaze. "It's a skill I've never seen before. It seems so, so…."

"Backward?" he finished for her.

Cardis kept her face turned so he couldn't see her expression. She'd held her tongue at the last because it seemed rude to insult him in his own home. But he continued to ramble around the tiny kitchen space as if her words didn't bother him. She gazed at the fire. Though using such a method for heat did indeed seem backward to her, she was forced to admit there was a strange beauty to the dancing light.

"I suppose backward is the word you were searching for. It would fit the rest of the comments you've made about this place."

Cardis stiffened, but she saw no point in starting a fight with him now, even though, for some reason, being reminded of her rudeness seemed rude on his part. Still, she should try for the high road. She was the civilized one after all. Plastering her most sincere expression on her face, she turned toward him.

"I apologize if I've been less than generous. My words were meant only as an observation. After all, I wasn't prepared for being here. This is the first time I've been to your planet and my visit was a surprise. What, um, information I have heard about Edaria has been perhaps biased."

"Gossip and rumors usually are."

"Look, this whole situation is rather awkward, and it was your choice, not mine. I'm sure you love your home and can see all its virtues. But you have to admit, there are certain, uh, unaccountable differences between Edaria and most of the realm. Differences that appear more from choice than circumstance."

"And our choices make us backward, is that it?"

Cardis shook her head. "You're deliberately misunderstanding me. I mean, look around you and try to see it through my eyes. There are no amenities, not even any simple conveniences that one would expect. I'm wondering why you and your people choose to live this way when it would be so easy to make life less difficult."

"So we should suck up to the Council, do whatever they want just so we can have these amenities you think are so necessary, huh?"

Cardis rolled her eyes. "Okay, I give up. No more comments about difference. And I will try to keep the word backward out of my conversation."

"That's okay, I can see it on your face."

"On my face? Are you saying you can read my thoughts by looking at my face?"

"Well, not exactly read your thoughts like I would know them word for word. But I can get the general idea. You have one of the most expressive faces I've ever seen."

"Really?" Cardis didn't know if that pleased her or not. It certainly made her feel vulnerable.

"Yeah, really."

He grinned at her as he moved toward her. Cardis had a sudden thought that the heat that moved toward her from the front would rival the flames in the primitive fireplace behind her. Both blazes could get out of control easily.

Still, she couldn't keep her eyes off him as he sauntered over to her. For a barbarian, he moved well, with a lithe grace that came from a man who knew his own body and was comfortable in it. *How comfortable would she be with that body in three days?* Something about that thought suddenly seemed way more appealing than she cared for.

A tiny voice in the back of her head nagged at her. Could it hurt to enjoy what was coming rather than being terrified? After all, think of all she could learn. The memory of their time by the river caused a blush to move up her cheeks. From what she could tell, Stellan knew things her mother hadn't included in the lessons. Maybe the next three days wouldn't be a complete loss after all. A pity though, that such a hot body would end up dead or enslaved, but that was the body's poor luck for housing such an ego. She had given him a chance to back out and that was all she could do. Still, it would be a shame to waste such a talent for pleasure. Cardis remembered an auction she'd seen on Rial Four. The memory had her smiling.

"See, like now." Stellan moved in front of her and lifted a hand to her face. One finger traced her lips as he stared at her. "I can tell you just thought of something, probably something that ended up with me in a less than flattering position."

"Oh, I don't know about that." She shifted away from him enough to keep his finger from her skin. "It could be considered very flattering. What's more, you might like it.

113

And it would be a rather interesting position. Maybe you can't read me as well as you thought." She grinned.

He looked at her with suspicion. "What are you thinking, princess?"

Cardis gave him a wicked smile. "That maybe I should sell you to one of the pleasure houses on Rial Four when you lose this challenge."

"Pleasure houses? You mentioned those before."

"Sure. They're all over the outpost there. After all, the women of the realm need some R&R every now and then."

"So they buy men in these pleasure houses?" Stellan wasn't sure whether he was horrified or intrigued.

Cardis shrugged. "Yes, I guess. I suppose the men don't exactly volunteer."

"So Edaria isn't the only barbaric planet in the realm."

"I suppose not. But, it would be better than ending up dead. You move well and aren't too bad to look at. And after your little demonstration at the glen, you'd probably do real well in a place like that. So long as you keep your mouth closed, you could be a most pleasant companion."

"Well, I'm glad you enjoyed my little demo. But as to your pleasure houses, although there are parts of that I have to admit I find interesting, I don't think I like your basic description of my qualifications. You make me sound like a trained puppy."

"More like an untrained one."

"This from an ancient virgin."

Cardis sighed. "He has baited me with that for years now."

"In the hopes you'd take the hint and face a challenge?"

Cardis blushed. "Perhaps, though I think it was more my mother's harping on my unmarried status that he wanted to end."

"You know, princess, you keep harping on what you don't understand about Edaria and how backward we all are compared with Adena. But I have to tell you, I don't understand the men on your planet either."

"Why, because they see their women as more than property to attach to the best provider they can find.

Because they allow a woman to make the choice that affects her most of all."

"And she has to base that choice on physical skill, on sexual intimacy."

Cardis blushed. It was a part of the challenge she didn't understand herself. "Passion is a part of marriage." Her mother would be proud she'd remembered that line. "It's important that two people be compatible in that area if they are to mate for life. Otherwise, there may be reason to upset the harmony of the home."

"You mean to stray?"

"Yes. The challenge deals with the messy aspect of choosing someone who will be a good partner in every way."

Stellan shook his head. "Okay, let's say I buy that for now. Answer another question for me. Are the men on Adena all nobility?"

"All nobility? I don't understand."

"Well, let's face it, there's more to this challenge than knowing the two of you'll be happy between the sheets. I mean, you yourself said as much."

She frowned at his reminder of her cynical judgment of her suitors. "Yes, I did. Although you seemed to think then I was too jaded in my conclusions."

"Jaded, yes. But I can still see where you're coming from. You're a beautiful woman, don't mistake me, but you're right, that's not the only reason you're known as a prize. And you tempt a man, with your looks and with all your, how shall we say, accessories."

"My accessories?"

"You're a package deal, darling, like it or not. So I'm wondering, how does a woman like you avoid a challenge for so long? You offer a man a chance. Surely there's some poor slob slaving away as an underling in somebody else's business who dreams of having his own freighter or of creating his own empire. So why not challenge for a rich woman?"

Cardis felt a small pang of disappointment at his words. So much for stroking her ego. "I wondered when we'd get around to this again. Thanks for the compliments but you can keep them, buster. I know it's not my fair skin or sexy body that's got us alone in this godforsaken place. It all boils down to what I bring to the table, doesn't it?"

"Don't get yourself in a snit, princess. This is your custom, not mine. You're the one who keeps comparing the two places. I'm just following your train of thought, so to speak, just trying to understand how civilization works. I mean, we might be backward I'll admit, but I'm beginning to think your men might be a little slow on the uptake too. They've got a golden prize right in front of them and they let her get away? Doesn't sound like men who are right on top of things to me. Are Adena's men not strong enough to take what they want, what they need?"

"You forget, we virgins come with protection."

"Okay, I meant confident enough to go after what they want."

"There is a courtship ritual, a time leading up to a challenge where the two people assess how things might go between them. There are families to consider, likes and dislikes, the issue of compatibility."

"Back to that compatibility thing again, huh. Do you ever think two people could be too compatible? I mean, harmony's good and all, but it can be overrated. And sometimes it takes a little spark now and then to keep a steady flame going. You make this challenge sound kind of boring, more like a trial run on a business merger than three days of hot, sweaty sex."

Hot sweaty sex? The image derailed Cardis' retort for a moment. Seduction seemed a mild term for what those words conjured up. A sudden view of the two of them, their naked bodies plastered together in an embrace that involved slick skin and that musky scent of his made Cardis' mouth go dry. She ignored the mental pictures and focused on a spot somewhere around the top of his head. Surely looking at his hair wouldn't inspire lust.

"A smart man simply doesn't walk up to a strange woman and propose a challenge that could end his life should he lose it."

Her blatant implication made Stellan smile. "Seems to me a smart man wouldn't ignore an opportunity, a golden opportunity at that, when it drops in his lap." He shrugged. "Maybe Adena's men aren't so smart after all."

He raked a hand through his hair and Cardis found

herself remembering the feel of those gold-streaked strands against her neck when he drew close. Her fingers itched to thread their way through all those waves. *Get a grip on yourself, woman.*

"Maybe Adenan men aren't desperate." *Unlike me, apparently.* Cardis struggled for control. Maybe temper would be the best tool to use now. "Life on Adena is not so bad nor so backward they're willing to risk their lives on an impossible challenge."

"You mean, they don't know how to want something bad enough. Or could it be you and the rest of the noble families on Adena make sure they know what not to want? Do you make sure they know the rules of the game, princess?"

"Stop calling me that. I've told you, I'm not a princess."

"Could've fooled me, darling."

"Well, it doesn't take much to fool a fool. For your information, Adena is a republic, with an elected council, not some sort of feudal kingdom that keeps the populace oppressed and put upon. Unlike those in some places I could mention, our people don't have to want for those things that make a good life. The government makes sure those things are all available to them."

"Keep 'em warm and fed so they won't notice what's missing, huh? Still sounds boring." He laughed when she rolled her eyes. "Well, I'm glad you didn't take on any challenges. I prefer to think fate was making you wait for me." He gave her a wink then laughed again at the scowl on her face. "Speaking of warm and fed, maybe I'll take a tip from your civilized government and feed you. It did seem to work real well before."

Cardis blushed as she remembered what followed the meal at the river.

"There's a bathing room through there," Stellan jerked his chin in the direction of the doorway, "if you'd like to wash up while I fix us something to eat.

Nodding, Cardis headed for the door.

****

It took Cardis four tries before she got the water to come on in the strange contraption. Voice commands did nothing but leave her standing in the middle of the room feeling silly. Undaunted, she pushed and prodded every spot she could think of until she coaxed a small stream of cool water into the basin. Listening for a moment to make sure Stellan was still occupied in the other room, she wiped much of the sweat from her face with the cloth she'd found in the tiny closet. The cool cloth on her skin felt so good she stripped off her top and used the sweet smelling soap in the tiny dish by the sink to quickly wash the rest of her. The heat hadn't reached this room yet so she hurriedly toweled off and tugged her top back on. It wasn't a full shower but it would have to do. Maybe any leftover smell would dim Stellan's ardor and he'd leave her alone tonight. *Fat chance, especially after she'd warned him the clock was ticking.*

Cardis heard him rummaging around in the other room. The fool was whistling. A sudden pang of nerves made a shiver run down her spine. She was completely alone with a total stranger, a man as far removed from the men of her people as he could be. Even in all her travels Cardis had never encountered a world so different, a man so different as this one. A man so capable of manipulating her with a simple touch. He'd proven she had reason to be wary of him. Tonight she wouldn't let him slip through her guard so easily.

Cardis turned the thought over in her mind. She wanted to be fair to him, to the challenge. In that sense, her honor was at stake. But then, he hadn't exactly played fair with her. It wasn't fair that she'd even ended up in this predicament. She shook her head, trying to clear her mind before she faced him again. This was a game, albeit one with some serious repercussions, and he'd been warned of the consequences. If he courted danger, it was from his own reckless choice. She didn't have to take the responsibility for him. After all, his reasons were hardly ones of love or honor. He'd made that clear a few minutes ago.

She knew why he would want her. It wasn't ego for her to know that. Her wealth and her lineage did indeed make her a prize, a fact that had been pointed out to her by others. A fact that had brought her to this rough shelter and a strange man.

"Front room's warming up some."

Cardis jumped to find him so close to her. She hadn't heard a thing. It wasn't a good sign that the man could be so sneaky. Or that she could be so distracted.

"Hmm? Yeah, I guess I'm about finished in here." She turned to face him.

"You're probably pretty chilly back here." Stellan moved closer to rub his hands up and down her arms. "Later, I'll fix the water heater and you can take a shower. After things have warmed up."

Stellan smiled, wondering if she'd catch his meaning. He had no intention of letting much more time pass before he got his hands on her again. She'd fled to the bathroom like an army was after her.

He'd harbored the hope she would've stripped to wash. The thought of all that creamy skin open to view made his mouth water. But then he was glad she hadn't. The shower could be a perfect place to play. That vision had him contemplating a myriad of delicious ways to enjoy touching her. Then he caught a glimpse of those beautiful golden eyes. There was definite fear in them, no matter the sneer on her face.

Stellan had never traveled out of his own world, never spent any real amount of time with someone who didn't share his background, his culture. What must it be like for her to stand here in a strange place and know what he wanted from her? And on top of that she was a virgin. That was the whole point of the prize. He never dealt much with virgins, knowing that those in his world would have marriage in mind. To the women of Edaria, that seemed the only compensation for sex. And Stellan enjoyed pleasuring a woman, something more likely to happen with a woman of experience than a frightened virgin. Gentling the need that shouted for him to touch her, take her, he stepped toward her.

"I think Alberta left some extra clothes for you."

"Oh? It'd be great to get out of these dirty ones."

As soon as the words were out of her mouth, Cardis blushed. She'd already chastised herself for flinching as he came near her. The oath she'd taken meant he could come near her, real near her and she had to allow it. But this was the first challenge she had ever faced, the first man to put his hands on her in such a way. She swallowed hard.

"A shower would be nice. Thank you." *No way in hell was she stripping all her clothes off voluntarily, not so long as he was anywhere near.*

"Great. I'll get the heater kicked on after we eat."

"Okay."

Although she really had no appetite, Cardis moved past him into the front room. Spread out on the roughhewn table was a small feast, cold meat and cheese, dark bread and some red fruit that resembled the wineberries that grew wild on Adena. She was startled when Stellan pulled out a chair for her. They sat together for a while, staring at each other across the food. Neither of them seemed interested in any of it.

Stellan noted the way she hugged her arms in front of her, the way fear glistened in her eyes. There had to be a way to relax her or this night would prove nothing. He rose, noting the slight jump she made at the movement. As he walked past her, he smiled. She watched him with a puzzled look on her face as he carried their plates to the sink.

"It doesn't look like either one of us is hungry." *At least not for fruit and cheese.* Stellan turned back to clear the rest of the table.

"No, I suppose not," Cardis murmured. Though her choice would've been to sit and stare at each other all night, part of her needed to get on with this before she exploded. At least if she started it, she controlled it. Or so she hoped. Wondering if she'd truly lost her mind, she stood up.

"So now you propose that I strip my clothes off and let you have at me with all the skill your people devote to such things?"

He paused to stare at her on his way to the sink. Something twinkled in his eyes that was part lust and part amusement. "And is that what you think I want to do with you, have at you?"

Cardis folded her arms across her chest. "Of course. That's the whole reason we're here in this godforsaken place, so that you can get your hands on me and dazzle me with the supposed skill you have in luring women into your bed."

"Darling, I'm beginning to see how you got rid of your other potential challengers. You've got a tongue that can make a man walk away in a hurry."

"And yet I couldn't drive you away. More's the pity."

"Maybe being a backward barbarian gives me an edge on your fancy Adenan men. Although my risk does seem kinda pointless when you glare at me that way."

"I've told you all along it was pointless. But you're too stubborn to listen."

"Actually, I've never been told I was too stubborn. More often, not stubborn enough. Maybe you know me better."

"I know nothing about you at all."

"No, you don't, do you?"

He stared at her a moment with a thoughtful look on his face. Then he walked back to the table and lifted his chair. Cardis froze as he carried the chair over by the fire. *Was the man going to tie her down?* She tried to remember her mother's talks on foreplay. Had any of them included a chair?

Stellan stopped and lowered the chair to the floor before he turned back to her. She could read nothing in his expression when he looked at her. He patted the chair and motioned for her to come over. Cardis looked from the fireplace to Stellan, wondering which blaze was the most dangerous.

"Well, maybe there's something we can do about that, darling."

Chapter Ten

Stellan walked back and picked up the other chair. He carried it to where the first one was, turning them to face each other. Then he glanced back over at Cardis, who stood rooted to her spot by the table, one hand gripping the edge. Boy, did he hope this worked.

He patted the chair in front of him. She didn't take the hint. Stellan walked back over to her, prying her fingers away from their death grip on his table. He feared there would be scars in the wood. As he tugged her toward the fire, he gave her an encouraging grin.

"Neither of us really knows anything about the other. Our, I guess you'd call them interesting, circumstances haven't exactly been conducive to that. And we certainly haven't gotten off to a very good start." He sat down in one of the chairs. "Well, maybe there's something we can do about that. How about playing a little game with me, darling?"

He reached up a hand and tugged her down onto the other chair.

"A game?"

"Sure."

She looked at him with suspicion. He grinned at her.

"You know what a game is, darling, where you play."

The memory of what he'd termed foreplay at the river sent a chill through Cardis. Or was it heat spiraling up in her already? Whichever, she fought it and him with a sneer.

"Play? Play is for children. I thought, since your time was limited, you might be interested in more adult pursuits tonight."

"Oh, there are all kinds of games that can be nicely adapted for adults." He winked at her. "We tried some of them just a little while ago, remember?"

Damnit, he remembered too. She gave a yawn, and plastered what she hoped was a bored look on her face. "Yes, I believe you tried to call it foreplay. I think you don't quite understand the definition of that word."

Stellan chuckled. "Let's just play for a little while, have some fun. Later you can analyze my definition and whether or not it lives up to your expectations."

"Yes, that's what I'm supposed to be doing, isn't it?" She gave him a smile. "After all, I do get to judge this little contest."

That ought to put the ball back in my court. If her ploy worked, she couldn't tell it by Stellan's expression. The fool just kept smiling at her.

Stellan found it hard to concentrate on any of her words. The thought of what he got to do tonight sent his lust meter into overdrive. Vaguely aware she was talking, he reached for her arm, needing to touch some part of her body before his senses exploded.

As she babbled on, he pushed the fabric up slightly so he could wrap his fingers around her bare skin. Busy trying to intimidate him with words, Cardis didn't seem to notice. Disappointed at first, Stellan then decided it just might work to his advantage to keep her off guard. If he worked at it, he could probably have a few items of clothing off her before she knew it.

"Are you listening to me at all?"

He looked up in time to catch her frown. "Uh-uh."

Stellan pulled her to him and gently touched her lips with his. Her honeyed scent filled his nose and he wanted to bury his face in her neck. Reluctantly, he pulled back, pleased to see Cardis' face was flushed. So much for not distracting her. She cleared her throat.

"So you want us to have some fun, is that it?"

"Yeah, some fun, darling."

And just for fun he let his lips roam down the side of her neck this time. When he pulled back, it was harder to leave the taste of her skin. Other things were getting harder as well. The reward for his suffering came when she cleared her throat several times.

"And we're going to do that by playing some stupid game."

"Uh-huh." He gave her another quick kiss, just to keep the taste of her on his lips. "This game's real simple so you should catch on quick." He smiled at her sharp intake of breath.

"You're the idiot, not me, so I would expect the rules to be simple."

"It wasn't an insult, darling, just an observation. I don't believe you play much, at least not with men."

"Wouldn't that be the whole point of being a virgin?"

He laughed. "Yeah, I guess it is. Especially one who avoids any challenges the way you have."

For some perverse reason, the snarl on her face pleased him. Stellan leaned in close, traced the outer circle of her ear with his lips, let his mouth trail across her cheek to the edges of her eyes, eyes that watched him warily, as if he would strike before she could defend herself. Which was exactly what he intended to do, only not in the sense she believed.

He'd watched her the whole time they'd been alone and he'd learned one thing. This woman in front of him had more than one shield. Though the magic one could kill him, the other one kept him from getting inside her. And he found he very much wanted to get inside her, to see what made a woman like her tick. And what made her burn. Something told him the cool, aloof package she wrapped herself in concealed more passion than any woman he'd been with. He continued his assault on her senses as he tugged her against him.

On reflex Cardis closed her eyes and he planted a gentle kiss on them. When she pulled back, she opened them again. Wariness had been replaced by confusion. *So far, so good.*

"I believe we had this discussion earlier, about the way Edarian men must prolong childhood." Her voice was throaty and breathless.

"Yeah, maybe, but like I said, this isn't a game for children, not the way I've adapted it."

Stellan let his hands rest on her shoulders for a moment as his lips brushed her chin. She shivered against his tongue and he hardened. It wasn't going to be easy to play with her knowing there might not be anything in it for him. The rules of the challenge left it up to the woman if she chose to do any seducing of her own. Wald had made a point of sharing that tidbit with him. Stellan feared Cardis had a long time of celibacy in mind for him. But no matter. Watching her wouldn't leave him completely unfulfilled. There were ways to get satisfaction. He adjusted himself with one hand, trying to ease some of the pain. Cardis watched his movements and her eyes widened. She licked her lips and he smiled.

"There are things grown-ups do to play that can make a game really worthwhile."

She rolled her gaze up from his hand. Stellan let his fingers trail up her arms until his hands slid around to cup her breasts. Through the fabric he brushed her nipples, delighted to feel them harden under his touch. Never taking his heated stare off her face, he reached for her hand. Splaying her fingers out against his chest, he placed his hand over hers and moved them both down until he pressed her palm to his swollen cock. If he was going to die, he was going to die happy. Her eyes got even wider.

"I can touch you, you can touch me. This is most definitely a game for grown-ups, princess." Her hand slid the length of him and Stellan feared he might explode right in her palm.

Breathing deeply to control his growing need, Stellan placed his hands back on her, let his thumbs trace slow circles around the sensitive tips of her breasts. "Want me to tell you the rules?"

"There are rules to this game?" This time there was a definite rasp to her voice.

Stellan kept his hands moving. He didn't think she was even aware of the fact that she moved closer to him, leaning into his touch.

"Well, I'm actually kinda making them up as I go along, but we can call them rules if you want. You strike me as the type of lady who likes rules and order."

Cardis took several deep breaths before she gazed at his face. She realized her hand still lay on his cock and she jerked it away. When he chuckled, she tried to sneer at him again, but her breathing was still a little off.

"Does this game have a name?"

"Not really. Here's how it goes. You get to ask me a

question and I get to decide if I want to answer it. If I answer it, you have to take off one piece of your clothes."

"And if you don't answer it?"

"Then you don't take off anything. Then I get to ask you a question."

"And the same thing happens?"

"Yep. If you answer it, I have to take off some of my clothes."

"And if I don't?"

"Then you don't get to see anything, darling."

Cardis shook her head. "I can ask you anything I want?"

Stellan nodded. "And I get to decide if I want to answer it." He winked at her. "And if I get to see anything. I'll even let you go first."

"Gee, thanks." This time she did sneer. "And you have to answer honestly, right?"

"Right. Or don't answer at all."

"How will I know you're not lying?"

He shrugged. "I guess there does have to be a little trust. But, since I'll be dead if I lose the challenge, if there's any answers you plan on using against me, it won't matter anymore. And, when the more likely outcome occurs, where you and I are saying marriage vows, I figure you won't want to use any incriminating information against your new husband. So either way, there's no point in my lying."

Cardis tugged at her lip as she thought about his proposal. In a matter of minutes the man had undone all her resolve and she hadn't lost any of her clothing. There was no telling what he could get her to do if she were naked. Talking might postpone the total meltdown of her brain. Surely she could prolong the questioning until it was too late for him to do much to her. After a long enough time she could plead fatigue and put anything else off until the morning.

"All right, I'll play. And I'll accept your offer to go first."

Stellan gave her a mock bow. "Ask away, princess."

"How many poor unsuspecting victims have you and your brothers lured to this place so you can rob them?"

Cardis leaned back in her chair and gave him a smug

smile. She felt certain he wouldn't want to get into that topic, no matter what he said about not caring if he incriminated himself. Yes, indeed, they both were likely to remain clothed for quite a long time, maybe throughout this whole bloody evening.

"None."

Stellan reached for the buttons on her top. Cardis slapped his hand away.

"You have to answer honestly."

"I did." Stellan grinned.

"You did not! I know our ship isn't the first. The crimes Edaria has committed are legend among the merchants of the realm."

"Not crimes, darling, trade practices."

"Trade practices?"

"Exactly. Practices developed from the necessity of dealing with the constant damage from vessels that wreck here because they can't seem to keep themselves out of our airspace. Our boundaries are well known among those who belong to the Council, as are our welcoming policies. Yet we continually have to deal with the wreckage of Council vessels that violate our airspace. You asked how many we lured down here. Well, you've ridiculed our technology enough since you've been here. Have you seen anything that would lead you to believe we have the capability to lure a star vessel out of its orbit? Anything we could use to trick them into landing here? Hell, we can't even communicate with any of the vessels. Why do you think all their distress calls go unanswered?"

Stellan leaned back and folded his arms across his chest. "That was a completely honest answer. None of those were poor helpless victims, as you call them. Neither was your vessel. Your pretty little ship came down in our airspace without any help from us. You might even say we rescued your party."

"Rescued us? In no stretch of the imagination can you say you rescued us. But for the sake of argument, call it a rescue. How do you explain away your looting our cargo?"

"Not looting. The cost of doing business. Or rather the cost of rescuing. Like all the others, your father has the option of trading with us. If he wants the cargo we've recovered—"

"Including the crew and the passengers?"

Stellan nodded. "If he wants his property back, he will make a trade with us." He leaned forward in his chair. "And that was three questions, princess, all of them answered honestly."

Cardis glared at him. Then she gave him a cold smile. "Very well. Your honesty should be appropriately rewarded." She reached down and removed both her boots, tossing them into the corner.

"And the third?" Stellan smiled.

"Of course. I wouldn't want to deprive you of anything you're due." Cardis lifted one foot and carefully rolled her sock down and off. "Satisfied?"

"Not by a long shot, darling. But then, we're not finished either."

Cardis gritted her teeth. "No, of course not. We still need to play some more. I'm sure you're anxious to get the other sock off and have a look at the other foot. So what's your question?"

Stellan lifted her foot into his lap. "Not so fast. Maybe you're right, I'm missing an opportunity here."

"An opportunity for what?" Cardis' already fired temper spiked as he stroked a finger along the bottom of her foot. She didn't have an erogenous zone in her foot, she just couldn't. How fair was it that there didn't seem to be a spot on her body where the man couldn't heat her up by touching it? "Now you're going to start tickling me?"

"Maybe. Seeing you let loose with a real laugh might be worth it, especially since I think you've missed the concept on playing altogether. It's supposed to be fun, darling." Stellan's hand started up her leg. Cardis yanked her foot out of his lap.

"Uh-uh. There are rules, remember? You don't get to touch anything you haven't uncovered so my leg's out of bounds."

Stellan chuckled. "For now. I guess I'll have to get back to it shortly. Now to my question."

Cardis rolled her eyes as he tapped a finger on his chin. "Don't strain yourself."

"Worried, darling, that tonight won't be as much fun if I hurt myself? Why, that's so nice of you. I didn't think you cared. But my question's really simple, so don't worry.

At least, this first one is. Why have you avoided every challenge until now?"

"I would think that would be obvious. I don't want this."

"This?"

"All this." Cardis waved her hands. "All this focus on sex and seduction and how much pleasure a man and woman can have together. It's all a trap."

"Spoken like a true virgin. A trap? Now that's the way most men would see it, not a beautiful woman with every reason in the world to marry and settle down."

"That's it exactly. A trap, disguised by men to lure unsuspecting women into lives they never wanted in the first place. Men get to watch the stars go by, to see the whole universe and everything in it, women get to sit at home and watch their lives go by, until they wake up one day too old to dream anymore. It's a trap, using our own bodies, our hormones, our own needs as bait. And most women never know it until it's too late."

"Now how could the women of such an advanced culture not see something like that coming?"

Something about his tone of voice set off a vague warning bell in her head, but she was on a roll and couldn't stop herself. She'd never before had anyone to listen to her diatribe on this barbaric custom. Most of them ran before she could finish telling them what she thought.

"Because all of them, men and women, have bought into the idea that the challenge is a good thing, that it makes marriage more harmonious, more civilized. Hah! Oh, sure, it gets covered in a nice wrapping that makes the men of Adena feel all civilized. Why, their women get to choose their own mates, how advanced is that. They allow their women such freedom. What a crock. They call it freedom but what you don't get is the freedom to ignore their little custom."

"You get named the oldest virgin."

"Exactly. Try ignoring their little challenge concept and they go off the deep end. You're some kind of basket case if you don't run headlong into their trap. Well, I won't be caught like that."

Too late she slammed her mouth shut as she caught

the smile playing over his face. She couldn't believe she'd told him all that. What kind of magic did this man wield? It had to have been the feel of his hands on her. Or the fact her brain seemed to die whenever the man was near her. That was the only explanation Cardis could come up with for her loose tongue.

"Does that little diatribe mean the great and mighty culture of Adena might not be so civilized after all?"

"Of course we're civilized. That's not what I meant at all, I mean, I do get the choice. Nobody's locked me up yet. I have avoided any challengers," she glared at him, "up until now. It's not like I'm a teenage girl being bartered off to any old man who comes along. My dreams aren't irrelevant to my future."

"And what is it you dream of, princess?"

Cardis snorted. "Don't pretend you're not laughing at me. I've seen the state of the women in this place. The men here don't even bother to lay a pretty trap when they want to go after a woman. After all, she's just another piece of property, another thing to acquire."

"Just a prize for a man to reach for, is that it?"

Cardis gave a harsh laugh. "I doubt Edarian men consider any woman a prize. They wouldn't value her that highly."

"Maybe she carries more value than you think, darling, especially when he looks at the rest of his life. The stars aren't something even the men here get to dream of, so maybe they don't have much else to dream about other than the woman waiting for them at home."

Stellan tugged at the buttons on his vest, then pulled it off. "We don't get to dream much on Edaria. So we play games." He tossed the garment into the corner with her boots, then started to unlace his pants.

"Wait a minute, what are you doing?"

"Well, princess, you just answered four questions and it all sounded pretty honest to me. I'm just giving you your reward."

"Since it's my reward, don't I get to pick what comes off?"

Stellan paused, the sheer panic on her face almost comical. "I take it we have different rewards in mind."

"I mean, you need to take off your boots first, right?

You're gonna have to get them off before the pants anyway, and since you already took the vest off, then two boots, well..." Cardis' voice trailed off as her gaze landed on the line of golden hair revealed by his unlaced pants.

"Okay." Stellan bent to unlace his boots. "But I don't think you're gonna be seduced by us playing footsies all night."

"Well, you could take off your socks first."

He grinned at her as he pulled the boots off. "I'm not wearing any, princess. The only thing left is the pants." He tossed the boots into the corner.

Before she could protest further, Stellan tugged the leather pants off and tossed them in the corner with the rest. His confidence buoyed by the fact her gaze didn't rise above groin level, Stellan sat back down, stretching his legs out in front of him. *Wouldn't hurt his cause to give her the full view.*

Cardis felt the blood drain out of her head, likely to pool somewhere that was far more demanding. How was she to know the man wore nothing but pants and a vest. *She'd have stopped blabbing sooner if she'd known that.* Everything nature had given him was now displayed in front of her. And nature had been kind. The stars be damned, this man's body was the most heavenly sight she'd ever seen.

She shook her head to clear it, disgusted by her total lack of control. Just because every inch of his skin was the same burnished gold was no reason to drool. What did the man do, stroll around naked all the time? She had to get a grip. If all the man had to do was strip and she was toast, then she'd have to kill him after this. She couldn't leave any witness to what he was likely to have her do once her brain had shut off and her hormones ran amuck. She folded her arms across her chest and stared him straight in the eye.

"All right. So what would you dream of if you could?"

"The stars." Stellan answered so quickly Cardis couldn't doubt his words, nor could she ignore the hunger that filled his eyes. She knew it, recognized it, for she'd seen it often enough in those who chose the stars over more sane pursuits. And she'd felt its echo in her own heart when she pleaded with her father to take her with him on his interstellar runs.

For some reason his hunger for the stars made her feel more uncomfortable than his lust for her and that irritated her. She hadn't taken his dream away from him. It wasn't her fault he couldn't be out there flying around. But maybe she understood the risk he was taking. Cardis pushed the little voice away. The man was taking a risk with her future as well.

"Same as every other man. Men don't dream of home and family because they want to, only if they have to."

"A man can dream of a lot of things. Even about a woman's feet." He reached for her other sock but Cardis tucked her foot under the chair.

"Enough already. I'm not going to sit here and stare at you naked while you play with my feet."

He stretched that long, lean body, muscled arms over his head and all that golden skin right smack in her line of sight. Had she not feared he'd call her a coward outright, Cardis would've closed her eyes.

"Okay, darling." He tugged her bare foot into his lap and ran his finger down the arch, pleased by the tiny moan that escaped her. "I'm ready to start working my way up whenever you are."

Chapter Eleven

Torn between the screaming of her frazzled nerves and the heat from the fire his finger had started on her instep, Cardis didn't know whether to cry or moan. She would've sworn there were not that many erogenous zones on a woman's body. Her senses reeling from his assault, Cardis knew it was either time to do this seduction thing and get it over with or beat him over the head with the pot on the table and get the hell out of here, rules or no rules. If seduction was the menu for tonight, then they needed to get to it. And she needed to control it.

She folded her arms across her chest and stared at him, stifling the latest moan with more effort than she cared to think about.

"I guess that means you're through playing around then."

He laughed. "Oh, not by a long shot, princess. We haven't even really started playing."

Stellan slid her foot down his leg as he stood, the bristly feel of the golden hairs on his thigh against her sensitized skin bringing another moan she couldn't quite stifle. What was worse, the movement put certain parts of him practically in her face, parts that suddenly intrigued her a great deal. Her tongue stuck to the roof of her mouth as she stared, ensuring no words came out. A good thing, for the words that wanted to tumble out were ones like *please* and *I want*, which had replaced other more sane phrases in her feeble brain.

"But I think you still want us to get to know each other a little before we play harder." Stellan winked at her. "So I guess we need to think of other ways to do that."

He leaned close, placing a hand on each arm of her

chair so that he hovered over her, not touching but teasing her overwhelmed senses with the heat from his body. Hovered so close she could feel him breathe, close enough to bathe in the lust spiraling off him. Close enough to want with a mindless hunger she'd never felt before. Strands of his gold-streaked hair brushed against her face and when he spoke his warm breath shivered across her skin.

"Do you want to play with me, princess?"

"Huh?"

The one syllable managed to escape past her formerly frozen tongue, which now wanted to dart out and lick the drool from her lips. *Don't look down, just don't look down.*

Stellan closed the distance between them and she didn't have to look down, didn't have to imagine anymore. She felt him against her thigh, solid flesh, the whole length of him, hot and hard pressed against her skin. Cardis knew it was only the thin fabric of her pants that kept her from being scorched.

The smile on his face added to her irritation. Maybe there was something she could do to wipe that infernal grin off his face. She was no coward and it was time she stopped letting her fear and her inexperience rule the night. He wanted to play games, then maybe it was time she picked the game.

"Other ways, huh?" She tilted her head back and looked him in the eyes. "Let me see if I can think of one this time."

Cardis stood, her gaze never leaving his as he stepped back to let her up. She gripped the band of her trousers with both hands and pulled them off in one swift motion. Before she lost her nerve, she whipped the stretchy top over her head. Since she'd been sleeping when the *Venella* spun out of control, Cardis hadn't stopped to fully dress before running out to find out the trouble. She wasn't wearing anything under her clothes either. There seemed something karmic about both of them being prepared to strip down, but she chose to ignore that thought. Instead she opted for a look at his face.

"Wow."

Stellan let out a low whistle. Cardis eyed him

suspiciously.

"You don't have to flatter me. The rules of the challenge say I have to let you touch, so don't strain yourself trying to come up with compliments."

"Well if you won't accept them, then let me extend my compliments to your parents, cause, honey, you are a beautiful work of art."

She tried to ignore the hungry look on his face, tried to put his words down to an attempt to charm her. *Why did the fact he thought her beautiful give her a thrill?*

"I'm sure they'd be pleased with your assessment of my gene pool, but trust me, charming words aren't going to be enough to get you out of the mess you're in."

"The mess I'm in." He gave her a quizzical look.

"You're the one that risked your life on this great sexual skill you're supposed to have. So now you have to put up or shut up. And I'm not about to have you crying that I didn't give you a fair chance."

"Darling, I don't think I'm gonna be crying at all when this is done." Stellan sat back down in the chair and clasped his hands behind his head. "I don't think you will be either. Although women sometimes do tear up when they're happy. But I prefer to leave you smiling."

"Whatever you have to tell yourself. Just know there won't be any reason for excuses later."

"I appreciate your fairness."

Stellan's eyes twinkled as he stared at her, the look on his face one of complete satisfaction. No matter how blunt she was, there seemed to be no getting through that thick skull. Well, the consequences were on his head from here on out. He'd been warned.

Kicking the trousers to the corner, Cardis sat back down, spreading her legs wide around the sides of the chair. She leaned back, resting her hands on her bare thighs.

"Well, go ahead. Take your best shot."

As seductions went, it was crude, but effective. As far as Stellan was concerned it was a pity more women didn't use that approach. He wondered if he should be taking lessons from her instead of the other way around. Whatever her motivation, her moves impressed the hell out of him. Somewhere between the playing and the questions, his elegant princess had gone from reluctance to aggression. For just a second he wondered which question turned her around. But then, maybe it was his answer.

As he continued to stare at the gorgeous sight in front of him, what little oxygen was left in his brain exited with a whoosh. From the moment she'd tugged the shiny top over her head he'd had to work not to drool. Though he could tell from her remarks the woman had no idea how beautiful she was. And he had total permission to do whatever he wanted.

Not a man to waste a golden opportunity, Stellan lifted her legs and placed them on his thighs, keeping them spread wide so the view didn't change. It was a view he liked. Intrigued by the change in her, he watched those golden eyes as his hands roamed over her body.

Cardis bit her lip as Stellan's rough hands slid up the inside of her thighs, his callused palms oddly gentle against her skin. When his fingers brushed the edges of the dark curls over her core, she readied herself for his touch. But his hands moved up and skimmed around her hips to her back, leaving her edgy and breathless instead. With a tortuous slow pace, his hands stroked back to the front of her, brushing right by the part of her body that screamed for more as he circled around again, then lifted her hips to stroke his hands along her ass. The feel of him so close, the sight of the thickness of him laying like a heated flame before her, made her want to scream.

"Touch me."

The words leapt out of her mouth before she could stop them. Embarrassed through and through, Cardis hoped she wouldn't have to spell out where she needed that touch to be, where she had to have his fingers caress. There was no telling what words she'd use to do that.

He chuckled. "Oh, I'm going to, princess." He reached a finger around and flicked it across her clit. "But you're not ready yet. Not hot enough yet."

Cardis thought he must be crazy because she felt hot enough now to shoot flames out through her fingertips. Then Stellan slid those roaming hands up and cupped her bottom. With another chuckle, he pulled her onto his lap. The feel of skin against skin, of thick muscles bunched against her bare ass sent erotic chills up her spine. Her brain shut down completely as sensations she'd never encountered before flooded her body. For the first time in her life Cardis stopped thinking. She only wanted to feel. Throwing caution to the wind, she rubbed her buttocks across his legs, letting the friction stoke the pressure building inside her.

"That's it, baby. Let's see if we can't make you really wet."

Cardis could only moan her agreement as Stellan leaned in and took her breast in his mouth. His tongue teased and tasted her, his hot breath and moist lips making her delicate nipples hard and achy. While his mouth occupied the upper part of her, Stellan's hands roamed her lower half, his fingers caressing and stroking the fire in her core. He circled up and around her thighs, brushing his hands across her folds just lightly enough and quickly enough to build the want inside her. The dual assault of his tongue laving her breast as his fingers skimmed her clit had Cardis fearful she'd be reduced to begging soon. If the man wanted her damp, he'd sure been able to accomplish it. Cardis felt the slickness between her legs as her aching body cried for more. When Stellan pulled back from her, she gazed at his face and knew her hunger matched his own.

"So beautiful," he murmured as his hands continued to cup her breasts. He leaned back in his chair, tugging her with him as he scooted her bottom further up on his thighs. "What do you need now, princess?"

Cardis shook her head, certain her voice couldn't be trusted. And certain there were no words she knew to describe the need he'd built in her. All her mother's training was useless. This man reduced her to a mass of feelings.

Stellan kept her thighs on the outside of his hips, propping his feet on her chair and laying her back along his legs. Spread out before his hungry eyes, Cardis felt like the main course at an erotic feast. She glanced down and gasped at the size of him. He'd grown since she last looked. Her fingers itched to touch him, but her aggressive tendency appeared to have deserted her. Then he licked his lips and all sorts of things down low spasmed.

"Are you going to eat me?" She couldn't tell if her voice carried a tone of desire or fear.

Stellan waggled his eyebrows at her. He didn't think it a good idea to tell her exactly what he wanted to do to her.

"Don't you remember I said I was going to taste you all over?"

Cardis' eyes got huge and round as saucers. He chuckled. "But for now I want to feel you, princess."

With one hand he raised her up, while guiding his cock down the juncture of her thighs as he moved her. He slid her up and over, his cock slipping in the crack of her ass then back along the same tortuous route until Cardis thought she would scream. His hands spread her so that her most intimate part lapped at his member as he gripped her hips and sent her up and down again. She tightened her thighs around him, used him to ease the growing ache pooling in her. Without thought, she moved faster and faster, gripping his shoulders as his hands cupped her bottom to keep the rhythm building. When she thought the need would surely eat her alive, Stellan thrust his penis over her clit one last time and she exploded.

Waves of sheer pleasure had her gripping him to her body, tightening her thighs around him until she felt his release, felt him spill his seed against her skin. She collapsed onto his chest and let the tremors run their course. And for a moment, she let him hold her.

"Okay, so your game was better."

Cardis couldn't stop the laugh. Stellan still sounded breathless, a fact that pleased her. She hadn't lost control of this challenge, not yet. And she didn't plan on it.

****

Cardis heard voices in her head. At least that's what she thought when she woke in the dark to find herself alone in a strange bed. Disoriented, she looked around the unfamiliar room. Starlight shimmered through the sheer curtains over the window. The green tint of the Edarian moon glowed in the darkness. In spite of how exhausting the day had been, she'd probably only been sleeping for a couple of hours. A quick glance next to her told her she was alone. Now where would he have gone in the middle of the night?

Wherever it was, it didn't matter. She was exhausted. Cardis lay back on the bed, wishing sleep would claim her again. But her mind had other ideas. Thoughts of what she had done this evening played like a vidreel in her head. Despite her attempts to take control of the situation, the barbarian had reduced her to a mass of feelings, to a sexual quandary. By the time he was finished moving those skilled hands over her body she felt well and truly used.

And satisfied. That result still left her perplexed. Who would have known such a man, the product of such a brutal and primitive culture, could find so many ways to give pleasure. He'd touched, stroked, teased and stimulated every inch of her skin. By the time he was done, Cardis swore even her hair pulsed with the orgasms he'd induced. Then they'd gotten in the shower. By the time she slipped into the soft red gown Stellan's friend had left for her, Cardis wondered if her skin would ever stop tingling or her breathing ever return to normal.

But it wasn't only the physical. He'd joked with her, teased her as if they were old friends. How did a stranger become so comfortable to talk to? The whole experience persuaded her of one sure thing. The man was far more seductive than she would've ever given him credit for. She needed to get away from him and fast.

The voices murmured in the dark again and Cardis realized one was Stellan's. Was the man talking to himself? She shoved back the thick quilt and swung her legs over the side of the bed. Then she remembered she'd crawled into the bed naked at Stellan's insistence. Though he claimed it was because she'd be warmer that way, Cardis figured that was a lie and refused to snuggle with him as he'd wanted. Standing now in the cool room, her more truthful side was forced to admit she had kept warm, even without his body heat.

The fire had died down. Cardis shivered with the chill of the wooden floor beneath her feet as she struggled back into the red gown. Once again the sheer difference of this place, and the sense of how vulnerable she was in it, assaulted her. Even the elements carried something to worry about. It was a warning she needed to keep foremost in her mind. Nothing here was controlled, nothing structured, not the temperature inside, not the living conditions, and especially not the man she'd crawled into bed next to. No matter how much physical pleasure this man made her feel, she couldn't forget the circumstances that had brought her to this place. This whole incident would go down under a learning experience. And boy, was she learning.

Cardis slid her feet silently across the floor until she reached the door. Slowly she cracked it.

"How could you, Stellan?"

It was a woman's voice. Cardis struggled to listen and understand, for the woman spoke what must have been a dialect of Edarian. But there was no mistaking the agitation she expressed. The voice held a tone of more than simple aggravation. There was an edge of fear and of despair. Perhaps Cardis was about to learn a truth about her challenger that would make the warning stick in her head for good.

She couldn't make out much about the woman's face in the dim light from the fire. Her garb was simple, but of good quality, woven in an array of color that shone even in the dark. Her light-colored braid wrapped around her head in what could have passed for a crown. Cardis remembered the braid Kara wore. Was the hairstyle a mark of womanhood on Edaria? She stood slightly hunched over, as if cowed by Stellan. Were all Edarian women frightened of their men?

From the shape of her Cardis knew this was no young girl who stood before the fire. Did Stellan have a woman on the side, one who might take offense at his challenging for her? That thought certainly put a cap on the evening. Whoever she was, she couldn't be a wife, that much Cardis knew. The magic wouldn't have allowed the ritual of the challenge to be completed had there been a bondmate for one of them. But that didn't mean he wasn't promised to someone. Cardis almost felt sorry for the woman.

But as the object of her pity moved further into the firelight, Cardis realized she was much older than Stellan, the light hues of her hair silver and not blonde.

When the woman turned to pace in front of Stellan, Cardis realized the leaning she'd taken to mean fear came from the cane in the woman's hand. Now facing Stellan, the woman leaned heavily on the walking stick. Though she must have been a great beauty in her youth, her elegant face was now lined with the years. Perhaps this woman was the family Stellan spoke of.

"Shh, Alberta. She's asleep right in the next room."

"Asleep? What is she doing sleeping when you've put so much on the line? Get in there, boy."

Stellan laughed. "I thought you didn't approve of my challenge."

"I don't. It's likely the craziest thing you've done and that's saying something. But from what you say, it's done and can't be undone, so get in there and make sure this turns out well."

Stellan's voice took on a teasing tone. "Don't you have faith in me, Berta?"

The old woman smacked him on the shin with her cane.

"Ow! I take that as a no."

"Of course, I've got faith in you, boy. More than most, as I know better than most what lies inside you."

Stellan leaned over and gave her a peck on the cheek. "I brought you something."

He walked over to the table where his pack lay and dug inside. Cardis gasped when he pulled out the five medkits and handed them to the woman.

"Ah, Stellan." The old woman shook her head. "You can't keep stealing for me."

"If it keeps you breathing, I can do it. These kits have loprinimine in them, and the injectors. You're probably about out of the last batch I got you."

"The risk is too big for an old woman, Stellan. If Hakir finds you've pinched something he thinks he can make a coin or two selling, there'll be hell to pay."

Stellan shrugged as he tucked the kits in Alberta's apron pockets. "I've taken risks before."

"And I've nursed you through the consequences before. And doctored the wounds." She tapped the scar next to Stellan's eye.

"Oww, Berta!"

"Then don't go telling me you got a spot in your brain that makes a Merovian star-rider look sane, like it would be news to me. How well I know you've taken risks before."

He winked at her. "But I got Ferrin's sow for you."

She glared at him. "And nearly lost an eye doing it. Sooner or later your luck isn't going to be enough. Neither are your good intentions. You need to start being careful." She slid a weathered hand along his cheek. "Stellan, just because some fool puts a challenge in front of you doesn't mean you have to take it."

Cardis' concern for the old woman took a slight tumble at the fool remark. If anyone had been foolish it was Stellan.

"Berta, this was a chance I couldn't pass up. It's the chance of a lifetime."

"And that's what it may end up costing you, Stellan, for if you've told the truth of it, losing this time could cost you your life. You've been reckless enough with yourself at times, but this tops them all. You've no business being so careless."

"It's a gamble, I know, but..."

"A gamble? It's a fool's dare, that's what it is. A gamble's when you might lose a few coin, or a piece of your pride. This, this could cost you your life, Stellan."

"It doesn't have to be that. Death isn't the only choice should I lose."

"Oh, you think losing your freedom is better? Either way, you're gone. For those of us that have a modicum of love for you, in spite of yourself I might add, do you think we'll be more content knowing you're slaving away on some strange planet mining ore for the rest of your born days? You gave no thought to the rest of us, boy."

Stellan shook his head as he reached for the old woman's free hand. "I took this chance for all of us, Berta."

"And if you lose this gamble of yours, where does that leave the rest of us?"

She gripped his hand and tugged it to her heart. Stellan pulled her into an embrace.

"I can do this, Berta, I know I can."

"It leaves us at the mercy of those sadists you call

brothers, that's where it leaves us. And mercy is a quality that pair holds in short supply."

The woman pushed away from Stellan, her cane tapping out a rhythm on the wooden floor that matched her agitation. When she paused, Cardis caught the glint of tears on her lined face, though the drops trailed across a look of pure frustration.

"Your father, despite his greed, at least managed to see that the people didn't starve, that their basic needs were met. Those two, they see only their own needs, only what they can take from this land, from the people." She turned and pierced Stellan with a look. "We won't survive them, Stellan. This land won't survive without you."

Stellan threaded a hand through his hair as he avoided her gaze. "I did this for all of us, Berta. With the resources I can gain, things will really change around here. The dam, the water, we can fix it, make it good again, safe again. The resources this woman will bring to us can make more difference than I'll ever make with words."

Her gaze dropped to the floor for a long moment and her voice was soft when she spoke. "And you think those resources will survive your brothers?"

"They will. I'll see to it." Stellan took her hand in his and patted it. "It'll be all right, Berta, you'll see. I'll make it happen."

She raised her weathered face up to his. "I pray you're right, boy, I pray you're right."

The old woman clomped to the door. "It's not you alone who'll pay the price if you're wrong, Stellan. You didn't just risk your own life. You risked us all."

Without another word, she went out the door into the night. With the scolding ringing in the air around her, Cardis closed the door softly and padded back to the bed. For a long time she lay there, pondering what to do with a man she couldn't figure out at all.

Chapter Twelve

Cardis felt the slow, moist lap against her skin. Would the man not even leave her alone in her sleep? She turned over and snuggled deeper under the covers. Any more seduction would have to wait until she'd had a decent night's rest.

The tongue glided down her cheek and across her neck, hot breath and crisp hairs tickling her ear as it moved, leaving an inordinate amount of slobber behind as it trailed across her skin.

Slobber? Cardis blinked slowly, then jumped as dark eyes stared back at her out of a furry silver face. She'd barely registered the size of the creature moving toward her when the behemoth barked at her. Cardis scrambled as far to the other side of the bed as she could. It followed her, its enormous feet dipping the bed precariously on one side.

"Oh, no you don't. I'm already sharing the bed with one barbarian."

Cardis shoved, barely getting one huge paw to budge when the other took its place. She jerked on the blanket to throw the creature off balance but the beast only tugged playfully on the other end of the cloth.

"Get off!"

Cardis tried for her most commanding tone, not an easy feat to accomplish sitting naked in a bed. It sat back on its monstrous haunches and grinned at her.

"Oh, you've got to belong to him. You're wearing the same goofy grin."

With an answering bark, the creature leapt over her head in one swift movement. Cardis had no time to duck and the scream caught in her throat as the rush of fur cleared her head by only a fraction. Without the slightest

144

hint of apology, the animal snuggled down on Stellan's pillow, its furry back turned to her.

"What, did I take your place in the bed?"

Content to ignore her, the beast nestled its head on one huge paw and started to snore. Cardis rolled her eyes as she untangled herself from the covers. Welcome to Edaria, home of the weird, the bizarre and the just plain silly. So much for Stellan's desire to take her somewhere quiet and secluded. For an event she'd hoped to endure alone, this place seemed full of visitors.

The thought of visitors conjured up the image of the woman's face from last night, followed by a twinge of guilt. Her comments echoed the reasons Cardis had avoided any challenges up until now. She didn't want this one to happen, hadn't asked for it and it wasn't her fault he'd risked so much on a dangerous custom not even his own. She'd warned him, her father had warned him, hell, even his brothers had warned him. The risk was his own choice. Still, the look of despair on the woman's face continued to haunt her.

She'd feigned sleep when Stellan came back. Without a word to her, he slid under the covers. For a moment Cardis held her breath, wondering if the old woman's admonishment would drive him back to his need to seduce her. But he turned away from her instead and soon she heard his even breathing. After a few minutes she'd closed her eyes tight and found her own rest.

Cool morning air had Cardis shivering as she inched out from under the covers. She'd forgotten there was no regulator for the temperature in this place. *What kind of people just lived with whatever temperature nature offered them?* Hopefully, Stellan had started one of those fires he liked to create in the other room.

She reached for the red gown at the foot of the bed. With a yawn, the dog turned a bleary-eyed stare her way.

"Hey, turn those eyes around, buster." Cardis gripped the gown in front of her. "Only one barbarian in this place gets to see me naked."

With an answering yip and what Cardis swore was a twinkle in his eye, the dog continued to stare. Ignoring her audience, she tugged the gown over her head. As she shoved both feet into the soft boots Stellan had left for her, she returned the stare.

"Now you can go back to sleep. Show's over."

As if he'd understood her, the beast rolled back over onto the pillow. Cardis shook her head as she walked from the room. Talking dogs, babbling fools and distraught women. If yesterday was any indication, she didn't even want to think about how this day would go. Or what strange creatures would appear once she left this room.

As she entered the front room, a wondrous smell and a puzzling sound greeted her. And a sight that topped them both for getting her attention.

Stellan stood by the counter with his back to her, his hair wet and wearing only a towel. A small towel. Now that she knew what lay hidden under that tiny piece of cloth, Cardis couldn't control the blush. Or the lust that shot straight through her. The man had left her body a veritable minefield. Her thoughts had nowhere safe to rest anymore.

Still, she enjoyed the view so she watched for a moment as he moved around the kitchen mumbling to himself. It fascinated her to know the lengths he had to go to just to fix a simple meal in this place. No wonder no one had time to improve Edarian technology. It took all the time in the day to cover the basics.

He juggled the containers on top of an ancient hunk of metal with flames shooting out of it with the ease of familiarity. His golden hair streamed down his back, making a tiny puddle by his feet. Still humming under his breath, he stretched that lean body across the counter and Cardis groaned at the muscles rippling beneath that bronze skin. *Thank the fates she was facing his back.* As if he read her thoughts, he turned to her. She managed to keep her focus on his face.

"Good morning." He smiled at her as if every woman woke to a mostly naked man rambling around her kitchen.

Cardis pointed to the puddle at his feet. "What, did you shower again without me?"

She tried to fake disappointment to cover the glee at not having to face that trial to her control again. Trapped in the shower with him, she'd sworn he had eight hands. And she'd wanted all of them on her, a desire she found embarrassing in the light of day.

"Huh?" He stood holding a pot that wafted the wondrous smell she'd caught when she entered the room. The steam rose around him, making the golden hairs on his chest glisten.

"Your hair, it's wet." She pointed to his head.

"Oh," he rubbed a hand through the damp mess, "yeah. I got caught in the rain. I had to scrub Ryjah down before I could let him in."

"Ryjah? About eight feet high, with four trees for legs, and a silver face with a goofy grin that matches yours, would that be Ryjah?"

"I take it you've met."

"Not a formal introduction, but enough for him to let me know I was taking his place in the bed."

Stellan winced. "He's not that good at sharing. Usually it's just me and him."

"Did you chase him away for last night?"

"No. He likes to stay with Alberta when I'm gone. She feeds him really well and her grandkids make over him. I guess he booked it over here when she let him out this morning. I'm surprised, 'cause he doesn't like the rain."

"The rain?"

"Yeah." Stellan pointed to the roof and Cardis realized what the sound was that had caught her attention when she entered.

"So that's what the noise is. I thought maybe your home was by a stream or a waterfall. Weird."

"Weird?"

"Sorry. I'm not used to so much, stuff I guess you'd say, going on around me. To so many smells, so much noise everywhere."

He gave her a puzzled look. "How do you get unused to stuff going on around you?"

"I don't know." She shrugged. "These days, I spend most of my time traveling. The *Venetta* has background noise, I guess, but most of it's deliberate, you know, like machinery or the comset. Some people use music chips while they work, but those are mostly meditation rituals or chants meant to soothe and relax. And even that's kept to a minimum. Most of the time it's quiet."

"And when you're not on the *Venetta*?"

"Our house has a filtration system, for noise, smells, things like that, so that no toxins get into the air system."

"Toxins?"

"You know, poisons, bad stuff."

He arched a brow. "You have a lot of bad stuff on Adena, do you?"

"No. Well, I mean, of course there are some things that aren't so good, a few less than healthy aspects. Every society has those."

"And you screen them out."

"It's important for the health of the people that certain pollutants be regulated. A good air intake system will ensure the right balance to create a safe environment in the home, in the work place, the right mixture for optimum health."

He grinned at her. "Are you selling something, princess?"

Cardis gritted her teeth. "No, I'm not selling anything. I'm trying to explain why it's important to filter out the more harmful aspects of the, well, of the outside world."

"Like toxins?"

"Yes."

"And noise?"

"Yes."

"Because noise is a harmful aspect."

"Well, no. I mean, yes, it can be. Noises have definite effects on people, on their moods, their productivity, things like that."

"So you filter them out?"

"Not all of them. My mother programs the system to allow for certain recorded noises that can be conducive to relaxation or meditation or that are pleasing to the ear. It's important to have some background noise. Total silence would be, well…"

"Boring?"

She glared at him. "Nonproductive. People work better with certain sounds around them."

"So when you stare out the windows, the sounds don't match the view."

"We don't have windows."

"No windows." She heard the shock in his voice. He shook his head. "How do you let the air in?"

"The filtration system. Windows create a rift in the system."

"You never look outside?"

Cardis gave him an exasperated look. "Of course we do. We even go outside from time to time. There are gardens, parks, plenty of places to be outside when we want to be."

"And plenty of shelter when you don't."

"Exactly." She gave him a pleased smile, happy to know he understood the wonders of her home. Maybe now was a good time to share some of the ideas she'd mulled over while sitting outside the tavern. Surely it would ease his mind to know that no matter how things turned out, she planned to share the benefits of Adenan technology with the poor people of Edaria.

Stellan shook his head. "So that's why you're a control freak. It's inbred in you."

She gaped at him, outrage chasing away her former calm. Idiot! No wonder this place stayed backward and primitive with a moron like him in charge.

"Excuse me?"

"Just an observation, darling. You do tend to like things your way."

"My way? If things had gone my way, I certainly wouldn't be here."

Realizing her voice had reached screaming pitch, Cardis held her hands out in front of her and took a deep breath. "I'm not going to get in an argument with you. We have two days left together. I believe we can get through that time with a modicum of civility."

He laughed. "See what I mean? Control the situation, don't let anything get out of hand."

Her voice got an octave higher. "Good manners and harmony are not telltale signs of a control freak. Not in any civilized context." She growled the words at him. He smiled at her.

"You know, if you keep gritting your teeth like that you're gonna bite clean through your lip."

Cardis struggled to find her center. *I will not give in to him, I will not give in to him.*

"You're doing this deliberately, aren't you?"

He shrugged. "You make it too much fun, princess."

"I must warn you, since you don't seem to know it, pissing a woman off is hardly a good tactic for seducing her."

"I don't know, darling. I'd say that depends on what kind of fire you want to get going. Sometimes it takes a bit of friction to stir a good flame, to get things to a good boil." Something in his eyes made her blush all over again. She looked away.

"Speaking of bubbling over...." Cardis pointed to the stove where the now frothing pot stood. Stellan snatched it off the fire. "Looks to me like too much of a flame equals disaster."

"Not a disaster, not when you know how to fix what bubbles over." He winked at her as he stirred the pot.

Cardis decided retreat was the best tactic. "Please, don't let me interfere with your domestic chores."

"Simple cooking, darling, that's all." He set the pot back on top of the metal box. "Sneer at me if you like. Without a woman here to do this for me, I'm left all on my own. And, since I tend to be kind of picky about what I eat, I've been forced to get good at it."

"Aw, poor baby."

"I'm touched by the deep pity you feel for me. And well you should feel sorry for me. It's just another drawback of my primitive and barbaric surroundings, surroundings I'm planning on you taking me away from in a very short time. Until then, I have to live with the basic truth that if I don't cook, I don't eat. Pretty backward, I know, like most everything else here."

"More of a poor choice, I'd say, something you really have no reason to whine about. After all, the technology for food preparation is so simple and so adaptable. A food dispenser offers well-rounded, healthy meals with little time investment and the capability to use any local cuisine. It frees up time, thereby allowing for familial interaction to take place."

"Familial interaction, huh? No more slaving away in the kitchen. Are you advertising again?"

"No. But I feel we should at least talk about how various improvements could be made to Edarian society. I mean, no matter how our, situation, turns out, I believe my father and the rest of the Merchants Association would be willing to negotiate a trade, so to speak, of technology for security."

"Thereby opening up a whole new market for them."

Cardis stiffened. "They are businessmen, with families of their own to care for. And good businessmen understand the need to look to the future, something it doesn't seem your brothers understand at all."

"You got that right. It would take a marketing genius to get Hakir to believe he'd be better off with a box that spits food out to him than a woman he can yell at about the results."

"Your brother would be a challenge."

Stellan grinned at her as he moved toward the table. Cardis stepped closer to peer into the pot he held. In spite of the marvelous smell, it looked like a lump of mud.

"What is that?"

"It's taeras wheat."

Cardis wrinkled her nose. "How can it smell so good and look so...."

"Disgusting?" He tapped her nose with the spoon. She scowled as she swiped the mess from her face.

"Because looks can be deceiving, princess. Taeras is a plant that grows wild around this valley, and it tastes as good as it smells."

"If you can get it past your eyes."

"Ah, careful or I'll do what my mother used to do to me when I wouldn't eat what she'd fixed." The grin turned wicked.

"And that was?"

"Make me put my hands over my eyes while she force fed me."

"How mean. Remember I've got a magic shield against that kind of cruelty."

"Don't be a wuss. You can't hide behind that shield for everything. Life's tough, princess. And most parents don't like taking no for an answer. Besides," he walked past her to the table and set the pot down. "It got it into my mouth and let me know how wonderful it tasted. Sometimes we've gotta be pushed into doing something before we know how much fun it can be." He lifted a spoonful of the sticky stuff and waggled it at her.

Visions of last evening danced in Cardis' brain. His play on words brought yet another blush to her face as she remembered how much fun having his hands on her had been. The man had reduced her to a babbling, blushing mess. She couldn't even hold a conversation with him without being embarrassed. Cardis took another look into the pot.

"You'd better be right about this."

"I was right before, wasn't I?"

Cardis glared at him. He laughed.

"Trust me, princess. You're gonna like it."

Still scowling at him, she clapped both hands over her eyes and opened her mouth.

She felt the heat of him as he moved closer, the scent of the taeras steaming around her. Her mouth watered as he drew near her and for a moment she wasn't sure if it was for the food or for him. The thought made her scowl deepen. He moved closer still and her nerves danced under her skin. Stellan hovered behind her, making her wonder what he was up to. When his hand slid down her cheek she worked hard not to jump. His breath stirred her hair as he whispered in her ear.

"Open wider for me, princess."

He purred the words against her already jangled nerves and things spurted all over her body. Cardis swore everything inside her, especially those things lower down, turned to liquid as sheer lust pooled below her belly. He stepped closer, the hard length of him pressed against her from behind as the pad of his finger stroked her lips. Cardis' tongue darted along the hot trail his fingers left and he chuckled.

"That's a good girl."

Grasping her chin, he tugged her mouth down and slipped the spoon inside. He was right, it was heavenly, decadently sweet on her tongue. She rolled the taste of it in her mouth as Stellan bent over her shoulder to plant a kiss on her neck.

"More, princess?"

He pushed against her to emphasize his words and Cardis thought her knees might fail her. She caught the edge of the table with one hand to steady herself. Stellan covered her hand with his own, taking the other one and curling it around the edge as well. Cardis felt the towel brush her as it dropped to the floor.

"Hold on tight, darling."

With those words he lifted his hands and pressed the heel of one of them against her core. Slowly, carefully, he worked the fire he'd started there, first with his fingers, then as he rocked her back against his erection.

Cardis' breath burst from her lungs in short gasps when he tugged her dress up around her hips, then slipped a hand back down to her core to continue massaging her. The rough pads of his fingertips tangled in the hair of her mound. From behind, she felt his cock against her bare ass, the hot, heavy feel of it like a brand against her skin. He thrust himself down the curve of her cheeks as his fingers peeled back her folds to stroke her.

Caught in a mindless swell of feeling, Cardis gripped the table and moaned. All of her was on fire, even her brain cells. She couldn't think, she could only feel, only wait as the pressure built and built. When her climax came she screamed and bucked as Stellan continued to milk her body for every fragment of pleasure.

When at last he stepped away from her, Cardis took deep gulps of air until the tremors subsided. She couldn't feel her legs, any of her body for that matter. She was sure she was numb, that all of her nerve endings had simply electrocuted themselves. Stellan wrapped one arm around her waist and pulled her down into the chair. Grateful, she rested her head on the table.

"Ready for breakfast yet, princess?"

Though it took more energy than she had, Cardis couldn't choke back the laugh. She leaned back in the chair and looked at him.

"It's going to take a whole lot more than a little bowl of grain if the rest of the day is going to be anything like this. I'm going to need protein, and lots of it."

He gave her a slow, wicked smile. "I hunt, you know."

"Really?" *Now why did she find that visual erotic?*

"Yeah. I'll have to arrange some raw meat for lunch."

"I haven't even made it through breakfast. I'm not sure I can even think about lunch."

"Don't think, darling." He winked at her. "Just let me

worry about all the details. Put everything in my hands."

Cardis shook her head. "Putting everything in your hands is the reason I'm here now. I don't think that's my safest bet. Besides," she gave him a sideways stare. "You haven't even attended to the little detail of putting some clothes on."

"And not attending to that little detail made breakfast all the more fun. All the more reason to put everything in my hands."

"For fun?"

"Yep. Why I'll bet already that I'm the most fun you've ever had. And speaking of fun," Stellan rose and pulled her up by one hand. "I thought we'd get out of here, have a little fun outside."

Memories of the river made Cardis wary. "Outside? Why do you want to go outside? Besides, it's raining."

"Nah, the rain's cleared off for now, princess. It should hold off long enough for us to take a little walk."

Cardis groaned. "Another walk?" *Did the man never rest?*

"See, I can tell by the look on your face how excited you are. It won't be a long one, I promise. There's just a little errand I need to run, then we have the whole day for fun."

"Running errands? You do remember you made a stupid challenge, don't you?"

"Just a quick one. And it's on our way. We might even find a way to have a little fun there, too."

He winked at her. At least he didn't mention any toys. She didn't want to know what kind of games he would play outside.

"If you keep exercising me like this, you really are going to have to feed me more." Cardis could've bit her tongue as he grinned at her double meaning. "I'm not used to walking you know."

"Exercise is good for all kinds of things. But as to the food part, I've already got that covered, darling." He pointed to a basket on the table. "I know this nice, secluded picnic spot where you and I can have our own private feast."

"Picnic spot? I thought you were going hunting, you know, providing the delicate damsel with protein."

"Oh, don't worry, darling, there'll be meat for you. I'll make sure of it."

Stellan wiggled his eyebrows at her as he shoved another spoonful of the cereal into her gaping mouth.

"So, eat up."

Cardis yanked the spoon back out of her mouth as Stellan walked off whistling. What in the hell was she going to do? Never in all of her imaginings had she thought she'd have this reaction to a challenge. It seemed like such a simple task when looking at it logically. You're not attracted to a man, so turning him down is no problem. How had such a simple thing become so complicated? Did this man have some sort of magic of his own, some crazy form of technology that rendered a thinking, intelligent woman incapable of reasoning coherently? She had to pull herself together and quick.

Cardis sighed as she laid the spoon on the table. So they were going walking again, huh? Well maybe at least the fresh air would give her dying brain enough oxygen to make it work again.

Chapter Thirteen

"If you knock me down, I'm taking you with me." Cardis glared into the furry face as she bent over to retrieve the last of the leavings from their picnic.

A few hardy rays of sunshine peeked through the dark clouds. Behind them, rain still threatened and blustered along the sodden sky.

Stellan's comments on Ryjah's dislike for the stormy weather appeared to be true. Pulled from the bed by Stellan's whistled command, the dog seemed hell-bent on getting back to some form of shelter. Since his pace depended on his two-legged companions, the beast obviously felt the need to herd them along. Ryjah alternated between jumping up to place all four monstrous paws on Cardis' shoulders and barreling down the rocky path at breakneck speed. If the dog hoped to convince Cardis to hurry up, he was as mistaken as his master. She had already threatened Stellan with bodily harm if he didn't let her set the pace.

"Ryjah, down!" Stellan gave her a sheepish look as the dog continued to lick Cardis' face. "It means he likes you." He reached over and tugged at the silver fur around Ryjah's neck. With a yip, the dog bounced down and ran off.

"So his sudden desire to lick my skin has nothing to do with my not bathing this morning?"

Cardis wiped the drool from her chin. Even at her slower pace, sweat dripped off her, making her wonder about her choice to turn down the chance for a shower Stellan offered. Her refusal came after he'd made it clear he intended to join her there. She wanted her legs steady if she was going to be doing any more hiking.

"Not at all, darling." He winked at her. "You know us

barbarians, we're not that particular."

Cardis stuck her tongue out at him. "Anyway, I'm blaming it on you."

"Not that that surprises me, but blaming what on me?"

"I figure you put him up to it, since I wouldn't get in the shower with you before we left."

"Well, I would've been good company."

"Some things are best done alone."

"We're gonna have to work on some of your concepts, princess." Stellan laughed at the snort she gave. "But it does leave open another chance for me to help you wash up after lunch. Sure was fun when we did that last time. That must be why you wanted to skip the shower."

Cardis felt her face grow hot under the memories. *So much for keeping her legs steady.* But it wasn't only her legs that shook. Something about that easy smile on that killer face made her heart tremble as well. *And when had she gotten so comfortable with his teasing?*

There were too many things she was getting comfortable with. One of them was having his hands on her. It was somewhat of a relief to find she could enjoy a man's body, that she could respond to a man's touch with pleasure. She'd avoided challenges for so long she'd begun to wonder about herself. But how did she convince him that getting comfortable with sex didn't make a favorable outcome of the challenge a given?

Cardis felt her heart turn over as she realized her worst nightmare had come true. She had carefully planned out the path she wanted her life to take. And that path didn't include a husband, even one who could make her melt with his touch. A friendship might be possible. She certainly enjoyed Stellan's company, a fact which completely surprised her. But how do you send a friend off to a lifetime of slavery? *Why oh why did this challenge come with such rigid rules?*

"Come on then."

When Stellan reached for her hand, Cardis tried not to flinch. Instead she let her growing discomfort turn to anger. After all, he was the one crazy enough to start all this. He tugged the basket out of her hand.

"We'd best get going if we want to have time to play."

His words irritated her rising temper. She didn't have time to be playing with this man. She shouldn't be in the middle of this whole mess. None of it had been her choice. Her friends and family were in trouble and she should be back there helping her father put things in order instead of strolling around playing nature girl with a stranger. Suddenly his easygoing manner grated on her nerves. With an annoyed glare, Cardis tugged back as he twined his fingers with hers.

"Uh-uh. No running this time." *It would be enough of a struggle to get through the next few hours. No point in hurrying.*

"Oh, yeah. I promised to go easy on you, didn't I?" Stellan winked at her and Cardis gritted her teeth. With effort she calmed herself and faced him.

"That's right. Today, you follow and I lead." She brushed past him, hoping the walk would work off some of the temper she felt.

"Whatever you say, princess. The back view's as good as the front. After you." She glanced back to see Stellan's gaze plastered on her backside. With a grin that was becoming way too familiar firmly in place, he waved her on ahead of him.

Cardis stomped off, vowing not to hold any more conversations with the man. It was his own choice to be here and she was under no obligation to be pleasant about it. If he wanted to stare at her butt all day, it was no skin off her nose. She could ignore the man's foolish antics all day if need be. He'd get no easy response from her this time. *And didn't that lie collide very quickly with the fact she swore she felt him staring at her ass as she walked.*

Heat spiraled through her, making her sweat even more. By the time they reached this dam he kept talking about, she'd probably strip off her clothes and throw herself at him. The man simply shredded any semblance of control she had the moment he put his hands on her. Or, apparently, just by looking at her. She caught sight of the empty basket swinging from Stellan's fingers and felt the rumblings of another hunger. Between the energy she burned walking and the toll Stellan's seduction was taking on her, she should be thin as a rail when these three days were over.

As she shoved her way through a patch of dense overgrowth, trying to get her mind off the feel of Stellan watching her butt, Cardis let her own look wander around the landscape. Wasn't there something she could do with her time here that might prove useful? She might hate the circumstances that brought her to this place but if she focused at least a bit she could also learn a few things about a land mostly shrouded in rumor. While she was here, she had the rare opportunity for a good look around at Edaria. There might not be the physical amenities she considered basic to a good life, but, if she suspended her need to see technology, she had to admit there was beauty here, albeit a strange and faintly dangerous beauty.

The rain had left a glistening sheen on the landscape, highlighting the deep green of the trees and the vivid colors of tiny wildflowers along the trail. The plants tilted and swirled under the watery assault of the straggling drops. Beneath her the ground grew spongy and pliant as it soaked up the puddles left behind by the storm.

Each step they took brought them deeper into a mystic realm of wooded color. Cardis couldn't help but marvel at how different this patch of Edaria was from the rocky canyon they'd crashed in. No wonder Stellan preferred to make his home here instead of closer to his brothers. The difference pointed out all over again what a contradiction Edaria was, one minute a barren, lifeless desert and the next a forest haven. The land was as confusing as its inhabitants.

"What is it?"

Cardis came out of her reverie to find Stellan staring at her face. She hadn't realized she'd stopped walking.

"What is what?"

"Why did you stop? You have a funny look on your face. What's wrong?"

"Nothing." Cardis glanced around her. "It's just that, well, it's rather pretty after all, at least in an untamed, uh…"

"Backward sort of way?"

She frowned at him. "I was going to say a wild sort of way."

He chuckled. "Well, I appreciate the attempt at civility. And you're right, it is beautiful. I think you're mellowing, princess."

Irritation shot through her again, fueled by embarrassment. "Hardly. I've been many places where the land is beautiful. It's the people who generally mess things up."

Stellan chuckled. "Okay, okay, I take back the compliment about civility. Didn't mean to insult you with it. Growl at me all you like, but tell me what looks beautiful to you." He reached for her hand and pulled her with him down the trail.

Cardis tried to ignore the warm feel of his skin against hers. Her control was fragile enough without giving in to the least little touch from the man. She concentrated her thoughts back on her surroundings. "There's more color here than I think I've seen in all of Edaria so far. Granted, I haven't seen that much of Edaria. But still, it does seem unusual compared to the rest."

"Not really, not if you know a little about it."

She gave him a puzzled look. "Such as?"

"The color is deliberate. It's a product of those who nurtured it. This place began as an artist colony."

Now she viewed him with suspicion. "I thought you said it started off as some kind of hermit's fortress. You gave me that whole cockamamie story about it."

Stellan laughed. "Cockamamie story? Are you casting aspersions on my storytelling ability?"

"No, only on your truth-telling ability."

"Oh, but that was the truth. You're going to have to learn to trust me more."

Cardis snorted. "So if that was the truth, then what's this story about an artist colony?"

He laced his fingers through hers, enjoying the feel of her skin against his. Truth be told, he enjoyed it every time he touched her, even when she was snarling at him.

Sex had never been a complication for him. It was a need, pure and simple. He took his own pleasure, gave as good as he got and moved on. But the last few hours had sated none of the want in him where this woman was concerned. In fact, the need had grown. And so had the rather surprising need to share things with her, to have her know him in a way he'd avoided having anyone know him for a very long time. He wondered if that might be the biggest risk he was taking. The question was how much did he really want to risk on this challenge. He looked into her face and feared he might already have lost too much. Would it hurt or help to tell her more? He shook his head and tried to grin.

"That's the truth, too." He did grin now, perversely amused by her suspicious glare. "You're a very black and white woman, aren't you?" He tugged on her hand as he started walking again. "Things can be more than one way, Cardis, and places can hold more than one secret. Both stories are true, just at different times. Years after the poor soldier passed on—"

"Leaving all his wooden guards behind." Cardis wasn't sure she was up to more twists and turns. *Wasn't anything in this place the way it seemed?*

She should be viewing everything out of his mouth with suspicion, especially the tall tales he liked to tell about this barbaric place. But some latent inner child within her became mesmerized when he started his stories.

"Yes, leaving his legacy of carvings behind." His smile seemed to recognize the same inner child she was chastising. "A group of people, artists, thought the rather humorous history of this place was a good omen for their kind. The soldier had made a fortress out of his talent. Surely they could make a living with their art in a place that got its reputation from exactly the kind of talents they possessed."

"More carvings?"

"And other kinds of artwork. They, the ones who came here long after the soldier was gone, saw the community they wanted to build as a kind of retreat for those who wanted to focus on their art. Many of them, my great-grandparents included, came to these hills and found they couldn't leave, so gradually the town grew up around them."

"An artist colony? That's, uh, interesting. I didn't think, well, to find such a place, here."

"Once upon a time, there was a lot of beauty on Edaria. Art, music, the weavings of Lyre that could rival any with their intricate designs. Edaria hasn't always been a bastion of poverty and backwardness. We do have a history, one we used to be proud of. We had storytellers who could recite that history back to the first peoples who crossed the Sajaran mountains into Edarian territory. Now no one wants to listen."

A faraway look came into his eyes and Cardis wondered where his memories had gone. She slowed the pace, fascinated by the change in his demeanor. The cocksure grin and rogue manner were gone, replaced by what she might almost call a hunger. But for what? For the past? It seemed to her Edaria couldn't go any further back and still sustain life on this rock-hard planet. Despite the warning bells coming from the vicinity of her heart, she found she wanted to know more.

"So your grandparents settled here?"

"Great-grandparents."

"Artists, huh? So your family were artists?"

He stared at her a moment before the easy grin slipped back in place. "On my mother's side. I hear a note of disbelief in your voice, princess. Does that mean you haven't noticed my artistic bent yet? I'll have to try harder."

"Are you telling me you're responsible for the cabin? For the colors, the flowers, all that?"

He laughed. "Now I really hear disbelief in your voice. I don't suppose it would do any good to lie, for you wouldn't believe me anyway. All that is Alberta's touch."

"Alberta?" Cardis wondered if that was the older woman's name.

"Later we'll head into town for some more supplies. You'll meet her then."

"Oh. Is Alberta a relative?" The sudden thought of a possible familial connection made her nervous. She'd assumed more of a friendship from the conversation she'd overheard rather than family concern. Yet this was his mother's home place. It wouldn't be unlikely for Stellan to have other family here. *And what would that mean for how they saw her?*

"No." Stellan shook his head. "A longtime family friend."

"I'm sorry." Cardis paused, hesitant to prod the conversation on to too intimate a ground. Best not to get into areas like family and longtime family friends.

"Well, I appreciate the sentiment, but, as I said, it was a long time ago." He squeezed her hand and smiled. "And no, I'm not an artist, only an ungifted relative of artists. But I respect talent. And this place. My mother brought me here often when I was a boy, when we, when she needed to get away from my father. It was the only place where she could completely relax, where she laughed and smiled."

Something in his eyes gave Cardis pause. The memories were difficult for him she could tell. She had enough of those herself to try and give some comfort.

"She must have loved being here very much. Home is like that for some people. It must have been hard to leave here when she married your father."

He paused for a long moment and Cardis wondered if he wanted to let the conversation slip away. Then he nodded. "I don't know how he persuaded her. She was young and, at the time, much in love."

"At least she could come back to visit." She gave him a quick grin that she hoped would lighten the mood.

"Yeah. She loved coming back." He gazed around him. "We spent days wandering the riverbank, looking for colored stones or anything special she could use in her latest collage. Then at night we sat under the stars and listened to the storytellers. And sang. She had an incredible voice."

"You must have loved the storytellers." He chuckled and Cardis' tension eased somewhat. Maybe it was best if they kept from getting too personal. *And what they'd been doing last night and would likely be doing once again when they stopped wasn't personal?* Cardis opted to ignore the mocking voice in her head.

"So your mother was an artist?"

He shook his head. "Only here. At home, she never seemed to have the time for wandering, or for art, or for anything except what she'd call the drudgery."

A spurt of irritation surfaced again. "But it was part of her. She should've made time for it, if it was truly important to her. Why should she have to give up what she loved simply because she'd wed?"

"She had my father, and me and two stepsons to care

for. It wasn't easy. But here, here she could free that part of herself. At least that's what she told me."

Cardis bit her tongue before her opinion of his father could tumble out. She glared at him instead, her temper at war with the thought that he wasn't responsible for his parents' actions.

He shrugged and his obvious discomfort with the memories muted some of her temper. She reminded herself that they weren't friends, that he wasn't one of the men she'd been able to skillfully shift away from any sort of challenge. Warning bells went off inside her head again, telling her to let it drop, to keep their relationship on a purely physical basis. A basis that would be easy to walk away from when the time came. But her natural curiosity, the trait that most often got her in trouble, prodded her tongue. That, and what she recognized as pain in his eyes.

"That's why she had to get away every so often."

This time the pause was even longer. Cardis had begun to believe he would let it drop when Stellan nodded. "Yes. I could tell when that fire was building inside her. She would get restless, forgetful. Or sad."

"And your father let her come?"

Stellan shrugged with a nonchalant air Cardis recognized as reluctance. She'd used the gesture often enough herself to discourage more intimate conversation. A small, selfish part of her felt relieved at leaving the intimate conversation behind.

He dropped her hand and whistled for Ryjah. Just when she'd relaxed into the silence, he spoke again. This time there was no mistaking the pain in his voice.

"She came because she had to. At least that's what she told him when he would arrive here, when they argued about it. I always knew it would be only a day or so before he would come to get us."

"Did he never come with you?" The words were out before Cardis could stop them.

Stellan snorted. "He wouldn't even spend the night here. He hated this place. Even if dark was coming we'd leave rather than staying till the morning."

It said a lot about his relationship with his father that Stellan had chosen to live in this place his father had so obviously hated. She wondered if he understood the meaning behind his choice. Feeling a little like an eavesdropper or a nosy stranger, Cardis tried to put her best spin on his words. Berating his father or his culture now smacked of unnecessary cruelty.

"And yet he let her come, in spite of his dislike. That says something about the feelings he must have had for her."

"Until I was around six. They fought hard over it then because she wanted to keep bringing me with her." A dark look passed over Stellan's face. "I think that was the first time he'd ever hit her."

He took her hand and started walking again. Stunned by the casual revelation, Cardis let him lead her down the trail. She shouldn't be surprised, should have expected violence to be behind his reluctance. After all, she'd met his brothers. And Edaria was a barbaric society, especially for its women. Still, a part of her heart ached for him, for what the child must have felt at seeing that violence so close at hand. What had that moment changed inside him?

They walked along in silence and Cardis wondered if he would speak again. When he did his voice was strained. "After that we didn't come back. She died maybe a year or so later." Lifting his head up, Stellan searched the rumbling sky. "Looks like those clouds are getting ready to open up. Our picnic just might get interrupted. We'd best get to the dam before the rain starts again. There's a shelter there."

"The dam?"

"Well, the beginnings of one. We haven't gotten it completed yet." He gazed up at the darkening sky again. "Last night's rains were pretty steady. I want to see how the levees are holding up with all the new water pressing on them." As he tugged on her hand she noticed he'd picked up the pace. "Come on, princess, it's time to hurry whether you want to or not."

Chapter Fourteen

Cardis kept quiet as they headed down the trail. Stellan worried as he walked, fearful of what the expression on her face meant. He couldn't believe he'd let himself run off at the mouth like that. What in the hell had he been thinking?

The truth was he hadn't been thinking, hadn't been keeping his guard up at all. He'd begun to relax way too much with this woman. And it had become way too easy to talk to her. Maybe it was because she was a stranger, someone who didn't know anything about him, or his family. Or maybe it was because it had been so long since he'd had anyone he could talk to, anyone who wasn't looking to him to fix things for them.

The rain only added to his miseries. Most of the huge drops had slacked off, leaving only a slight mist now and then, but both of them were damp from the storm's earlier efforts. It probably would've been closer to turn back to his cabin, but Stellan needed to check the levees. With as much rain as they'd had overnight, the fragile structures were likely strained to capacity.

Beside him, Cardis stumbled. With the kind of ripe oath he was coming to expect from the elegant princess, she gripped his arm. The woman knew more curse words than a Maltenese trader.

"Sorry," he mumbled. "Guess I was trying to hurry us too much." He grinned at her. "But I didn't want you to melt, sugar." Stellan dropped his pack and reached his hand out to stroke a finger down her cheek. He couldn't seem to go very long without touching this woman. Wasn't that a surprise?

Cardis glared at him as she shook away his touch. "Ending up face down in the mud isn't much of an alternative." She swiped at the rainwater misting on her face. "How far is it to town, anyway?"

"Not too much further."

Stellan grinned at her as he drew his hand through her black curls, sending drops of rain back across her face. She frowned at him.

"We're just taking a little detour, princess, so I can check out the levees. Before you know it we'll be snug and warm and out of the rain. I've got some new games to show you."

Cardis snorted. "And we're going to be playing them in the middle of the town square? I don't think so. No matter how many artists live in this place, I'm not being anybody's nude model for some porn statue."

"I don't think I'd be too hasty, darling. A nice bronze would make a great wedding present." He glanced over at her. "You know my mother used to tell me if you gave people those kind of looks your face would freeze that way."

Cardis lifted her middle finger in an obscene gesture and he chuckled. The woman never gave an inch. It was a quality he was surprised to find he admired in a woman.

"I still say you ought to reconsider, darling." Stellan reached for his pack, hefting it onto his shoulder. "Some of the folks in town are well-known for their artwork. It could be a very valuable piece. A good merchant like you shouldn't pass up that kind of opportunity."

Cardis rolled her eyes at him. "A golden opportunity, huh?"

She let her emphasis linger on the word golden and was rewarded by the smirk on Stellan's face. The man had the thickest skin she'd ever seen. Shaking her head, she decided surrender might at least throw him off.

"Do they still let anyone who wants to come and work on their art stay here?"

She was surprised when Stellan frowned. "It's been years since art was the main focus of the people who live here. In fact, many of them have laid aside their talents altogether."

"Why would they do that?"

"Many reasons, mostly economical. The community did well at first." Had done well for a long time, he thought. Until his father got a hold of it. But he kept that tidbit to himself. He'd revealed enough personal information for one day. Stellan shifted his pack onto his back as he started walking. He didn't glance over when Cardis stepped up beside him. The woman was far too capable of getting him to spill his guts with her questions. Best he keep quiet. Keeping her in the dark about the less savory aspects of Edaria could only help his chances of winning this challenge. If he had any chances left.

"So what happened?"

Stellan sighed. Looked like he wasn't going to get any extra chances after all. "Things changed a few years back. If you've noticed, Barron's Fort is, um, different in many ways from other parts of Edaria. More isolated, different climate, terrain. There were those who thought an artist colony was a waste of good farmland. Too much of it left idle, to their mind. A waste of perfectly good land that could be developed for other uses."

"Something more basic and less aesthetic, I take it. Pretty trails and idyllic scenery might be great for an artist's muse, but it doesn't bring food to the table, is that it?"

Stellan nodded. "The people in town found their work was less, appreciated I guess you'd say, than before. As the whole realm changed, things got more sophisticated, at least in other places. And Edaria grew more and more isolated, making it harder and harder to survive."

"And the market for pretty artwork or carvings of wooden soldiers dried up as Edaria isolated itself from the rest of the realm."

He nodded. "With Edaria's economy struggling and without some richer planet to buy their goods, that's pretty much what happened. Something like a fancy painting or a tapestry became a frivolity, a useless indulgence that fewer and fewer people could afford. And there were, um, problems with developing the area for agriculture. The town's struggled to stay alive for the last few years."

Cardis shook her head. "Were the problems insurmountable? I mean, economic development is a possibility pretty much anywhere given the right investments. Whatever problems there are, surely there are answers to go with them, if not here, than somewhere else in the realm. Edaria doesn't have to stay so isolated."

Stellan shook his head. "It's not just that. To develop you have to have something others want. We're stuck at the survival point. Staying alive is all most people can focus on right now. Edaria's climate is changing. Our food supply isn't what it used to be. The water has, um, problems. We can no longer use the river to irrigate."

She stopped and turned him to face her. "Problems from the rush to develop all the land, right?"

He nodded. "The development sounded good, probably would even have worked like they thought it would over the long-term."

"But the people who complained about the land left undeveloped didn't want to wait for long-term results."

"No. And our technology wasn't prepared to mitigate the short-term problems."

"All of that can be dealt with, Stellan. I won't say it's easy or that it's a fast result, but it is doable. The Council developed the technology to adapt climate control eons ago. And a purification plant would take care of the water issues. These are simple enough problems to solve. It would only take—"

Stellan cut her off. "You're forgetting one very important flaw in your plan, princess. The Council doesn't deal with us. We're the backward bogeyman, remember."

"An image you and your brothers have done nothing to dispel."

"Whatever the reason, the fact is Council merchants don't bring trade goods this way, much less their precious equipment."

"Stealing from them is hardly a way of saying 'welcome, please include us in your market'."

He turned and started walking again. Cardis gritted her teeth in frustration as she stared at his retreating back.

"You know walking away from a problem insures you won't find a solution."

He stopped at her words, but didn't turn around.

"Talking it to death won't bring a solution either."

"Now there's a sentiment your brothers could appreciate."

He turned and glared at her. "Okay, princess, if you want to talk, we'll talk. Even if your precious Merchant's Council would bring us the tools we need, no one here knows how to use them."

"And no one here is teachable?"

Though his glare heated up, she took a step toward him.

"Stellan, no matter what I might think about Edaria, or its inhabitants, it doesn't make sense for you and everyone else to just stick your heads in the ground and wait for your own extinction. Or are you deliberately baiting the Council to invade so you don't have to wait for it?"

He arched a brow at her and said nothing. His lips tightened as he folded his arms across his chest. Watching the ripple of muscle play under the bronze skin, for the first time Cardis felt a little frightened of him. What was she thinking? She was alone out here with a strange man. Perhaps making him angry wasn't the best use of her time. After all, he had to get close for her shield to come to life. If he chunked a rock at her she'd be out cold before the shield could be any help. Still, she'd never settled for being a coward.

Cardis focused on his face. He wasn't the first stone wall she'd run into. She'd never backed away from any of them. Her courage hitched a little as he continued to stare her down, the look on his face designed to intimidate. But her own stubbornness, not always her best trait, egged her on.

"If you'd only look at the long-term, it would be a simple task to...."

"A task my brothers have no interest in."

The words came out in a clipped tone that grated on her last nerve. Frustrated by the rain, the trauma of everything that had happened and the obstinance of the stubborn man in front of her, Cardis felt her control begin to shred. With supreme effort, she tamped down on the temper threatening to take over. She would be reasonable, logical, she wouldn't give in to the baser instincts driving her murderous thoughts. But it was a challenge to keep her voice even.

"But surely even they must see the importance of it,

to their own survival if nothing else."

"Hakir isn't particularly farsighted. I'm surprised you didn't pick up on that in the short time you were around him. His stance is there's meat in the woods and wild grain. A man needs no more than that unless it's a woman to cook it. He doesn't see beyond today, princess, not for himself, not for any of us."

Stellan turned as if to dismiss her. All her desire for reason and logic turned with him as she thought of his brothers and the treatment her father's crew received at their hands. Temper replaced frustration. How many years had she spent arguing perfect logic against male stubbornness? How many times had she nearly bitten her tongue clean through trying to remain rational and calm in the face of patronizing and condescension? Well, no more. She was through being patient with the male gender. And Stellan looked like the perfect scapegoat for her accumulated wrath, standing there arguing against her totally sensible suggestions. The words exploded out of her as she gave in to her temper. If he chunked a rock at her, she'd just find it and chunk it back at him.

"Or he's taken to stealing to get what he wants that Edaria can't supply, so to hell with the rest of it."

When he turned, the look on his face made her wonder if she should reach down for a rock first. Stellan took a step toward her, murder in his eyes, both hands fisted by his side. Maybe at least now they'd get some of the passion that sparked between them out of their systems without her having to get naked again.

Stellan stopped and Cardis watched, fascinated, as he struggled for control. He took a couple of deep breaths before he spoke.

"We need to get moving, princess. I'm sure you want to get in out of the rain."

He turned and started walking. Cardis' temper peaked at being denied the fight she was itching for.

"So you've just given up. Is that it?"

Her jab was rewarded by a spark that shed any form of patience from his careful expression. As he turned back to her he stalked her with a focus that brought all her fears back to her head.

"You have no idea what I have or haven't done. I

171

believe I said something before about not judging things you don't understand."

Cardis shook her head. "You're right, I don't understand simply walking away from your problems when there are solutions to be had."

He unfolded his arms as he edged closer toward her. She watched his fingers curl together and briefly thought about running. His words were soft and low and Cardis felt the threat in them.

"Sometimes the solutions aren't as easy for the rest of us as they are for rich folk, princess."

He growled the endearment. Cardis lifted her chin. Let him think he could intimidate her. It'd take more than one angry male to make her back down. No matter how tough he thought he was, she could out-stubborn him any time.

"It's easy to blame a lack of money for giving up."

"Nobody said anything about giving up."

Stellan's fisted hands lifted and Cardis had a brief image of him throttling her. Damn, why couldn't she remember if her shield would protect her against any other threat besides rape. But it didn't matter, for there was no stopping her quick temper. Going with the growing anger inside her, Cardis let her gaze travel up and down Stellan as she sneered at him.

"No, you've just done it. At least nobody can say you're all talk."

Stellan pressed his fingers to his eyes then blew out his breath. Cardis stared at him, wondering what to expect next. The man played like he was so laid back you couldn't find his temper with a map. Had it all been a facade, an act designed to seduce her? Well, maybe she'd melted enough times for this man. Maybe it was time to show him exactly how difficult it could be to seduce her. She stared at him coolly, rewarded by the red flush moving up the tips of his ears.

Stellan smiled through clenched teeth. "You know you're just not catching on to the idea of playing, princess."

The word came out as more of a curse than an endearment and Cardis mentally congratulated herself. Stellan flexed his fingers and stared at her neck.

"We came out here to have fun, not to fight. There are better things we could be doing with our time." He moved up close to her, letting one finger stroke down her cheek. His smile deepened as he leaned in to kiss her.

"Oh, that's right, you made a challenge." Cardis smirked at him as she planted her hand in his chest before his lips could reach hers. "How's that working out for you? Ready to walk away from it yet? I mean, you've probably reached your limit of effort by now. Three days is a long time to focus on a task. Wouldn't want to tax yourself too much."

Stellan's hands curled into fists again as he took a step back. This time Cardis felt him staring at her neck. "You know I'm beginning to see the true challenge in spending time with you, princess."

"What, you don't want to touch me anymore?" Cardis gave him a wide-eyed stare.

"Oh, I want to touch you all right." Cardis figured his throat hurt with the effort she could tell he was putting into not shouting. "As a matter of fact, darling, there's a spot in particular my fingers are itching to touch right now."

"Well, come on, then. The challenge time isn't up." His clenched fists lifted and she chuckled. "I dare you."

For a moment she thought he'd take up the dare. Then, with some effort, he lowered his hands and stepped back.

"What, and give you the pleasure of ripping me apart with that fancy shield of yours?"

"Coward."

Stellan snorted. "Just a thinking man, darling. And I'm thinking there's an excellent chance for you to continue to be the world's oldest virgin."

"Oh, really?" For some reason the jab hurt and the blow to her pride fueled her temper. Cardis stepped toward him, pleased to see his hands curl back into fists. About time he started worrying about defending himself. "Well, I'm thinking I wouldn't even have to use my shield. A man gives up as easily as you apparently do couldn't put up much of a fight. I could handle you with my bare hands."

Something flashed in his eyes as he stepped closer

and Cardis feared she'd pushed him too far. Her mother chided her often over her penchant for danger but Cardis thought she might finally be about to learn what it meant to play with fire.

"You want to put your hands on me, darling?" His mocking tone added fuel to the fire. "Then let's play, princess. But we play my way."

He moved toward her again and an electric surge of plain old lust shot through Cardis, a reaction she found so stupid she didn't even want to consider it. That certainly hadn't been in any of her mother's lectures. Her burning desire to fight with this man suddenly flooded her brain with vivid images of knocking him to the ground and wrestling those clothes off of him. She realized too late the danger of memories as the knowledge of what lay under those clothes pounded want through her veins that drove all particles of common sense out of her head. Then he took another step closer and she licked her lips. Stellan leaned in close and let the challenge in his voice graze across her taut skin.

"Well, come on, darling, let's see what you can do. Now I'm daring you."

As he leaned back, he whipped his shirt over his head. "You don't want me to think you're all talk, do you?"

All talk? Who could get words out with the sight of all that golden skin in front of them? Steamed beyond anything she'd ever known, and hotter than she'd thought possible, Cardis found she did indeed want her bare hands on him. And her tongue, and her teeth and some other body parts she didn't even want to think about. With a low growl, she threaded her fingers through the golden hairs on his chest and pulled.

With an answering jerk, Stellan slammed her against him, his large hands gripping her hips as he lifted her up. Cardis wrapped her legs around his waist and let her fingers stroke the hot flesh they itched to touch. She licked and nipped and teased, satisfied beyond measure when she heard the breath catch in his throat. The red gown was wedged up around her hips and Stellan's hands roamed unhindered, making her writhe with the feel of his hot hands.

Anxious to burn off the flames spiraling through her,

Cardis tugged at the laces of his pants, her fingers digging into his flesh. An answering grunt from Stellan made her work faster. Each touch made her hotter, until she thought she'd expire on the spot. Her only salvation lay in satisfying the growing need to touch the body parts under the tight leather.

Stellan's hands stroked and teased her skin as he pulled the gown up to her waist. His fingers kneaded her butt as his mouth covered her breast through the gauzy fabric, the touch of his wet mouth sizzling even through the thin shield. Desperate for more, for what her body now knew was coming, Cardis clenched her thighs tighter around his waist as she rubbed herself against him, letting the friction of leather against skin stoke the fire building in her.

Spurred by her own cravings and caught in the scent and the feel of the man she was stripping, Cardis lost all sense of her surroundings. She become the most basic of creatures, driving need seeking to sate itself. So deep into the fever burning through her, she almost didn't hear the voice behind them.

"Well, I suppose this answers any curiosity I have about the visitor Alberta told me about."

Chapter Fifteen

Murder wasn't her normal way of dealing with problems, but a primal part of Cardis she hadn't known existed urged her to kill whoever had distracted her. Need that screamed to be filled burned a hole through her skin as her feeble brain tried to register the noise humming behind her. Over the roar in her head, she turned to see who or what had interrupted them.

Three wasn't exactly a crowd, but it was definitely more people than Cardis cared to see staring at her right at the moment. Nor were they far enough away to have missed much. The woman politely kept her focus on restraining the wiggling child in her arms. The man gave her a foolish grin and a small wave. The grin was way too familiar.

Cardis couldn't decide if she wanted to bury her face in Stellan's chest and pray they'd go away or turn around and run. Stellan made the decision for her when he gently unwrapped her legs from his waist. She slid down with a groan, unable to keep the blush from her face as she tugged the gown down below her hips. Stellan kept his hands on her to steady her but she shoved him away. She frowned up at him, disconcerted further by the grin on his face.

"Exactly how much did you tell people about why I'm here?"

She hissed the words at him, afraid she already knew the answer. But she hadn't thought to wonder what other people would think of her appearance there with Stellan. Up till now she hadn't had time. Last night at the tavern she kept to herself. With the exception of Nathan and his sister, she hadn't spoken to anyone but Stellan. But, come to think of it, anyone who saw them together would have to know why they were together. Everyone back at the crash site knew why she was alone with Stellan. And what they were doing. Word of the challenge probably traveled pretty quick. She might as well be wearing a sign that said hello, my name is Cardis and I'm being seduced.

As if in answer to her thoughts, Stellan gave her a wink and said, "Sorry, darling, but it's not as if everyone doesn't know why we're here."

"Everyone?" Cardis covered her face and groaned.

Stellan nodded as he confirmed her worst fears. "Pretty much. This is a small town, news travels fast."

Her embarrassment deepened at his words. She suddenly felt exposed. *Great, they might as well be doing it as a spectator sport.* Another thought occurred to her as the old woman's words came back to her. *She might need a bodyguard to get off this planet in one piece after she turned Stellan down.*

Stellan stepped in front of her, giving Cardis a little more time to adjust herself as the family moved toward them.

"Stellan, you're back." The man pulled Stellan into a bear hug. "It's always good when you're here, cousin. Alberta must be smiling wide today."

"Well, I don't know about that." Stellan turned to her. "Cardis, this is my cousin Lavin. Lavin, this is Cardis. She's, uh, visiting for a spell."

Cardis found her hand gripped and shaken. The man was handsome, though he didn't resemble Stellan at all, except for the grin still plastered on his face. His dark wavy hair fell past his shoulders with thin braids down each side. He wore a linen shirt over leather pants that matched the heavy leather boots on his feet. His blue eyes twinkled as he shook Cardis' hand.

"Ah, yes. Alberta mentioned you had a visitor."

"Stellan, it's good to have you back." The woman tugged on Stellan's shoulder and he bent down for her to kiss his cheek. Then she turned to Cardis. "And good to meet your friend."

Though inane sparks of jealousy flared when the woman touched Stellan, Cardis found herself gazing into warm friendly eyes of deep brown. The woman barely came up to her shoulder and Cardis felt like a clumsy giant next to her delicate frame. Fine-boned features accented her heart-shaped face, surrounded by sleek waves of chocolate brown hair. She was every inch the dainty female.

Lavin turned to the woman and smiled as she reached for Cardis' hand. "My wife, Dinah."

Cardis did her best to handle the situation with some sort of dignity. "Nice to meet you, Dinah. Nice to meet you both." She looked at the little girl, who hid her face in her mother's neck. "And this would be?"

"Chiara." The woman chuckled as her daughter squirmed in her arms. "Who never seems to remember she has her own two legs."

The man turned back to Stellan. "I didn't expect to see you out and about." Amusement glinted in his eyes. "We'd heard you were...occupied."

Cardis wished she could expire right there on the spot. Or better yet, commit murder. She glared at Stellan. He carefully avoided her gaze.

"Fresh air's good for a lot of things."

If he heard Cardis' growl behind him, Stellan gave no notice. She might have to kill him after all. As she noticed the smirk on Lavin's face, Cardis reconsidered. She might have to take out the whole planet. Best not to leave any witnesses.

"Besides, I thought after all that rain, I'd better check out the levees."

Dinah leaned over to Cardis. "That's what's got us out in this weather too."

"Things needed taking care of, Dinah." Lavin's chiding tone had his wife blushing. He turned back to Stellan. "We've just come from the levee. Though the water is straining its bounds, so far it's holding. We can only hope it will continue to."

"We've shored it up before and it held." Stellan glanced at Cardis. "Lavin's in charge of the town's utilities."

"Oh." Cardis gave him a smile. "Then I should talk to you as well."

"Talk to me?" He gave Stellan a puzzled look. Stellan shrugged, but the look he gave Cardis carried heat and warning. She gave him a sweet smile.

"Yes. Stellan has told me some of the complications your town is facing. I believe there are some things the Council could do that would be helpful to your situation here."

"Oh, really?" Cardis thought the man's brows couldn't go much higher. She smiled at him.

"Yes. I believe it would be a fairly simple project and one that would enable you to upgrade your systems over a relatively short period of time. You see—"

"Well," Lavin cleared his throat. "I'm sure it's quite an interesting proposal you'd have. Perhaps later. Stellan?"

Lavin gave his cousin a questioning stare. Confused, Cardis looked from one man to the other. For some reason, Lavin seemed quite uncomfortable with talking to her. A quick look at Dinah told her he wasn't the only one. The woman avoided looking at Cardis, her pretty cheeks stained a deep red. What did she have to blush about? Cardis had never understood jealousy, but maybe the woman thought she was flirting. Sometimes her own gender made her as confused as the opposite sex did.

"Yes." Cardis kept her tone as businesslike as possible. "I think I can detail some of the solutions that might work best for you. If you'd like me to lay out a plan for you to share with the others, I'd be happy to do that."

Lavin continued to look at her as if she'd grown two heads.

"Lavin," Stellan's smooth interruption gave no hint of the temper she saw boiling in his eyes. Guess their fight wasn't quite finished. She didn't think he had such an ego, that her polite offer of help would bruise it like that. "We can talk when I get to town."

"Of course." Lavin winked at her. "I shouldn't want to interrupt your, um, outing."

Stellan cleared his throat. "If you want to get the elders together, it might be good if all of us went over what preparations need to be made."

Lavin nodded, relief on his face. "I will speak with the others. I hope your news will be good."

"As do I."

"We'll see you tonight then. Dinah." Lavin grasped his wife's hand.

Dinah winked at Cardis. "I apologize for interrupting your time here, Cardis. It was a pleasure to meet you, but I'm sure you and Stellan are ready to have some fun. Perhaps we'll see you later, at the sing tonight."

"Yeah, sure," Cardis mumbled, her confusion growing along with her temper.

The couple walked off as Stellan glanced over at her.

"What was that all about?" She glared back at him as she tossed her question out.

"What was what all about?" Stellan turned to pick up his pack. Cardis grabbed his arm and turned him back to face her.

"The quick brush-off, that's what. That man never heard a word I said."

"It wasn't a quick brush-off. It just wasn't the time to be talking."

"Oh, really? Not the time to be talking or not the person to be talking to?"

"Look, things are done differently here."

"You bet they are. Do you think I'm stupid enough to have missed the look those two gave me? Oh, wait. Of course I'm stupid enough. I'm a woman. How could I possibly understand the nuances of man talk?" She glared at Stellan. "That's why you're not yelling at me, isn't it? I mean, you can't hold a woman who hasn't been taught her place responsible for not knowing what she was doing was wrong, now can you?. That wouldn't be fair. After all, I come from some crazy culture that gives women all kinds of strange ideas, like the fact that they have a brain just like men. So you're being polite and not ranting at me for my foolishness. Isn't that it?" Cardis gave a short laugh. "And to think I was worried that woman thought I was flirting with her husband. She was just embarrassed for me."

"Dinah would never be rude."

"Oh, of course she wouldn't. After all, she knows her place."

"That's not it. Dinah—"

"Oh, yes it is. I know the type, that adoring look and absolutely no will of her own. Yes, dear, whatever you want, dear."

"Dinah just knows if her man's happy, then he'll

make sure to keep her happy." Stellan reached for her, leaning in for a kiss. "She knows what her man can do for her to make her happy."

Cardis jerked back before his lips could make contact. "Oh, so that's the way it goes. I can't be happy unless my man's there to keep me happy, is that it?"

"Well, now, you've had a little taste of what a man can do to keep you happy." Stellan brushed his hand over her hair as he winked at her. "It hasn't been too bad, has it?"

Cardis took a step back as she shoved his hand away. "And of course, that's all it takes for a woman, right? I mean, what more can she ask for."

Stellan sensed a trap somewhere in the words but he couldn't quite find it. "There's still a whole lot more in store, darling. We haven't officially gotten you out of that virgin status yet." He leaned in once more.

Cardis planted her fist in his chest. "You think because you do a few tricks, that we got down and dirty for a bit and my body responded the way it's designed to that I'm supposed to roll over and play dead?"

"I know the challenge isn't over yet, if that's what you're getting at." Tiny strains of temper edged his voice this time. "But you have to admit, princess, those few tricks as you call them didn't exactly have you dying. Although you did seem to be doing a lot of gasping for breath."

Stellan took a deep breath of his own as he struggled with his temper. Now wasn't the time to give in to his anger. He knew she thought her words to Lavin were helpful. And he was willing to try and understand her point of view, to understand she came from a place with very different customs and attitudes than Edaria. But the woman had a stubborn streak that could drive a man over the edge. And her words seemed designed to pick a fight. *Had he really thought he wanted a woman with passion?*

"And that's supposed to be enough?" Cardis' words interrupted his attempts to calm himself. "I guess that's what you think, huh? After all, I'm just a woman, doesn't matter where I'm from, what I might want. No, the big strong man just needs to give me a few breathless moments, tell me some cute little stories then he can tuck me into his bed with a pat on the head like a good little girl. Easy as can be."

"Hey, this is your weird custom, not mine." Stellan threaded his hands through his hair in frustration.

"Exactly. Different worlds, different ideas." She shook her head. "You know, you've picked at me this whole time for being narrow-minded in how I viewed Edaria. But your mind certainly isn't wide open. No matter how many cute stories you tell, or how laidback you pretend to be, that macho core is still there, isn't it? Was it all an act to get through the challenge? Did you really think I was that stupid?"

"Darling, it ain't your intelligence blocking the way here. I noticed how stubborn you were right from the start. You're not exactly an easy woman to be around."

"If you wanted easy then you should've picked one of those simpering little blobs you call women here, all adoring smiles and nodding heads."

In the back of his brain Stellan registered the warning that he should keep his mouth shut. But his tongue and his brain conspired to dig him deeper into trouble.

"And if you wanted to give up that precious virgin status your people see as such a prize then you'd stop seeing everything through that stubborn head of yours and start thinking with an organ a little lower."

He jerked up his pack as she sneered at him. "And no, I'm not talking that low. I meant your heart. Supposedly you do have one. But I guess that organ's not nearly as important as your brain. After all, the point is to prove you're as capable as any man, right? That you're smarter, stronger and faster than anything male. Where's the worth in proving you can feel, or that you can show any tenderness? Or, worse yet, that you might be able to love?"

Stellan swung his pack over his shoulder and stared at her. "But don't worry, princess. This'll all be over in a few hours. I'll become just a bad memory and you can go on being Adena's queen bitch."

He turned and walked away, leaving her standing in the rain, staring after him.

Chapter Sixteen

The drops grew harder as they walked, a change Stellan actually found himself grateful for. It kept Cardis from talking. Or rather from yelling at him anymore. *What in the hell had made him say those things? Had made him talk about love, of all things?*

In one short conversation he'd undone any progress he'd made on convincing her he was the man of her dreams. Or at least of her fantasies. From the scowl she'd given him he'd bet he couldn't even audition for her nightmares now. Unless he could repair the damage their argument had done, she'd leave and never look back when the time was up. And never wonder what became of him.

By the time they made it to the edge of town they were soaked to the skin. A covered bridge led them across the river, giving them a brief respite from the downpour. As they made their way over the rickety wooden structure, Cardis peered over the fragile railing to stare at the roaring water below. No more than a hundred feet wide, the water nipped at the surrounding land as if straining at the boundaries the banks imposed. Stellan's heart sank. The half-completed walls of the dam system would be easy prey to the surging depths. Beside him, Cardis shivered against the chilly spray.

Before she could complain further, Stellan gripped her hand and pulled her off the bridge. The rain hit them in the face as a rumble of thunder shook the sky. Big drops hit the ground with a fury.

"Uh-oh." Stellan urged her on past the tavern.

"What do you mean uh-oh?" Cardis tried to see where he was dragging her.

"This one looks like it means business."

"What one?" She dodged a group of children and their

183

ball. *Didn't they know to get in out of the rain?*

"This storm. It's been worrying itself into a real gutwasher for days now. I think it's finally arrived."

The drops got heavier and Cardis heard the rumble of thunder follow the deluge. By the time they arrived at the tiny cabin both of them were shivering. Without knocking, Stellan pushed open the door and ushered her inside. The first thing she saw was the woman from last night.

"Oh, Stellan, praise be you're here. I've sent Merritt to look for you."

"What's wrong, Berta?" Stellan crossed to the woman, taking her hand in his and pulling her toward Cardis.

"The rain, Stellan, the rain. The levee won't hold, you know that."

Cardis stood there uncomfortably, not knowing what to do. The warmth of the room made her want to relax and sink into it, the cheerful fire taking some of the gloom off the world around her. A quick glimpse of the place confirmed Stellan's earlier confession that Alberta had been the one to decorate his home before her arrival. Flowers and bright colored stones sparked against the muted background of wood and stone. The room formed a tiny oasis of harmony and imagination. She'd never given much thought to the skill it took to weave care and comfort into one's surroundings, but this place gave her pause. Had she neglected to learn such a simple thing in her quest for the stars?

Cardis held her tongue both from fear of breaking the comforting spell the room wove around her and from a deeper sense of being the outsider. The woman's agitation didn't appear to include her and she didn't want to intrude. But before she could relax too much, Stellan pulled her forward.

"Cardis, this is Alberta. She was my mother's best friend and now she's my guardian."

"Guardian? Oh, well, it's nice to meet you." She took the old woman's hand in hers and bowed stiffly.

Alberta shook her head. "Don't be so formal, girl. What this idiot really means is I'm his keeper."

Cardis laughed. "Now that's a term I understand. Especially when it applies to Stellan."

Alberta glanced at her, then back at Stellan. "Well, I was supposed to be his keeper, the one who kept him out of trouble. But I guess I didn't do a very good job, at least not the last couple of days."

Cardis flushed, not sure how to answer that statement.

"He has taken a big risk."

"Indeed." The sharp old eyes filled with remorse and something else Cardis couldn't define. Or maybe she just didn't want to. "I know he has only limited time to win this gamble, girl, but right now we need him. I don't want him to lose, but if he doesn't see to that levee we've all lost anyway. If this rain turns out like I think it will, this whole town's going to lose."

Stellan put a finger on Alberta's lips. "No one's lost yet, Berta. You ought not give up before the fight's even begun. I came back to see if the old radio worked."

Alberta nodded toward the alcove next to the kitchen. "It's in there. But, Stellan, it hasn't worked for a year or more now, you know that."

"It has to work, Berta. We need help and we need it quick."

Stellan crossed the room in long strides, Cardis right behind him. He moved to a small table in the alcove that held the oldest piece of radio equipment Cardis had ever seen. The thing should've been in a museum. As she watched him fiddle with the huge dials and strange knobs, she wondered if the thing had ever worked.

"What is that piece of junk?"

Stellan gave her a glare that should've set off warning bells in her head. Ignoring her words, he turned back to the decrepit radio. He pulled the backing off the thing and tugged at the wires inside. Then he cursed under his breath as the pathetic object refused to offer him so much as static.

Cardis leaned over his shoulder. "Maybe if you try to put the...."

"Leave off, woman!"

This time the glare had her closing her mouth. She stepped back and folded her arms across her chest. He didn't have to look at her like she was a total moron. After all, she was the one acquainted with technology, not the one from the most backward planet in the known universe. But did he move aside and let her look at the thing? Of course not. Maybe he figured the antique was so outdated it wouldn't matter what she knew. But surely there had to be some similarities, some basic operations she could figure out from her knowledge of newer models.

The radio sparked, then made a sizzling noise. Stellan jerked his hand back.

"Ow! Sonofabitch!"

Cardis rolled her eyes. "Okay, macho man, if you'd just let me look at it...."

"Not now!" he hissed at her. With another oath, he yanked the back of the radio off and jiggled things around. This time the sparks ignited. Grabbing a towel, Stellan smothered the tiny flame, then picked the whole thing up and threw it against the wall.

"Well, that should teach it who's boss."

The words were out before Cardis could clamp her lips down on them. She was surprised flames didn't shoot out of his eyes as he glared at her. He started to say something, seemed to think better of it and grabbed her hand.

Before Cardis knew what he was doing, he pulled her close and kissed her hard. She stumbled slightly when he let go. He gave her a self-satisfied smile, although it didn't mask the bleak look in his eyes.

"Stay here with Berta." He gave her a gentle push away from the door. "She's probably got some goodies already baking. You'll need to eat to keep up your strength for later." He gave her a weak grin as he headed back to the door. It wasn't hard to see the worry behind it.

"Excuse me?" Cardis jerked hard on his arm, spinning Stellan around to face her. "Where do you think you're going?"

He patted her on the arm. "I told you, darling, I'll be back. Don't worry, we've shored up the levee before and it held. We'll do it again this time." He moved to Alberta and kissed the weathered cheek. "You'll see, it will be okay."

"Oh, I see." What Cardis really wanted to tell him was she was seeing red. Instead, she managed to clip out the words, even though her hands balled into fists at her side. "I'm supposed to cower here in the shelter with the womenfolk while you go out and save the world. Or maybe I should, say, bake a few goodies so you can keep your manly strength up."

Behind her, Alberta snorted as she bustled around the room. Stellan frowned at her.

"I really need to go, Cardis. You'll be safe here."

Cardis rolled her eyes. "You just don't get it, do you?"

Alberta came up beside her and handed her a stack of burlap sacks. "You're probably gonna have to spell it out for him. And you're gonna need these out there. Fill 'em with sand and they'll help hold back the water."

Cardis nodded. Stellan reached for the sacks and she slapped his hand away.

"Let me put this in simple language, Stellan, words you can understand. I am a trained medic. I've dealt with storms of every kind under conditions of every kind. And just because I'm not used to walking everywhere I go, don't get the impression I'm out of shape." She hefted the bags onto her shoulder and walked to the door. "Now, we need to stop talking so we can get out there and start helping."

Without another word, Cardis strolled out the door, leaving Stellan gaping behind her. Alberta laughed.

"You know, boy, maybe you've found another keeper."

The frown still plastered on his face, Stellan stomped out the door.

The rain had pushed the tenuous hold of the riverbanks to the breaking point. Driven apart by the sheer force of the surging water, the fragile levees threatened to crumble, sending the river careening over the banks and into the town. For a moment Cardis stood and stared, mesmerized by the wild intensity of the muddy stream as it shoved its way through brush, stone and trees, taking whatever came into its path along for the ride. Then it sank in. Not only was the water taking debris with it, it was taking people.

Cardis watched in horror as the raging torrents sucked at the feet of the men who battled it, tugging them off balance to be carried away by the force of the stream. A man fell and quickly bobbed downstream, his head dipping and rising above the swirling water. His shouts brought the others to the bank with ropes and ties to try to pitch to him. Cardis held her breath as each lifeline slipped by him, his flailing arms unable to catch hold. At last he caught the floating line and, with a cheer, the rescuers pulled him to safety.

But even as they tugged their friend onto the muddy banks, the levee broke completely apart, the raging river taking a large chunk of the stone and debris right out of the middle of the embankment. The roar of the water swelled to a victory yell as the straining mass plunged free of all restraint.

"It will carry off everything!"

Cardis startled at the sound of the voice next to her. She'd been so caught up in the drama before her, she'd forgotten about anything else. The woman was about the same age as Cardis, her thick red hair tied off her face with a fancy white ribbon. Her eyes brimmed with tears as her gaze fixed on the ever-moving water.

"We'll lose it all and we'll starve."

Her hands covered her face and she sank to her knees. Cardis knelt beside her, not knowing what to do, what to say. Awkwardly, she patted the woman on the back. Then she heard a scream that chilled her very blood. The sound carried more pain than Cardis would've thought possible to bear.

"Chiara! My baby!"

From behind her, Dinah surged toward the watery inferno, her hands frantically reaching as if to pluck something from the moving stream. Cardis' heart leapt to her throat as she stared at the pretty face of Stellan's cousin. She reached for her arm, struggling to hold the distraught woman.

"What is it, Dinah?"

Dinah's sobs tore at the air, breaking through the sound of the rushing water. Almost frantic herself, Cardis scanned the area, finally spotting Stellan's broad back among the others. She shouted his name, hoping he would hear over the pounding noise.

Cardis turned her attention back to the frantic woman in her arms.

"Tell me what's wrong, Dinah. Where's Chiara? Where's Lavin?"

Dinah pointed a trembling finger to the water. "I only let her down for a minute. I wanted to help carry the bags. She was gone so quick. I grabbed at her, got hold of her, but the water, it took her from me." Dinah sank into a heap on the ground. "It just took her from me."

Cardis felt a sense of relief as Stellan came up behind her. She had no words to comfort the woman in front of her.

"My baby!" Dinah wailed louder as Stellan wrapped his arms around her. "She's in the water. It took her from me. Oh, Stellan, it pulled her out of my arms. I grabbed her but it pulled her out of my arms. Lavin went in after her but the water, it swallowed them both." She gripped his hands in hers. "Oh, Stellan, you've got to find them!"

Without another word, Stellan shoved the distraught woman toward Cardis and headed back to the river. As she pulled Dinah into her arms to comfort her, Cardis watched Stellan move down the embankment. He waved to a group of men gathered around the remains of the levee. She heard their shouts over the noise of the flooding but the grim words disappeared in the roar of the water.

"Here, bring her over here." The red-haired woman reached for Dinah, crooning to her softly. "Come, darling. They'll find her for you. Lavin's a good swimmer, he'll catch up to her. And when he brings her back she'll need her mama to be waiting for her, so let's sit down here."

She guided Dinah over to the trees lining the edge of town. Cardis paced beside them, watching Stellan as he moved up and down the crumbling banks. Her heart caught in her throat as he slipped down the steep slope, relaxing only when he caught himself on a limb. She started toward him as he took another tumble, only to be jerked back by a strong grip on her arm.

"Here." It was Alberta. She shoved a rough cloth sack into Cardis' hands, one of the ones Cardis had dropped when the waters mesmerized her. "We need to get fuel."

"Fuel?" Cardis stared at her blankly.

"For the fire. We need to get wood. It'll be wet and we need to get it indoors where it can dry, else it'll be days before we can use it. And I don't want to go days without a fire. Cleaning up after this mess will be tough enough as it is." Not waiting for an answer, the old woman grasped Cardis' hand and pulled her off.

Two hours later Cardis could locate every muscle in her body. This newfound knowledge came from the fact that all of them ached. Alberta had led her up and down the sides of the river to look for enough wood to last a while. They'd had to fight the rain for it, and her hands were covered in dirt from the messy pieces. Her back protested the slightest movement. Every inch of her was soaked through to the skin. Still Alberta pushed on, keeping the both of them busy with the task at hand. They spread the wet branches out along the tables set up in Alberta's shed behind her house.

Tired and filthy, Cardis had just closed her eyes when Stellan walked in. As he came through the door, she looked at him hopefully, the unspoken question clear on her face. The grim set of Stellan's face gave her the answer.

"There's no sign of them. We've walked the bank on both sides for the last two hours. It's too dark, really, to see much. Maybe with the dawn...." He let his words trail off as Alberta patted his arm.

"I'll fix you something warm to drink. I'm sure you're frozen through." Without waiting for an answer, she turned toward the kitchen.

He stared around the room as if he couldn't quite remember where he was. "We got the river contained. The rain's stopped and the sandbags should hold, at least for the night."

Cardis stepped to him. "You must be exhausted. You need to sleep, at least for a while. Maybe in the morning you can..."

Stellan shook his head as he cut her off. "By morning I don't know what will be left. Probably nothing. The water's headed downstream now for the most part, but the mud is still a threat. And a good many people lost their homes. We'll have to set up some shelters or they'll be spending the nights out under the trees for quite some time."

"Surely there's a way to get some help here, a way to contact your brothers and let them know what's happened."

"Maybe. I sent half the men home to rest. The others will take their turn in three hours.

"Come on." He yanked her up and she stumbled against him.

"Hey, slow up."

Cardis dug her heels into the floor and tugged her hand out of his grip. Stellan leaned against the doorway and took a deep breath.

"Hell, I'm sorry, princess. Look, I need to get back out there. There's a room, out behind the tavern. It's warm and dry and you can bed down there. Alberta's only got the one bed and I thought that'd be easier."

"Okay. But I really could help."

He shook his head. "Just let me grab a few things and I'll take you there."

Sighing, Cardis followed him out of the alcove.

Chapter Seventeen

They walked along the tiny path in silence. Cardis racked her brain, trying to think of some words, anything that would bring some measure of comfort. As they neared a rough structure on the edge of town, a figure moved quietly out of the shadows. Cardis barely muffled her scream as Stellan pulled her to a stop. The man moved to Stellan, his voice low and racked with pain.

"A moment, Stellan."

The man glanced at Cardis uneasily. Stellan nodded, his hand tightening on Cardis' arm.

"It's all right, Daniel. Tell me your news."

"We've found her, the babe, that is."

"Alive?"

Cardis held her breath as the man nodded in response to Stellan's question.

"Aye, she's alive. We found her in a tree by the far north bank." He hesitated as his gaze shifted from Stellan to Cardis and back again. "She said her daddy put her there."

"And Lavin?" Stellan's voice was but a whisper.

The man shook his head. "We've found no sign of him. The baby said he kept playing in the water."

The sob tore at Cardis' throat as she tried to stifle the sound. She looked at Stellan's face, but his features could've been carved from stone for all the emotion that showed on them.

"Thank you, Daniel. I'll be back out in a bit."

With a brief nod, the man faded back into the shadows.

"Stellan, I'm so—"

"I need to get back to the river." He tugged at her arm. "The sooner I get you settled, the quicker I can do that."

It was on the tip of her tongue to tell him she could settle herself very well, but the dark set of his features kept the words in her mouth. Instead, she nodded. Maybe she was learning a little about courting danger after all.

Stellan led Cardis into the small cabin. The place was primitive even by Edarian standards. A fire was going in the narrow firepit, illuminating the room with its flames. A tiny cot stood in one corner, a table in the center. There was little else in the way of furnishings. A shower and a sink stood in another corner.

Cardis glanced over at Stellan. The silence between them was somehow more awkward than any conversation they'd had. Grief, she knew, could strip away every form of protection a person had, leaving them raw and pulsing with hurt. She'd thought her tears would never dry when Stefan died.

The heat from the fire gave blessed relief from the numbing cold. Cardis moved to stand by the flames, anxious to get both the chill and the images of the last few hours from her mind. Out of the corner of her eye she watched him as he moved about the room restlessly, like a caged animal. Though he'd said he wanted to go, he paced back and forth as if he'd forgotten his intent. Or as if he needed to work off some energy before he went back out to his people.

Repressed fury radiated from him. Cardis felt she should say something, give some kind of comfort. She opened her mouth and hoped the right words would come.

"Stellan, I'm sorry. I know Lavin...."

"No, princess, you didn't know Lavin." He cut her off so swiftly she could only stand there gaping at him. "You don't know me, you don't know anything. So save your pity."

The bitterness in his voice surprised her. She'd expected grief, not anger. Grief she could understand, could deal with.

"Look, I'm sorry. I know this whole situation is tough for you."

"Tough?" He gave a laugh that held many things, none of them humor. "Why, princess, we go through this every spring. We barbarians learn to live with this kind of

193

situation. It's our lot in life. Tough is the way things are for us. Our backward culture has taught us to accept it."

Cardis frowned at the sarcasm in his tone. Hurt and anger leaked through every word. She shook her head in frustration.

"Okay, so you don't want my sympathy. But there are ways I can help, you know."

Stellan tossed his knapsack to the floor and strode to the sink. "No thanks, darling. Not your problem, not your mess."

He turned on the water in the sink and ducked his head under the stream. Cupping the flow in his hands, he rubbed his face.

For some reason his words cut right through her, slammed her into the wall that all their differences made between them. He was right, this wasn't her problem. But how dare he dismiss her attempts as if they were an insult to him. Temper rose in her as she watched him stomp his way to the door.

"You'll be all right here until I get back."

He tossed the words over his shoulder as he shoved his streaming hair out of his face. The drops glistened on the gold strands, the firelight making them shine. He stood, silhouetted by the flames, and Cardis couldn't take her eyes off him. Danger filled the very air around him, yet the sight of him beckoned to her. The primal roar inside her head dared her to take a step closer while her common sense screamed at her to run. Maybe she hadn't learned how to stay out of danger after all. Down low she felt the dampness and remembered his words from the river.

You'll stare at me across the kitchen and feel yourself grow wet, know that you're waiting for me to give you the pleasure that only I can.

Cardis felt like she'd been struck by an ion storm. *By all the stars and planets, she wanted this man. Wanted him desperately.* What in the hell had happened to her? Now was hardly a time to be feeling the kind of lust that was spurting through every inch of her.

"There's food and plenty of ways to keep warm." Stellan pointed to the pile of blankets on the sparse bed and turned to go.

She felt she had to make one more try, to make some kind of connection with him. The notion struck her as silly, but she couldn't let him walk out like this. "Stellan, I...I'm sorry for all this."

When he turned to her, Cardis wanted to step back. She had grown accustomed to the grin he wore. There wasn't a trace of it now.

"For all this?" He took a step toward her and Cardis did move back. His whole being radiated a force she instinctively knew could consume her if she let it.

"All this mess, you mean."

Stellan moved toward her again, giving Cardis the wary feeling of being stalked. She suddenly felt like prey, trapped but helpless to move away from the danger in front of her.

"No. I mean yes. I mean about what's happened today. I feel badly about Dinah and her loss, about the way the village will have to deal with the aftermath of all this."

Cardis knew she was babbling but the look on his face frightened her. There was an intensity about his manner she hadn't seen before. It was more than grief, more than anger. There was hunger written all over him. Did he feel the same lust that was consuming her? All the danger she'd sensed in him when she first saw him was boiling out of his wild green eyes.

"Do you?" Stellan took another step toward her.

"Yes, of course."

"Pity isn't the same as a real feeling. Do people like you really feel?" His voice was hard and his face even harder. "I wonder if you can."

"People like me?" A spark of temper caught at the lust, mixing it into a potent brew.

"Rich, used to the things your money can buy, the power it gives you to make the rest of us dance to your tune. Living in your oh-so-carefully constructed ivory towers, looking down on the rest of us."

Temper brought the mixture to a boil. "That's hardly the way it is. My family has worked hard for generations to get where we are."

Cardis bit her lip. She wasn't going to defend her father to this man. And she wasn't going to indulge in any misplaced notions of love either. His actions proved how futile that would be. All she had wanted was to extend a little sympathy to him. If he couldn't accept that, then so be it. As for the rest, his words pointed out their differences better than she could have. Whatever physical attraction there was, it wouldn't be enough to overcome the mountains between them, no matter how potent the lust the sight of him inspired.

Stellan's hard stare caught hers and she matched him glare for glare. But this time he was the one with the sneer on his face as he spoke.

"You and your kind look down on the rest of us, call us thieves and beggars for trying to grab a little of that power for our own, for trying to make things a little better for ourselves."

Stellan stepped so close Cardis swore there was green fire in his eyes. Every angle of his face hardened and he stared at her with a hunger that bordered on feral. For a moment Cardis couldn't move, transfixed by the difference in him. Stripped of even a veneer of civilization, Cardis realized the man who stood before her had none of the trappings of culture so prominent in the men of Adena. What stood before her now was raw male, primitive and primal in a way that fascinated and aroused her. The tiny scar below his eye, the golden stubble on his cheeks, the green fire in his eyes. All of it stirred her in a way she wasn't sure she wanted to examine too closely. The man was insulting her, and not only her but her family, her people. She should be angry, not aroused. Words that would put him in his place rattled around in the back of her brain, but no matter how hard she tried, she couldn't get them past her frozen lips.

Stellan gripped her arms and jerked her close.

"You end up here through your own ignorance, your own misfortune, yet you cast the blame on us. You tell us we should just graciously hand back the things you've scattered across our land without so much as a thank you. That we should be humbled, that the pat on the head should be enough of a reward for lowlifes such as us. That we should be grateful for the chance to even touch such things, things we can never aspire to have as our own.

He leaned into her, the heat of his body steaming its

way across her already sensitized skin. Cardis stared at his mouth, unconsciously wet her lips as she waited for his to claim her. She might as well kiss rational thought goodbye for she felt sure if he didn't touch her soon she'd explode. Stellan tightened his grip on her arms and shook her ever so slightly.

"Well now you can't deny me, princess, at least not for the next few hours. I get to touch as much as I want. Maybe you're right, maybe I'll end up paying for it with my life, be it slavery or death. But that only pushes me more to touch now, to take what I can before it's denied me again."

Before Cardis could release the moan forming on her lips, he captured her mouth with a possession that should have scared the hell out of her. And she was sure on some level it did. But it did other things to her as well, things that had more to do with want than fear.

He gave her no quarter to resist him, no room to maneuver his touch to any safe haven. He gave her absolutely no control as his hands shoved at the clothing barring his way to her skin.

From some faint distance the sound of the red gown ripping echoed over the roar in her head. As he tore at the fabric Stellan backed her up against the wall. His hot hands on her bare skin fired her nerves so much Cardis barely noticed the feel of the rough wood at her back. They tore at each other with the fury of temper and need driving them to throw away any inhibitions, any gentleness.

Stellan's teeth nipped at the soft skin of her breasts, tugging and tightening her nipples with his tongue as he grazed his mouth over them. With one hand he shoved her thighs apart, used his fingers to part her as he sought her clit. The friction of those calloused fingers against that sensitive spot drove her up and she undulated with his movements, stroking the fire inside her as he pushed her closer and closer to the edge. Her vision blurred as the climax started. She thought she might have screamed his name, but her breath caught in her throat when he lifted her hips and wrapped her legs around him, rubbing the sensitive flesh between her thighs against the taut leather. Over and over he stroked her, until the tiny thing she'd thought was her climax burst into a flame that consumed her as she rode him down to the floor in a tumble of leather, flesh and sex.

Chapter Eighteen

Cardis woke to the first rays of dawn coming through the tiny window. She lay alone on the cramped bed. Stellan had left her as she drifted off to sleep, but not before he made good on his promise to touch her. He had touched every place on her with those rough hands, had brought her to climax over and over until she thought she would burst apart from the intensity of each one. Her skin still tingled at the thought of his hands on her in places and ways she would never have known possible. Or pleasurable. But they were. He hadn't paused or stopped his assault on her for a moment, bringing her to the edge with ruthless skill each time.

And she'd done it as well. She'd fought him, licked, teased and touched every part of him, until she thought she might know his body better than she knew her own. It was something she'd never expected to do, never expected to want to do. There had been times she'd thought of taking a lover, but none of her expectations matched the reality of Stellan's body in the slightest.

By the time she lay at the edge of sleep from sheer exhaustion, Cardis believed the man had found every nerve ending and pleasure center in her body. He had indeed touched her, there was no mistaking that. Touched every part of her. Lying alone in the makeshift bed, Cardis was forced to admit he had touched more than her body. The man had touched her heart. She had never been more frightened.

Her aches and pains hit her when she crawled out of the small cot. Perhaps pleasure came with consequences she hadn't thought of. She stretched as slowly as she could, feeling every bump and bruise on her body. Rubbing her arms against the chill in the room, she reached for the red gown. Thankfully, in spite of Stellan's rough treatment of it, there was enough material left in one piece for her to fashion a suitable covering out of it. At least she wouldn't freeze to death.

A peek out the window told her she'd slept longer than she thought. Sunlight poured through the opening, giving the world a rosy glow that chased away the lingering gloom of yesterday. But a look out the door told her things weren't as rosy as the sun made them look.

Mud and debris covered most of the village. Makeshift shelters had been set up along the trees. People milled about the shelters, starting cooking fires and shoveling at the mud. Cardis closed the door and turned to the tiny sink. Maybe there was something she could do to help with the cleanup. Surely that would be considered woman's work and no one would have a problem with her helping.

As she gazed in the mirror above the sink, she thought she should first start with cleaning up herself. Her hair could use a brush and her face needed a bit of soap and water. Those would do for a start. She let the water run into the basin, scooping it up in her hands and scrubbing at her face. The feel of soap and water was heavenly after the mud and dirt of the last few hours. She reached for the bit of cloth hanging on a rack beside her, toweling off her face with it. A noise caught her in midmotion.

Startled, Cardis turned as the door opened, the towel still clutched in her hands as if she could use it as a weapon. She relaxed her guard a bit when she saw it was Stellan.

He was covered in mud, and some other substances she couldn't identify. The side of his vest had a large gash in it and his leather pants were caked with slime. Cardis wanted to ask him if the dam was fixed, but the look on his face stopped her. Or maybe, if she were truthful, it was something inside of her that gave her pause. The man fed a need inside of her just from a look at him. That fact should scare the shit out of her and it did. She dropped the towel and turned to face him fully. He looked away.

"Look, princess, I...I'm sorry." Stellan ran his hand

through his hair. He still didn't look at her, didn't turn to her.

"You're sorry?"

"Yeah, I'm sorry about last night. I had no right to take things out on you."

"Take things out on me?" Cardis moved to stand in front of him.

Stellan gazed down at her arms. "To use you the way I did."

"I thought that's what our being together was all about."

Stellan traced a finger along her arm. "I know you think we're all a bunch of barbarians, but I've never left bruises on a woman before."

Cardis grasped his finger. "I'm not sure you can take credit for the ones on me either. At least not all of them. Yesterday was a tough day." She wanted to ask about Lavin, about the levees, the town. And to give him some comfort. But he turned away from her again.

"Well, you have my apology, for what it's worth to you. Now I think I'm going to try to get some of the river off me."

He walked to the shower and turned on the water. Cardis watched his face as he shed his clothes. As much as she loved the sight of his body, she was more stirred by the pain that haunted his eyes. He had to be tired. Certainly she was. Cardis didn't think she had ever worked so hard in all her life.

And for what?

The thought came unbidden to her. There would be others like Lavin who paid with their lives for the neglect of those in power, for the scorn Hakir held for the quality of life his people lacked. It had to be what Stellan tormented himself with even now. The dam would never be built for his brothers would never help, maybe never even allow it. The people were no concern of theirs. Stellan and the others couldn't do it alone. This would be only the first of many floods this spring, the first of many losses that would weigh on him.

For she knew now it did weigh on him. Behind his simpleton grin beat a heart that cared for his people. Cardis didn't want to examine how much that surprised her, for then she would have to admit how much she had stereotyped him, had placed him in a definition of her own choosing. Today forced her to look at him in a new light. Or rather, to look at him as he truly was.

Stellan leaned against the shower stall, eyes closed. Water sluiced down the ridges of his back, dampened the crisp hairs on his chest and glided across the golden skin of his buttocks in a sensual waterfall. Cardis feasted her eyes on him, let herself really look at the body of the man who had spent so much of the last few hours making her hot.

Over the last two days she had let him touch her at will, had let him take her body in those large hands and use the skill he had to persuade her to become his lover. But she had not touched him, had not returned any of that skill with her own hands, on her own initiative. She'd touched him in the heat of the passion he'd stirred, but never sought that passion on her own.

She'd withheld that from him, as a test? A torture? Cardis wasn't sure which it was. Maybe only a way to keep from seeing him as he was, to keep from getting to know a man she planned to turn her back on and try never to remember when she left this place. Letting him know he stirred that passion inside her, that she wanted him might give him a sense of control that she didn't want to let go of.

But now, as she watched the defeated slump of his shoulders, stared at the hurt in his eyes, saw him wince as the water hit the cuts along his arms, something about withholding her touch from him seemed vengeful and mean-spirited. She didn't want to give him hope, resisted the idea that taking the initiative would give him the thought that he might win this challenge. But she couldn't keep from touching him.

Lost in his own bitterness, Stellan jumped when he felt her there with him in the shower. She had never come this close without his asking first, had never touched him without his touching her first. Now her hands slid around his chest as she stood on her toes and whispered in his ear.

"Lean back against me. I want to wash the mud off you."

Numbed by his own pain and needing the heat of her more than he cared to think about, Stellan leaned back gently, surprised, and grateful, to find her naked. It was likely the last time he would have to feel her skin against his own. It wouldn't have surprised him if she'd refused to let him touch her at all after what he'd done last night. Then again, maybe it was only pity that drove her to touch him now, pity at what lay ahead of him. One last crumb for a dead man.

Stellan bit back a sigh. If he'd gambled and lost, something that appeared more and more likely, especially after today, he would deal with the consequences when the time came. For now he would take what comfort she was willing to give without looking too hard at the reason for it.

In one hand Cardis held a cloth covered with creamy white soap that smelled of wildflowers and rain. He breathed in deeply, letting the homey scent comfort him. With slow circles, Cardis glided the soapy cloth across his chest as she let her fingers tangle in the golden hairs. Her hand moved lower and lower, until Stellan wondered that the cloth didn't ignite from the heat her strokes built under his skin. He kept still, fearful the slightest movement would make her leave him.

Cardis shifted her knee to push against him, spreading his thighs out wider. He felt her mouth move down his back as her knees lowered, biting and nipping against his skin even as her hand brushed down the front of him. She cupped him with the cloth, moving the rough fabric up and down his swollen shaft with a friction that had him biting his lip to keep from groaning. While she tortured him from the front, her mouth bit a trail of fire down the back of him. When her lips touched the crack of his butt, Stellan thought he might have to sit down. He started to turn and she shoved him back around.

"Lean over." Her voice was husky with the command.

Grateful for the wall in front of him, Stellan braced his hands against the shower frame. When he looked down, he saw her hands as they worked him, watched her fingers as they moved up and down his shaft with a rhythm that was driving him crazy one stroke at a time. Then she dropped the cloth and stroked him skin to skin, keeping the rhythm going while moving the other hand up the back of his shaft to cup his sac. She rolled the sensitive skin between her fingers while her tongue licked at the water coursing down his butt. As she pinched down on him, she thrust her hand down his shaft hard and fast. Stellan came with an explosion and a groan that nearly made him sink to his knees. But Cardis pushed him against the wall as she milked him, keeping the pleasure bursting through him until he felt all his insides must be pouring out into the water that slid down him. Spent at last, he leaned against the wall, his breath ragged as he waited for the room to stop spinning. Behind him, Cardis chuckled.

"You know, I'm not finished with your bath."

"I thought you weren't allowed to kill me off during the challenge."

"Not unless you attack me. Those are the rules."

"Do those rules say anything about you attacking me?" He turned around to face Cardis, still not sure he should move away from the support of the wall behind him.

"Yeah." This time she grinned. "They say you're supposed to relax and enjoy it. What did you think all the training Adenan virgins get was all about?"

"How to rip a guy's limbs off without killing him?"

Cardis trailed a hungry look down the hard line of his chest to where he was already semi-hard again. "Well, there are a few parts that they tell us are better left attached."

Cardis leaned out of the shower to grab another handful of soap from the small container. Stellan watched in fascination as she moved, her nude body glistening with the sheen of the water.

"Now kneel down," she instructed.

He pointed to the spot in front of her.

"Yes, there. I'm going to wash your hair. You have mud all in it."

Grinning, Stellan knelt in front of her, placing his hands on her waist, fingers spread across her hips.

"You know, this puts me in a very vulnerable position. I've never been in this spot before."

"I know."

"But," Stellan leaned forward slightly to touch his lips to her belly. "I'm beginning to see that it also has its advantages." His tongue licked a circle around her navel.

"Quit!"

Cardis smacked his shoulder, sending soap spattering in his eyes. He frowned at her as he leaned back to wipe his face.

"Well, that's what you get for distracting me. Now be still."

"Yes, ma'am." He gave her an unrepentant grin.

Cardis threaded her hands through the burnished gold strands of his hair. In spite of the mud, it felt silky and soft against her skin. She massaged his scalp with her fingers, smiling when he groaned.

"Lean your head back, so you don't get soap in your eyes."

"Then I'll get water in my mouth."

"Not if you keep it closed."

"You're a bossy woman."

"Sweet talk isn't your forte, is it?"

Stellan closed his mouth and thought for a moment. "No more than it is yours."

"But I'm not the one who has to be persuasive. Sweet talk might help your cause a little."

He stared at her. "Would it really? Or don't you already have your mind made up, princess?"

Cardis felt a pang of guilt at his words. Was she only playing with him, only using him? And did it matter? He brought this challenge on himself, hoping to enrich himself with her wealth, her lineage. He had no right to challenge for her and she had tried to warn him. Still, the thought of the consequences nagged at her.

Stellan watched the emotions play across her face. He had risked everything, more than Cardis could even know, on a gamble of life and death proportions. What would happen to the others when he was gone, he didn't want to think about. He smiled up at her.

"Maybe you were right, and all that's left to me is to relax and enjoy. So I think I will."

Stellan leaned forward again, planting a long slow kiss on her belly. He let his tongue dip into the soft indentation, filling his mouth with the taste of her. His hands tightened on her hips and he smiled when her fingers gripped his hair. No matter what he might lose tomorrow, she wasn't unaffected by him right now.

He tugged on her hips to move her forward, wanting more of her in his mouth.

"Spread your legs, Cardis. Let me taste you."

She clenched her fingers in his hair for a moment, then leaned over slightly and spread her long legs. Stellan took her in his mouth, gliding his tongue over the sensitive skin. She tasted like heaven, or as near to it as he had ever been. Her skin was soft and moist, the heat of it delightful on his tongue. He pulled and suckled, feeling the effect of his movements in the tremors in her legs. His hands roamed her cheeks, massaging them as he felt the tremors build. Her legs were shaking and her hands moved over his shoulders and his back, gripping his skin. She came with a cry that sent shivers through him as well. His tongue continued to lave her folds until she finally collapsed against him. He leaned back, letting the water wash the soap from his hair as he gave her a satisfied grin. With one of her own, Cardis reached over and shut off the water and stepped out of the shower.

"I think we've had enough. We're both gonna be wrinkled. And there's only one of those little cloth things you use." Cardis frowned at the small piece of linen on the rack. A minute or two in a drying tube would've had them both warm and dry with far less effort.

Cardis stretched her arms over her head in a lazy motion. Stellan couldn't believe it but he felt his body respond to the sight of her. She looked down at his cock and grinned.

"Really?"

"Don't worry, princess, it's used to not always getting what it wants. And right now, I think I'll be lucky to make it up out of this shower, so you're safe. For the moment. I'm not sure whether or not this challenge is a test of my seductive powers or my stamina."

"Both. Now stop talking and find a way to get us both dry. I'm getting cold and it's still a long way to the bed."

"Bossy woman."

Cardis squealed as Stellan wrapped his arms around her bottom to lift her, tossing her over his shoulder.

Bracing one hand on the wall, he managed to make it to his feet.

"I asked for help, not to be carried. Running me around naked in the breeze is a worse way of getting me dried off than using that cloth. Besides, you're not much steadier than I am. I don't want you banging my head on the shower thingy."

Stellan wavered, then managed to straighten. He stumbled out of the shower, grabbed the towel as he passed the rack, then with a whoop ran to the bed and deposited her in a heap.

"I think it's a little late for that thing." Cardis tugged at the towel in his hand. "We've soaked the bedsheets already."

"I don't think you fully appreciate the advantages of the towel system."

"Advantages?"

"Well, to start with there's friction." He pulled the towel out of her grasp and rubbed it over her breasts. His fingers molded to the shape of them as he worked the cloth back and forth over her skin. Cardis moaned.

"Friction's good, but there's a problem."

He brushed the cloth down her belly, gliding his fingers over her hips. "Problem?"

"Yeah. You're dripping on me even as you wipe me off. I told you that one little piece of cloth wouldn't cut it."

"Ah, but there's another advantage to this system, princess."

"Really? And what would that be?"

She caught a flash of his wicked grin as he lowered his mouth to her belly. When his tongue darted out to lick the drops from her skin she thought she'd melt right into the bed. As his mouth moved lower, his tongue laving her folds, Cardis was forced to admit there were some things technology didn't improve on. Still, she couldn't resist teasing him.

"I don't think your system's working down there."

He glanced up at her. "Why not?"

"Cause you're making me wet, not dry."

He grinned at her. "Then I guess I'll have to get some heat going and see if that works better."

Stellan lowered his mouth back down to her core and

stoked the fire he'd started. Cardis writhed beneath his assault, her fingers gripped in the bedsheets. The force of the orgasm hit her and she screamed his name. When the tremors finally subsided, Stellan eased up between her thighs, laying his head on her belly.

"Did that do the trick?"

Cardis laughed. "I certainly hope so. I'm not sure I can make it through any more tricks you might have up your sleeve."

He tapped his chin. "Well, you know there are games we haven't played yet."

Cardis clapped her hands over her eyes. "Please don't tell me. I need a breather before you show me any more of your tricks." She dropped her hands down to thread her fingers through his hair. It was damp and soft against her belly.

"If you want your nap, you'd best stop doing that."

"Why," she asked with a teasing tone, "do you like for me to touch you?"

"I would think I'd made that clear, princess. I like, very much."

She pushed him off her and flat on the bed, rolling on top of him. "Then I guess I'll have to do it again."

Cardis let her lips roam his face, his neck, breathing in the scent of him. He reached up for her and she gave him a wicked grin.

"After my nap." With that, she rolled away from him, turning on her side and closing her eyes. She heard his chuckle and snuggled against him, letting him hold her as she drifted off to sleep.

****

Stellan woke to the sound of tapping. It took a moment to orient himself in the darkened room. The noise was gone and he thought he might have dreamed it. Turning over to return to sleep, he winced. He tried not to wake Cardis as he shifted his aching muscles. Despite all his movements, she never opened her eyes. The look on her face was peaceful, satisfied and he couldn't help tracing a finger down her cheek. They had played until nearly midnight, using each other's bodies in ways he never knew existed. She was amazing, wild and vigorous one minute and soft and tender the next.

Stellan had never spent much time simply being in bed with a woman. Most of the time they stiffened under him, making him feel as if he should satisfy himself as quickly as possible and leave. He liked to give them a part of the pleasure as well, but most of them seemed only to want the whole act to be over. Never had he been with a woman as passionate, as demanding as Cardis. A woman who wanted her own pleasure and took what she wanted. There was something about the feel of her hands on his body that went beyond any sex he'd ever had.

He sighed as the thought went through him. His brother's voice echoed in his head. He was a dreamer, risking his whole life on a woman who wouldn't give him a second thought when she left. And leave she would. Though he knew he had given her pleasure, Stellan knew she still saw him as a barbarian, a ruffian whose touch she tolerated because of the rules of the challenge. What they had done these last few days would mean nothing in the long run, once she was gone. And he was gone.

He wondered if she would kill him, or leave him a slave for the rest of his life. The latter would be worse, for even if she shed her memories, he would remember. Maybe even see her from time to time, knowing all he had risked and that now he couldn't touch, would never touch her again. He would be left to watch another claim her, for surely some challenger would at last win her heart and make her his wife. The loss of his dream would eat away at him more than the loss of his freedom. He hoped she demanded his death.

The tapping started again and Stellan glanced toward the window. He nearly fell out of bed when he saw the face pressed against the pane. Stellan slid the window up with something near panic clogging his throat.

"Samuel, what are you doing here?" He hissed the question at the boy, not wanting to wake Cardis.

"I need to talk to you, Stellan." The sense of urgency in the boy's voice had Stellan's panic going fullblown. "It's important. It's about you and her." Samuel jerked his chin toward where Cardis slept.

Stellan cast another glance at Cardis before turning back to Samuel. Something told him his dreams were about to take another nosedive. He nodded toward

Samuel before closing the window.
"I'll meet you outside."

Chapter Nineteen

Stellan closed the door behind him as quiet as he could. Every squeak and rattle of the wind had driven him to the door, believing Cardis' father had arrived. Samuel's message of his brothers' planned betrayal of the compact should've reached him by now. And the Adenans weren't hampered by having to walk. Surely the man would get here before dawn. And then it would all be over.

Every part of him felt cold as he walked to the bed. Every dream he'd ever had, every desire he'd secretly cherished in his heart crumbled as he stared at Cardis lying there so peacefully. Outwardly he cursed Hakir and Martin while inwardly he grieved for the loss of hope. And the loss of the woman who offered the fulfillment of it. Of all that his brothers had ever taken from him with their greed and their indifference, she was the most precious.

She lay snuggled in Alberta's soft coverlet, wrapped as carefully as a prized jewel. Truly she was a prize, one he knew now he could never hope to win, a treasure beyond any the likes of him would ever know. She deserved wealth and comfort. All he could offer was the whim of fate and a bit of physical pleasure. Then he shook his head. He could offer her protection as well, and that he had done.

He'd watched her all the time since Samuel had left, torn between the desire to wake her, to have a few more moments with her to hold as a treasure in his heart and the wish to begin numbing his heart to her memory. He didn't want to think about the emotion surging through him as he watched this woman who had turned his world upside down. His stubborn pride kept him from calling it love. What good would it do to name the thing such a beautiful word when soon all he would feel was pain.

211

Sighing, he rose. Stellan knew he'd made the right choice. That would have to be enough to see him through what lay ahead. He stepped to the bed and shook her gently.

"Cardis."

She mumbled something in her sleep. Stellan tugged the cover off of her and she opened a bleary eye to glare at him.

"Wake up, princess."

Cardis blinked her eyes and frowned.

"It's dark outside. I swear, Stellan, I'm not playing any night games with you. You've already worn me out. The challenge doesn't require you to go at it every hour of the day. Letting me sleep will only aid your efforts, trust me."

She reached for the blanket but he held it away from her hands.

"Sorry, darling, but I need you up. We have to talk."

His seriousness must have penetrated the fog of sleep, for Cardis jerked up from the bed.

"What's wrong? What's happened? Oh, no, Stellan, it's not Lavin, is it, he's not..."

"No, there's still no word." Her concern touched Stellan deeply. One more reason to let her go. "That's not why we have to talk."

"Then what is it?"

"There's something I have to tell you."

Stellan tugged her to her feet and wrapped the blanket around her. "And it'll be easier if you're covered up. That way I won't have to think about what I'm doing."

"About what you're doing? What do you mean? What's going on, Stellan?"

"I've sent for your father."

Cardis gaped at him. "You did what? She peered over at the timepiece on the small bedtable. "Did I sleep longer than I thought? We still have hours before he comes. The challenge isn't over until the evening of the third day."

Stellan stroked a hand down her cheek. "Not for us, princess. Ours has to end now."

"You're sending me away? Before the time is up?" Her face clouded with suspicion. "What's going on, Stellan?"

Before he could answer, someone knocked at the

door. As he turned to answer it, Stellan called over his shoulder.

"You need to get dressed. I don't think seeing you half naked in my bed would make your father's day. Especially not with what I have to tell him."

Cardis jumped up and grabbed his arm, jerking him around. "Forget telling him. Tell me."

He looked at her and sighed. "I'll tell you both together. So get dressed."

Prying her hand off his arm, Stellan kissed her and went to the door. He took a deep breath and kissed his own dreams goodbye as he opened it.

Cardis' father had come alone in spite of Stellan's warning. With a nod, Stellan opened the door wide and Alden Oderean walked in. The older man looked around the tiny cabin and for the first time Stellan felt embarrassed of his surroundings. This man wouldn't even consider such a place an acceptable outpost during an ion storm. But then, Oderean would carry no affection for Edaria back with him anyway, especially with the knowledge of the treachery his brothers planned. No amount of propaganda would dress up their intentions to commit violence against a man they'd sworn an oath of cooperation to.

Oderean stood in the center of the room, no hint of his emotions on his solemn face. He folded his arms across his chest and stared at Stellan. Stellan cleared his throat. Best to get it over with.

"You came alone. I half expected to hear an army outside my door. Or to have my door blasted open with a laser."

"My daughter?"

Stellan pointed behind him. "Cardis is fine."

Oderean raised a brow at him. "Indeed?"

"Your daughter has not been harmed. I'd like you to know that."

"I know that already by the fact you are still standing and you're all in one piece."

Stellan wanted to tell him that nothing was still in one piece, that everything inside him had shattered into a million pieces. Something told him Oderean wouldn't sympathize.

"I hope Samuel told you everything."

Oderean nodded. "The boy was quite talkative. I don't believe he left anything out. He is your nephew?"

"Yes. He is my brother Hakir's son."

"And you trusted his word against his father?"

"The boy is illegitimate, and Hakir is not always kind. Besides, Samuel seldom lies. For one thing, he isn't very good at it, and for another he sees no reason for it. If he doesn't want to help you, he just doesn't talk."

"An interesting approach to life."

"Well, Samuel leads an interesting life." Stellan started toward the bedroom door. "Cardis should be almost ready to go."

"Cardis isn't doing anything until you tell me what's going on." Stellan turned his gaze to her, the trousers and tunic he'd first seen her in back on. The scowl she'd first worn was back in place as well.

"You haven't told her?"

Stellan shook his head. "She was sleeping. We've had a long day."

Alden Oderean crossed to his daughter. He hugged her then stepped back to look at her. "You are well?"

Cardis nodded, wrapping her arms around him again. As she stepped back, Stellan noted the tears brimming in her eyes.

"The others? They are well?"

Her father nodded. "Everyone is fine. As agreed, once you and Stellan left, a medlab was arranged and food secured for all of them."

"I don't mean to interrupt," Stellan moved to stand beside Oderean. "But you should get going."

"Uh-uh." Cardis glared at him. "I told you, not until you've talked."

"The deal is over, violated, princess. Your people aren't safe anymore. My brothers are planning to move on your father's encampment at dawn. If you don't get going now, you'll be trapped here."

Cardis clasped her hands to her head, threading her fingers through her spiky hair. "What do you mean, violated?"

"I mean my brothers don't plan on honoring the truce during the challenge. They're going to trap your father and his men here while they wait, hold them all for ransom instead of just the crew of the *Venetta*. They figure your father's a better package than his crew."

"Really."

Cardis stared at him and Stellan's heart sank as he saw the ice princess in front of him again.

"Yeah, really, princess. After all, you're dealing with barbarians, and our kind can't be trusted."

"So you lump yourself in that group?"

"That's my family, darling, and you know what they say, blood will tell. You had it right from the beginning, I'm a lowlife just looking for a chance to have some fun."

"Fun that will cost you your life? Or did you forget that part?"

"I haven't forgotten anything, princess."

Stellan didn't add that it wouldn't be possible to forget a moment of these last two days, that he'd never get her scent off his skin, or the feel of her body in his hands out of his dreams. He turned away from her and strode to the bed.

"But the party's over." He picked up one of the thick blankets. "It's time to pay the piper."

"Just like that?" Cardis stared at his face as he wrapped the blanket around her. "You risk your life for a challenge you're now willing to drop just like that."

Stellan turned his back to her, pain knifing through him. "Just like that. I'm a gambler and a man who gambles needs to know when to fold."

"You'll still pay the price."

Her cold tone ripped what was left of Stellan's heart. He should tell her he'd already paid the price, that what came next didn't compare to what he'd already done to himself. But how foolish would it look now to tell her he'd fallen in love with her. The only thing left to him was dignity and the knowledge she would be safe from his brothers machinations.

"I'll pay the price."

"You idiot!" She planted both fists on his chest and shoved. "First you drag me off to this godforsaken place, then you," Cardis glanced at her father, "spend time with me, and now you want to walk away, just like that."

"Princess, we can argue this all night and I know how

much you'd love to spend the next few hours ripping into me for my stupidity, but the fact is if you don't get out of here now and take your people with you, then I've just thrown everything away for nothing."

"I'm not running from those cretins, so you can take your magnanimous gesture and shove it up your ass."

Stellan gritted his teeth. *Why did the woman have to be stubborn now? Wasn't leaving what she wanted anyway?* "I'm trying my best to save your ass, darling, so you either run or my magnanimous gesture is a total waste."

"Just like that, you expect me to cut and run?"

"I expect you to do what I tell you. I started this challenge and now I'm ending it."

"Do what you tell me? Have you lost what little mind you have? Since when do I do what you tell me? And as for the challenge, I'll be the judge of when it's over."

He glared at her. "You've just got to have the last word, don't you? Well, you're not in charge here, princess. Unfortunately, neither am I. This is the way it is. Like it or not, those cretins control Edaria. What they say goes, and you better believe their men won't hesitate to do whatever Hakir tells them to. If they want to end this, believe me, they'll end it. If Hakir tells his men to move on your people, that's what they'll do."

"Even if what he tells them threatens to bring down the wrath of the Council on them, on their families and their homes?" Cardis folded her arms across her chest and glared at him.

Stellan tried for patience. "The Council is an unknown to them, a faraway bogeyman they've never seen. The wrath of a bunch of strangers doesn't compare in their eyes to what they know Hakir will do to them if they disobey. His wrath they've seen and believe me it's made a deep impression on them."

"So they become monsters themselves, become men without honor because of their fear."

"It's easy to judge them from where you're standing, darling, but they're not all bad men. They do what they have to do in order to survive. Survival isn't the easiest thing to accomplish on Edaria. I would've thought today might have taught you that much."

"Edaria's environment isn't an insurmountable problem, Stellan. There is technology that would make the harsher aspects of life much easier, so your excuse doesn't wash. The fact that it's so hard to survive here comes from their own choices."

"Sometimes the right choice means a risk. When you've got a family, it isn't always easy to take that risk. To keep their families well, they do what they have to do."

"Like you did what you had to do when you challenged for me?"

It was his turn to glare. "I took a risk. It's not going to pay off like I'd hoped. That's not what matters now."

"What does matter now?"

"Why are we standing here arguing about this? I've told you what's going to happen and what you need to do. Your father is here to take care of you and your people. You'll all get safely back to Adena."

"So we run, and reinforce the idea that your brothers are the strongest."

"You either run or I go down the tubes for nothing."

"You keep saying that. You can't guilt me that way, Stellan. I didn't ask you to save me. I don't need you to save me."

"You need somebody to save you, especially from yourself. You're the most hardheaded, stubborn woman I've ever met."

"Not exactly seductive words, buster. Don't think you're getting around me with them either."

"I don't want to get around you, I want to get rid of you. Can't a guy save your life without putting up with all kinds of grief?"

"You haven't begun to see grief yet. I'm just getting started. You think you can walk away from me like this? Where do you get off playing the martyr and leaving me holding the bag of guilt? I don't think so."

"You were planning to walk away anyhow. What difference does it make if it's this morning or this evening? Your guilt is your own so don't lay it on me."

"It makes a hell of a lot of difference. You're quitting, dumping me like a bad investment."

"Dumping you? I'm saving your life, princess, don't you get that?"

"I get exactly what you're doing so don't wrap it in some noble intentions. You made a commitment and now you don't want to see it through."

Stellan gripped his head in both hands. "You're giving me a headache. I can see now why you haven't had other challengers. My admiration for the men on Adena has grown by leaps and bounds in the last few minutes."

Cardis snorted. "Oh, don't even go there, lowlife. There's no changing the deadline. I'm not going anywhere until this is over."

"It's over now, that's what I'm telling you."

"It's not over till I say it's over."

"Ahhh!" Stellan strode past her and snatched open the door.

"Where do you think you're going?"

"To talk to my brothers. They've got to be easier to persuade than you."

"Persuade to what?"

"To see reason."

Cardis rolled her eyes. "Those two can't see anything past their own greed. They don't even...."

Slamming the door, Stellan stomped over to her and grabbed her chin. Yanking her against him, he planted his lips on hers, silencing her with a hard kiss. When he released her, he gave her a grim smile.

"I'm saving you, princess, whether you want me to or not."

With that threat hanging in the air, he stormed out the door.

Chapter Twenty

Stellan stomped along the trail muttering to himself, thankful the path was familiar. At least he wouldn't fall off a cliff from a misstep in the dark.

Before the thought had fully formed in his head, he tripped and fell, both hands flailing for something to hold on to as he went down. The ground beneath him sloped down and momentum tumbled him further down the hill. Finally he came to a stop by smacking into a boulder.

As he stumbled to his feet, he looked at the rip in his pants with disgust. He'd walked this trail in the dark millions of times before without mishap. Could Cardis' magic shield have sent him tumbling down the hill? He wouldn't put it past her to zap him from a distance just as a way to fry his ass because he'd ignored her words.

"Probably hoped I'd break my neck in the fall and save her the trouble."

Great, Stellan thought, now I'm standing here talking to myself. The woman has made me crazy. She had to be the bossiest person he'd ever run into, certainly the bossiest female he'd ever dealt with. Why that should make him smile he'd never know. Just another sign the woman had driven him over the edge. *And another thing about her he'd miss.* Sparring with Cardis verbally had been almost as much fun as getting his hands on her body. Almost. Her aggressive nature added a passion to lovemaking that he'd never experienced before, had never known existed. Stellan doubted he could ever enjoy the timid women of Edaria anymore.

A nagging voice in his head reminded him he needn't worry about that. He wouldn't be enjoying the pleasures of sex anymore anyway. His gamble would cost him that aspect of his life, if it didn't up costing him his life altogether.

The more he thought about it, the angrier he got. It was too easy to blame Cardis and her magic shield for the trouble he faced. She'd been honest from the start about his chances, so he couldn't in good conscience blame her now for how things turned out. No, there was someone else who did carry the blame, someone whose choices always seemed to override anything Stellan tried to do to make things better. Hakir. This time Stellan had taken a chance all of them could've benefited from and what had it gotten him. As usual, Hakir's greed overrode anything else. His brother's penchant for violence never ceased to amaze him. Cardis was right when she called him a man without honor. Honor had no value to Hakir, because it wasn't something he could spend.

And what had Hakir's greed cost the rest of them? Stellan thought about the broken dam and the destruction of Barron's Fort. He thought about Lavin. This flood wasn't the only one that would strike this season. How much higher would the cost go? With nothing to hold the waters back now, the town would be obliterated. All of the people would suffer because Hakir was too greedy to spend the money and the time rebuilding the dam system throughout the lower valleys. And more good people would lose not only their homes, but possibly their lives.

And what of the other problems? Cardis' words rang in Stellan's head. Hakir controlled the flow of wealth so tightly that they'd never really looked at the cost of purchasing equipment and materials from outside Edaria's borders. No one had the funds or the inclination to go against his brother's wishes. But Cardis was right. There was technology that would make things better for all of them. Medicine and healthcare that would keep so many of the little ones from dying. Equipment and materials that would ease the toil of food production, that would make it easier to provide for themselves and allow for times of rest for the people instead of the constant labor that kept them working from daylight to dark just to feed and shelter their families. What right did one man have to keep all the rest of them from a life that was good?

By the time Stellan had reached the edge of Hakir's encampment, his temper was out of control. All his past grievances culminated in this one, all the anger he'd kept so carefully hidden threatening to burst the seams of his control. If this was his last opportunity to say the things his brother needed to hear, then he planned to use it to the fullest. He strode past his brother's guards, ignoring their looks of surprise. Temper guided him as he flung open the door to Hakir's office.

"Where do you get off violating a solemn oath and putting all I've laid on the line at risk?"

Hakir blinked at him as he turned from the conversation with his men, as if shocked to see Stellan standing there. Then his expression turned menacing.

"I've got no time for your prancing about, Stellan. You'll have to take your hurt feelings to the women. Perhaps they can soothe your tears."

Stellan's temper rose at the smirks on the faces of those around him. Martin chuckled as Stellan took a step closer. Near blind rage rose inside him as Stellan realized he wanted to wipe the condescending looks off all their faces.

"My men and I have business to attend to." With a wave of his hand, Hakir dismissed him and turned back to the others.

"Betrayal to attend to, you mean."

In an instant Stellan was across the room. Without thinking, he grabbed his brother by the shoulders and rammed him against the wall. Through the haze of his temper he barely noticed the prick of the knife Matthias held at his throat.

"Back off, Stellan. Hakir told you we've got no time for this."

Stellan shook his head. "No way. Thanks to the two of you and your schemes, I've got no time left anyway. So you're going to listen to me and you're going to listen now."

"Put your knife away, Matthias. I can flick this flea off me without any help."

Grumbling, Matthias lowered the knife. Hakir sneered at Stellan and for the first time Stellan saw the raw hatred in his brother's eyes. "Best you back away now, boy, before I embarrass you by putting you down in front of my men."

His gaze never leaving his brother's face, Stellan shook his head.

"No. You forget, Hakir, I've nothing left. Your greed has seen to that. So a little embarrassment means nothing. If I'm going to die before this day ends, then you're going to listen to what I have to say now."

"Ah, boy, stop being such a pussy. You're making me sick. I won't let the woman kill you, so you don't have to be scared of her."

Behind him Stellan heard chuckling. Hakir grinned at him and Stellan pressed harder against his brother's bulk. The grin faded and Hakir shoved against him, surprised when Stellan's grip stayed tight. Stellan lifted one arm and placed it against Hakir's throat. With the other hand he pulled out the small blade he carried and laid it against Hakir's neck. He pressed slightly, pleased to see an edge of worry come into his brother's expression.

"You can't stop it, even though you're the one to blame. My death is out of your hands now." Stellan nudged the tip of the blade deeper into Hakir's skin. "Best you worry about whether or not I'm going to take you with me. It would ease my mind greatly to know I'd taken care of my people by removing you as their leader before I died."

Hakir snorted. "You haven't got the balls to push that blade any further. You're all talk, Stellan, that's all you've ever been good for. I've tolerated you all these years for our father's sake, but after this you won't have to worry about this magic shield or whatever fairy tale's got you all scared now. I'll hang you out to dry myself and after your bones are bleached no one will even remember your name in Edaria."

Behind him Matthias let out a cry. Stellan turned to see the man's blade drop to the floor moments before he would've plunged it into Stellan's back. Matthias's face held a look of complete surprise as he stared down at the blade embedded in his chest. Stellan looked up to find Alden Oderean standing in the doorway.

Oderean stepped into the room. With a hard thrust, Hakir shoved away from Stellan. "You just made your own grave, merchant," he growled as he stalked toward the man, "one I'll make sure you have a long time to think about before I put you in it. Seize him."

Before his men could move, Oderean stepped aside as twenty armed Council soldiers entered behind him.

"I would warn you men to reconsider. The Council's forces have taken control of this compound and of Edarian airspace. Reinforcements should arrive momentarily. Edaria has been placed under Council control for violations of the interstellar code of conduct and for generally being a menace to the rest of the realm. And you," Oderean stared at Hakir, "are under arrest."

Before his brother could bluster, Stellan watched the Council guards disarm everyone in the room and round up Hakir's men. It was impressive and quick. In only moments the Council guards had Hakir's men subdued. With a wave of his hand, Oderean motioned the guards to remove the prisoners from the room. Once they were alone, he stepped toward Stellan.

"I don't guess you need to tie my hands." Stellan sighed as Oderean simply stared at him. "I did that all by myself, didn't I?"

The older man nodded.

"Well, you sure got the Council people here quick. It gave you enough of a force to make the bluff about the Council taking over work."

"It was no bluff, Stellan. What I said about the Council is true."

Slowly the truth dawned on Stellan. "You knew."

Oderean nodded. "The day we arrived monitors were planted within your brother's compound. Each crewmember of the *Venetta* also wears a monitor attached to their uniform. It's one of the security measures I insist upon. They are of a common metallic alloy, hardly anything that would appear valuable. None of these were taken when your brothers captured them."

"Hakir wouldn't have even known what they were." Stellan laughed bitterly. "And since they didn't sparkle he had no use for them."

"Your brothers were hardly secretive about their plans anyway. They spoke freely in front of their captives about what was planned."

"Hakir would be that arrogant. He has no conception of anyone who would disobey him."

"Apparently not. Nor, apparently, any knowledge of how communication devices work. It was a simple matter to get word to Adena. The Council has sought for years to find a way to put an end to the raiding of vessels that stumble into Edarian airspace."

"Now Hakir has handed them a reason."

"Yes."

"Then the people here will be prisoners, slaves." Stellan felt such an ache in his chest he could barely get the words out. By saving Cardis he had condemned his people. Nothing he'd planned had worked out and now he was going to die while the rest of them suffered. Could he have failed any more miserably?

"Your brothers will face a tribunal for their crimes. The others who aided them will be held accountable for their actions as well. But the people, Stellan, will be treated fairly. On that you have my word."

"I guess that's all I can ask for." Stellan straightened his shoulders and took a deep breath. "It's going to be dark soon. I suppose I should prepare to face the consequences of the challenge."

"I have a transport waiting to take you to where the ending ceremony will take place."

They have a special ceremony for it? He hadn't expected to have to face a crowd for this moment. Stellan cringed at the thought of watching Cardis turn away from him once and for all, in front of all her people. The only bright spot was the hope that Wald would be there watching. The magic shield planned to kill him anyway so things couldn't be made worse by punching that twit's face in. And he probably wouldn't even have to make a move to do it. Stellan was sure the brat would get close enough to him just so he could gloat. The thought gave him a small amount of satisfaction.

Oderean spoke to the driver as Stellan waited. With a nod, the driver started the transport.

"He will take you where you need to be."

"And he doesn't care that you haven't tied me up? I mean, I could try to get away."

His words didn't faze the older man. "The magic

would find you, no matter where you went."

He doesn't have to look so happy about it. Stellan shrugged. "So it's pointless."

"You were warned of that from the beginning. Besides, you were the one who chose to end the challenge early. You've shown great courage up until now. I have no fear you'll run." Oderean motioned him toward the transport. "The driver is waiting and your time grows short."

With a sigh, Stellan got in.

Any other time Stellan would've drooled at the opportunity to get such an up close view of the transport. The thing went fast, far faster than Stellan would've believed it capable of. And the ride was smooth. Only the passing scenery through the small viewfinder let him know where he was. Seated in the plush chair behind the driver, Stellan would've sworn they were traveling over smooth cyberroads rather than Edaria's rocky terrain. The older models commandeered by Hakir years ago lacked the amazing control and maneuverability of this machine. With no replacement parts and no one with the skill to repair them, they had become more like fancy metal wagons. Stellan stifled the urge to ask the driver if he could take the wheel for a moment, sort of a condemned man's last request. No sense getting a taste of what he wanted only to have it torn away. He would never see the stars now.

Asking questions of the driver seemed like a waste of time anyway. Gray cropped hair and a uniform with enough stars and braid along the shoulders and chest to let anyone know he'd seen more than his share of fights were just the first clues to his military background. He had the tight control of a soldier as well. The man's face held no expression and he kept his gaze straight ahead. Not once had he even acknowledged Stellan's presence next to him. The quiet was driving Stellan crazy. He leaned back in the seat and closed his eyes.

Before long, the transport pulled to a stop. Stellan opened one eye, hoping he was in some isolated zone where they could shove him off the nearest cliff and be done with it. What he saw instead had him turning to the driver in surprise.

"What are we doing here?"

"I was told to bring you home, sir."

"Home?" Stellan pushed open the transport door, surprised further when the driver made no protest. He stepped out into the clearing around his small cabin, even more confused when the door behind him closed.

"Wait a minute." He banged on the heavy metal door. The driver opened it again.

"Yes, sir?"

"You're just going to drop me off here?"

"Those were my orders."

"And you're just going to leave me here alone?"

"No, he's leaving you here with me."

Stellan wheeled around to find Cardis standing in the doorway of the cabin. She wore a loose gown of emerald green, her bare feet peeking out from under its hem. Her dark curls crowned her head, setting off the porcelain glow of her face. Memories of the soft feel of her ivory skin assaulted Stellan like a knife in his heart. She was the picture of elegance, the embodiment of all the reasons his dream never stood a chance. Watching her stand against the pitiful place he called home made him realize how silly the dream had been to begin with. Yet the sight of her made him hard, made him want her all over again. His heart ached, along with most of his other body parts.

"You gonna finish me off personally, princess?"

"Something like that." Cardis waved to the driver and the transport roared to life. As it pulled away, Stellan started toward her.

"You don't want any witnesses, darling?"

"Not to what I've got planned."

Stellan knew he should've gotten the details on exactly how he died when he lost. Did he just have to stand there while the shield ripped him to pieces? He took another step toward her. Her demeanor was serene, completely calm. From the tiny smile playing around the edges of her mouth, he was certain she was enjoying toying with him.

"Not even anyone to help you deal with the body parts? I mean, after you rip me up with your shield, there's bound to be a big mess to clean up. And I'm gonna be real hurt if you tell me Berta's coming over to help you."

"Oh, I think I can deal with your body parts all by myself."

She stared pointedly at his crotch. His cock swelled painfully. *Great, stick it out there and wave it like a flag. It's probably the first part she'll tear off.*

Cardis continued to give him that same cool stare. Part of him wanted to reach out and grab her by the shoulders and shake her. Maybe then her shield would just kill him on the spot and it would all be over. But some perverse part of him enjoyed bantering with her.

"So what's next?"

"Are you ready?"

"As ready as I'll ever be, darling."

"Then come inside."

She moved out of the doorway into the cabin. Stellan followed her, wondering if she planned to cremate his remains by setting fire to his home. Maybe it was an Adenan custom to leave no remnant of your victim behind. Sort of like erasing his name forever.

He gazed around the familiar room, trying to keep his eyes off her.

"Over here."

It was obvious the woman had lost none of her bossiness. She stood by the fireplace, a blaze going in the hearth to ease the growing chill. As he glanced around the room, Stellan noticed other things. New flowers had been placed in the vases. Food was laid out on the table, fresh bread, cheese and roast fowl. A bottle of wine stood opened beside the bread.

"Have you taken up cooking, princess?"

Cardis snorted. "Not hardly. Alberta brought the food over."

"And the flowers?"

"I took a walk while you were gone. The others were so pretty I decided to replace them with fresh ones."

"Are you planning on living in my house?"

Cardis shrugged. "I like it here. It has a sort of rustic charm, much like its owner. My father will likely stay on for a while during the transition to Council control, so perhaps I'll stay as well."

Well, he thought, that ruled out being cremated. At least his house would survive this night.

Cardis nodded toward the window. "It'll be getting dark soon. We need to get this done."

"Should I close my eyes or ask for a blindfold?"

"No, just take off your clothes."

"Excuse me?"

"Take off your clothes." She enunciated each word slowly.

"What, are you saving them for a memento?"

She folded her arms across her chest. "Strip. Now."

"Yes, ma'am." Stellan tugged the vest off his shoulders and flung it aside. He watched her face as he unlaced his trousers. When he slid them down his legs and his erection sprang free, the hunger in her eyes was clear. He didn't know what game she played, but his body was obviously ready. Maybe he'd go out with a smile after all.

"Okay, darling, you've got my full attention." He folded his arms across his chest and tried to look dignified.

"Good." Cardis crossed to him until she stood only inches away from him. She laid her hands on his chest, stroked them down the hard muscles until they rested on his hips. Stellan groaned. She laughed then moved her fingers around the back to smooth them down his buttocks. She pressed her lips against his chest, tasting his skin as she kneaded his behind.

"Keep that up, darling, and you're gonna have me on my knees."

She stepped back and gave him a wicked grin that traveled up and down the length of him. Then she licked her lips.

"How about on your back instead?"

He pointed to the floor. "Right here?"

"Yep."

She nodded, watching every movement of his body as he stretched out on the rug in front of the fireplace. With her foot, she tapped his legs until he spread them enough for her to stand between them. Bracing her feet against his inner thigh, Cardis unlaced the front of the dress and pulled it over her head. Stellan swore he stopped breathing at the sight of her.

"I can die happy now, princess, just looking at you like this."

"Now why would you want to go and die? I'm not done with you yet."

She knelt between his legs, her knees pressing against his groin as she planted kisses in the sensitive area above his shaft. Stellan moaned.

"You take my breath away, darling."

"So you do have pretty words for me?" Cardis knelt back on her feet and grinned at him.

"I don't know if words would do you justice. You're beautiful, the most beautiful thing I've ever touched."

"And you want to go on touching me?" Her hands moved up his inner thigh where she let her fingers brush his sac.

"Forever." Stellan half swallowed the word as his breath caught in his throat when she cupped him. He was sure the room was spinning.

"Why, Stellan?" Her tongue touched the tip of his shaft and Stellan felt his eyes roll back in his head.

"Why what?"

"Why do you want to touch me?"

"Why do I want to touch you?"

She chuckled as he repeated her question. "Yes, why?"

He shook his head. "I don't know. I just know if I could go on touching you forever, I'd be the happiest man in the world. I guess I could even die now so long as you were touching me. It'd be better than going on living in a world where I didn't get to touch you."

"Why?"

Stellan choked out a laugh. "Darling, call me stupid all you want, but I can't hold up my end of the conversation while you're doing what you're doing."

"Then how about you just watch me?"

Cardis spread her legs outside his thighs and slid her core over him. She pressed his cock down with her hand and against her folds.

"Are you watching me, Stellan?"

He nodded, not sure he was even breathing still. Maybe he'd already died and this was some sort of nirvana. Cardis sounded breathless too. She lifted herself up on her knees over him.

"Watch my eyes, Stellan."

The world stopped as she impaled herself on him. Stellan felt his cock slide into her tight sheath and thought he'd definitely died. She rocked against him and he wondered that he didn't simply explode. It was too much to dream that the feel of her wrapped around him, holding him inside her was true. Then he saw her eyes.

They were a brilliant blue, like the clear blue sky on a warm day. She smiled down at him as he lay there stunned.

"You'd best finish this, Stellan, or I'm gonna be disappointed in my choice. And that you'd never hear the end of."

Laughter burst out of him as he flipped her over, keeping them joined as he moved.

A word about the author...

Debra Doggett has been writing since childhood. Keeping stories in her head while raising three daughters, pursuing her BA in History and working as a museum professional has kept the writer inside her alive. She has also written, performed and directed for the stage, her second love.

Visit Debra at www.debradoggett.com

Thank you for purchasing
this Wild Rose Press publication.
For other wonderful stories of romance,
please visit our on-line bookstore at
www.thewildrosepress.com.

For questions or more information,
contact us at info@thewildrosepress.com.

The Wild Rose Press
www.TheWildRosePress.com